Ebook ISBN 978-1-80162-537-1

Kindle ISBN 978-1-80162-538-8

Audio CD ISBN 978-1-80162-529-6

MP3 CD ISBN 978-1-80162-530-2

Digital audio download ISBN 978-1-80162-531-9

Boldwood Books Ltd
23 Bowerdean Street
London SW6 3TN
www.boldwoodbooks.com

B

Boldwood

First published in Great Britain in 2022 by Boldwood Books Ltd.

Cover Design by Head Design

Cover photography: Shutterstock

A CIP catalogue record for this book is available from the British Library.

Paperback ISBN 978-1-80162-535-7

Large Print ISBN 978-1-80162-536-4

Hardback ISBN 978-1-80162-534-0

For my Dad, thank you for starting my love affair with books and for always supporting me in everything that I do. You are the best of the best and I love you.

PROLOGUE

Autumn had cast a spell around the Dublin streets and the late September sunlight flickered through the sycamore branches and glinted off the car windscreen in white flashes as she drove along. The leafy green shades of summer had been replaced by rich, earthy crimson, mustard and ochre colours as the leaves clung desperately to their branches before a breeze would sweep them away.

She looked at him sitting across from her in the passenger seat of her Renault Scenic. She hadn't seen him since his wedding day almost three years ago – the day he had told the world that he had finally met 'the one'. Took him long enough. As he stood up on the altar, beaming with adoration for his new wife, that he had only known for six months, she couldn't help wonder what had been wrong with her? She had spent so many years wishing he would look at her like that, but he had never felt that way about her.

He looked well now, she had to admit as she risked another look at him. His athletic physique hadn't changed since she'd last seen him. Marriage obviously suited him, she thought bitterly. His short-sleeved T-shirt showed off his toned forearms, bronzed, she guessed, from all his time spent outdoors. He had never owned a car, preferred cycling everywhere. His wavy brown hair was longer now than it used to be, but it suited him like that. A faint shadow of stubble peppered his strong jaw.

It annoyed her to find that he still made her heart leap. She hadn't expected that after all this time. Tiny bubbles fizzed up inside her tummy; anticipation or terror, she wasn't sure which. Was she doing the right thing? She knew he was wondering why she had wanted to meet him again after all this time. She guessed that her message out of the blue last week asking if they could meet somewhere to 'talk' had made him uneasy. He had suggested meeting at one of his coffee shops – she had read a feature on him in one of the Sunday papers a few months back and he had a chain of them – quite the entrepreneur by all accounts, but she had suggested Sandymount Strand. They needed to be far away from people who might know them, so she had said she would pick him up from his office and they would go for a walk along the beach.

As soon as he had sat into her car that morning, she could sense that something had changed. The connection – that magnetic force between them that had once been so strong – had somehow dissipated and it made her sad now to find that their conversation was stilted, where it once had flowed. To think he used to be a vein of excitement cutting through the mundanity of her life and now it felt as though they had nothing in common – well, maybe not nothing, she thought, feeling an unpalatable lump of guilt stick in her throat.

They had caught up on their mutual friends, who was doing what, who was married now. She asked him if he had any children and he said he hadn't. She wasn't sure if it was her imagination, but she thought she had seen a sheen of pain in his eyes that told her there was more to that story.

'Mama, why is that man in our car?' Milly, her three-year-old daughter, who was strapped into her car seat in the back clutching her Peppa Pig lunch bag tightly, asked. She had started playschool a few weeks ago and was so proud of that bag and had even taken it to bed with her the first day they had bought it.

She should have been dropping Milly at playschool that morning but had decided at the last minute to bring her along with her. She had called her teacher and explained that Milly was going to be late, but now she was having second thoughts. Maybe this was a bad idea...

She glanced nervously at her daughter in the rear-view mirror. 'He's just an old friend, sweetie.'

'But me want to go to playschool!'

'We'll be going there soon, I promise.'

'Look, Rowan, can I ask what this is about?' he was saying. Now that they had got the pleasantries out of the way, he was getting impatient. He wanted to know the reason why she had contacted him again after all this time.

'There's something I have to tell you...' she said, hearing a crack in her voice. That was all she was going to say for now; the car wasn't the right place to do it, she would wait until they reached the beach, where Milly could play and they could talk without the risk of being overheard.

He was looking out the window now. She indicated and turned right onto the Coast Road.

'Mama, ook! The candy canes!' Milly shouted from the back seat, pointing to the red and white striped Poolbeg chimneys that had come into view in the distance.

'Yes, there they are, sweetie,' Rowan replied distractedly as she drove.

The sea shimmered silver under the low morning sun and in the distance a container ship was lumbering across Dublin Bay.

'Me like candy canes,' Milly continued chatting away.

Rowan's head was in a spin as she thought about the conversation that lay ahead. She had been over it so many times, what would be the best way to tell him? But the more she thought about it, she didn't think that there was a 'best' way.

'Mama?' She heard her daughter say, cutting through her thoughts.

She glanced in the rear-view mirror and she could see Milly's concerned face. 'It's okay, love, we're nearly there now,' she soothed.

'Mama!' Milly called again, more impatient this time.

'What's wrong, Milly?' She glanced in the rear-view mirror at her daughter once more.

'Op, Mama! Op!' Milly was shouting at her now.

'Jesus Christ, Rowan, *look out*!' his voice roared suddenly.

Rowan switched her eyes from the mirror back to the windscreen and suddenly saw what they were trying to tell her. The traffic had stalled, leaving her car impossibly close to the lorry in front of her. *Oh God.* She slammed the brake and tried to swerve, all the time knowing that it was too late.

'*M-ill-y!*' she heard herself scream as every syllable was stretched out onto the air between them in slow motion.

She was suspended there for a moment, just waiting, bracing herself for the impact. Seconds lasted an eternity until finally the force slammed into her, even worse than she had anticipated. She was shunted forwards against the airbag like a rag doll, feeling the seatbelt slice into her chest like cheese wire before being slammed back into her seat again. Her ears were ringing with the crunch and twist of metal so loud. It seemed to last forever, and she wondered when it might end. Finally the awful roar stopped and there was just deafening silence. The last thing she saw was a blinding flash of silvery light before darkness fell over her and she knew this was it, that it was her time to go.

She didn't hear the frantic cries of Milly calling, 'Mama'. She didn't hear him shouting her name over and over again. She didn't see the people helplessly watching the scene unfold from the footpath, the kind, shocked people who had rushed to assist them and dialled an ambulance. The people who tried to comfort a distressed Milly through the shattered glass, who was still sitting strapped into her car seat. She didn't see the stunned driver that they had crashed into, as he stumbled out from his lorry and realised that one side of the car had gone under his vehicle. He held his head in his hands before collapsing in a trembling mess on the side of the road.

She didn't smell the stench of cloying smoke and burning rubber. Rowan didn't hear the people who tried to talk to her through the wreckage, begging her to hold on. She didn't hear the people who prayed over her while she left this world.

1

HELENA

The day before everything went wrong had started off just like any other one. There had been no signs, no solitary magpie or black cat crossing her path to warn of what was to come. Helena O'Herlihy had got up that morning like she always did and gone to the Cara Family Practice in Rathmines where she worked as a GP. She had had a steady stream of patients that day; she had seen an elderly patient suffering with gout and she had prescribed antibiotics for a toddler with a chest infection, but when her patient Julie Carroll, a young mother of two, had broken down in front of her during her check-up following a recent miscarriage, something had erupted inside Helena. Something she had managed to keep suppressed and hidden for a long time. Helena hadn't even realised she was crying until Julie reached across her desk and handed Helena one of her own tissues from the box she kept there for her patients.

Helena had always prided herself on her professionalism. They had been trained in medical school on the importance of remaining sympathetic but detached from their patients' problems; it had been drilled into them that they must keep a professional distance and up until today she had always managed to achieve that. As a GP, she had seen lots of her patients break down in front of her over the years, but it wasn't meant to be the other way around – it wasn't a two-way street. Of course there had been times when she had shed a tear when a patient had died or when a child in her care had been diagnosed with a serious illness, but it had always been in private, behind the closed door of her surgery. She had never let the mask slip in public before, but Julie's pain had mirrored the emptiness inside her own heart as she herself grappled with the recent losses of her own much-wanted pregnancies.

As soon as she had taken the tissue proffered by Julie, Helena had realised a line had been crossed and had quickly pulled herself together. She began issuing harried apologies and mumbling things like, 'I don't know what came over me...' Julie had made sure she was all right, before standing up to leave, and Helena had mumbled more awkward apologies as she saw her to the door.

A few minutes later, there was a knock on her surgery door. 'Is everything okay, Helena?' Mairéad, their receptionist, had asked, as she came into the room. 'I saw Julie Carroll on the way out and she mentioned I should check on you?'

Helena was mortified when words deserted her as, once more, she was engulfed by tears.

'Oh, love, what it is?' Mairéad, a kind but efficient woman, had quickly closed the door behind her, before wrapping her arms around her in a motherly fashion, while Helena sobbed heartily onto her shoulder.

When Mairéad had suggested that Helena should take the rest of the day off, Helena hadn't even put up a fight. She had gone home and climbed into bed. It was after nine when her husband, James, had arrived home and he hadn't noticed there was anything out of the ordinary. He had left her alone and gone to sleep in the spare room. They had been avoiding each other lately anyway.

That had been yesterday and as Helena got up that morning and dressed for work, she already felt a lot better. She felt fortified by the dawn of a new day, if a little embarrassed by her outpouring the previous day, but it was out of her system now and she resolved never to let it happen again. She made a mental note to call Julie Carroll first thing to apologise for being so unprofessional.

* * *

She was the first one in the practice that morning and was just going through the backlog of paperwork which had piled up from her early departure the day before, when there was a knock on the door.

'Come in,' Helena called.

The door opened and she saw the friendly face of Ken, a fellow GP and the practice owner.

'May I come in?' he asked hesitantly. He was in his mid-fifties and dressed in his usual uniform of a tweed jacket over a shirt and tie. Helena guessed he had been dressing like that since he had been in college. He was a kind man, if a little socially awkward.

'Of course,' she said. 'Take a seat.'

He came in and sat on the chair at the end of her desk, the same chair that Julie had sat in the day before. He crossed his legs awkwardly and was fidgeting with the end of his tie, rolling the fabric up like a Swiss roll before unfurling it down again.

'Mairéad mentioned what happened yesterday...' he began. 'Are you okay?'

'I'm very sorry about that,' she cut across him straight away, wanting to end this conversation fast. She knew her colleagues would have had to fit in her appointments into their already overworked day and she felt awful for leaving them in the lurch. 'It never should have happened. I don't know what came over me, but don't worry, I'm going to ring Julie Carroll first thing this morning to apologise—'

'I've already spoken to Julie...' he admitted, rubbing his salt-and-pepper beard now. 'She was very understanding. She was worried for you.'

Helena felt herself bristle. She lifted a pile of paperwork and straightened the bottom edges against the desk. 'Well, I will call her anyway,' she insisted.

Ken cleared his throat before speaking again. 'I... em... think you should take a little time off, Helena.' The words were uttered so quietly that she wasn't sure if she heard him right.

'Sorry?'

'I know you're going through some... um... difficult... personal issues.' He took off his glasses and began cleaning them on his woollen pullover.

He knew about the miscarriages, of course; she had had to tell him as she had needed time off to recover, not just physically but emotionally too. But he didn't know that the fertility clinic that they had been attending for the last two and a half years had recently told Helena and James that they were unlikely to ever have a child of their own.

She should have known from the way their fertility specialist, Dr Bedford, wouldn't meet her eye when she had taken a seat across the desk from him that morning that it wasn't going to be good news. She had noticed him shift a little in his chair and her stomach had clenched as she'd waited for him to speak.

'Helena and James,' he had begun, 'I'm sorry but there is no easy way to tell you this.'

Icy sweat had broken out across her neck and her heart had started to hammer. James had reached across from his chair, his palm finding hers; it had felt clammy, like her own.

'Considering Helena's most recent miscarriage, I don't think it's in your best interests to continue treatment. Your body has been unable to sustain a pregnancy to date and I think you really need to consider other...' he'd stopped for a beat, '...avenues if you want to have a child.'

Helena had felt as though she was sinking through the floor. She hadn't been expecting that news coming to the clinic that morning. The losses of the last few years had been devastating, but she was slowly picking herself up again, like she had done so many times before, and she was ready once more to board that gruelling IVF train that would give them their much-awaited for baby.

'So what do we do now then?' she'd heard James ask, but she knew what Dr Bedford was saying. She was bracing herself for the impact.

Dr Bedford had continued, 'After six miscarriages, most of them quite early on in the first trimester, I suspect a hyperactive immune system is the reason your body can't sustain a pregnancy – your body is essentially attacking your own baby.'

'Surely there has to be something we can try? You must have *something* to stop it happening?' James had asked, and the desperate note in his voice had nearly finished her off completely.

'As you know, we have already tried immunosuppressant medication, which I had hoped would be successful, but unfortunately not...' He had paused and placed his hands flat on his desk. 'I am conscious of your age, Helena. At forty-three, time isn't on your side,' he'd said bluntly. 'All things considered, I think the best option for you both to have a child is through either surrogacy or adoption.' His gaze had switched between the two of them. 'I'm sorry, I know that's not the news you were hoping to hear today.' He'd exhaled sharply, making a little whistling sound through his teeth as if relieved that he had now said the words he had been preparing himself for, but Helena had felt winded, like he had just reached across his desk and assaulted her. A little rush of vomit had made its way up her throat.

She'd pulled her hand away from James's and balled it into a fist on her lap.

Dr Bedford had continued then, explaining about how he could put them in touch with a surrogacy clinic abroad, but Helena hadn't been listening. All she had heard were the words that she would never be pregnant. She would never carry her own child, she would never share her body with another, nourishing them until the time came to meet one another. She would never get to hold her baby as it curled its tiny fingers around hers and breathe in its newborn scent. It would never happen for them.

But I've been so good! she wanted to rage and rail. She'd done everything Dr Bedford had told her to do. She had given up coffee, forgoing her much-loved morning latte, she had tried meditation, acupuncture and reflexology, she had injected herself and taken so many drugs... but maybe she had missed some crucial step? Maybe if she had relaxed more... she'd always found it difficult... but, god, it was hard to relax when all your dreams were hanging in the balance. She knew life wasn't fair, but she really believed that, on some level, karma would see her right. If she was a good person on balance and played by life's rules, then it would all work out for them. But Dr Bedford's crushing words had told her that there wasn't a happy ever after for them and there never would be. As he had talked, she could taste the metallic tang of her own tears as they fell down her face.

They had returned home from the appointment both stunned by what they had been told. To be turned away as a lost cause really emphasised just how hopeless their situation was. Over the years in her job as a GP, she had met patients facing the same crushing news as they were, but it was fair to say that nothing could have ever prepared her for the awful finality of their own personal prognosis.

What Ken also didn't know was that she had had a huge argument with James when she had discovered that he had contacted a surrogacy clinic in Ukraine 'to get the ball rolling'. James couldn't understand why she was so angry. In his eyes, he was helping the situation by being proactive; he reasoned that the next logical step if they wanted to have a child of their own was to use a surrogate, but to her, he was being completely insensitive. She couldn't believe he was able to think about going down that road yet, while she was still grieving the fact that she would never carry her own baby. That she would never feel those first fluttery kicks as graceful as butterfly wings or the firm roundness of her baby growing strong inside her tummy.

She felt like a failure; carrying a baby was one of the most fundamental tasks of womanhood and she would never understand why her body couldn't do what generations of women had done before her. James didn't seem to understand the depths of her grief and so they had barely spoken to one another in three weeks. It was too hard to see her pain mirrored in his eyes. He was better off without her anyway. It was her fault that he would never be a father. His tests had all come back fine – he had joked about how his swimmers were the Michael Phelps of the sperm world – she was the only obstacle standing in his way of fatherhood.

It was a cruel irony that he was so good with children. Whenever they would go to the birthday parties of their nieces and nephews or their friends' children, James was the one tearing around the garden with the children, while the adults looked on, balancing paper plates of canapés and sipping wine;

he was always the biggest child of them all. Then they would plaster a smile on their face as they posed beside the birthday child for a photograph and nobody would ever guess the pain they held inside their hearts as she wondered when it might be their turn. When was she going to be the one standing taking a photo of her child blowing out candles on their birthday cake? Helena didn't know how they would move forward from here, or even if they could. The chasm between them seemed too much.

'But what about my patients?' Helena argued to Ken. 'I can't walk out on them! The practice is busy enough as it is.' How dare he suggest that she wasn't up to doing her job! She was a good doctor. Her job was all she had left right now.

'Come on, Helena, you know better than anyone how important it is to take care of our emotional well-being. Sometimes, as GPs, we spend so much time caring for others, that we forget to look after ourselves. This job can be very demanding if you're going through something in your personal life. Your health and well-being has to come first. We can get a locum to cover you.'

'I'm sorry—' Tears pushed forward once more and she tried to blink them away before Ken would notice. *Damn it anyway*, she cursed herself. Why couldn't she just hold it together? All the drugs and hormones in her body had turned her into a mess. She was mortified when he reached for a tissue from the same box that Julie had done the day before and handed it to her.

'Everything will be okay, just take a month out and give yourself time to get better,' Ken advised.

'A month?'

'It's for the best, Helena. You can't give your patients the best care if you're not taking care of yourself first.'

Helena blinked back tears. 'I-I'm a good doctor, Ken... I know I made a mistake yesterday, but I'm good at my job,' she pleaded.

'It wasn't just yesterday...' He paused and wouldn't meet her eyes. 'There was that issue with the prescription for Mrs Redmond last week too...'

Helena had prescribed the wrong dosage level for an elderly patient. Luckily, it had been picked up by the pharmacist, who had phoned the practice to double-check whether it was an error, but Helena knew it could have been so much worse.

She realised then that she didn't have a choice. The decision had already been made for her. Ken was right. She was a liability to the practice in her current state. When she wasn't breaking down in front of her patients, she was distracted and, lately, her brain was fuzzy and slow, her head was too full of grief to concentrate on anything. What if she made another mistake? One that wasn't discovered in time. Or if she misdiagnosed someone or missed a crucial symptom – for the sake of her patients she needed to get herself together.

'What will you tell people?' she asked quietly, resigned to her fate.

'We'll just say that you need some personal time – they don't need to know anything more than that.'

She nodded, too upset to speak. How had she let this happen? Her personal life had seeped into her professional life like liquid soaking through tissue paper.

'I respect and admire you greatly and I know your patients do too,' Ken continued. 'You are a much-valued member of the team here and I want you back feeling better. Okay?'

'Okay,' she sniffed as she dabbed the tissue at her nose.

Ken stood up then and left her alone.

As Helena gathered up her belongings, she took a moment to look around her office at all she was leaving behind. How had it come to this? She carried her GP bag in one hand and hooked her laptop bag over her shoulder, before she made her way out the back exit of the practice without saying goodbye to anyone. She got into her car and drove home to their red-bricked Victorian semi-detached house on Abbeville Road in Rathgar. She and James had bought it soon after they had got engaged. This house with its original fireplaces and timber sash windows where children scooted past on the leafy streets outside had seemed like the perfect family home. As soon as she had set foot inside it, she had already imagined laughter ringing between its walls. The house had a generous rear garden for this part of Dublin and was shaded with a large oak tree. They had had a whole future planned here – they would lie in bed together imagining what their children might look like. They both wanted at least two. She pictured James tying a rope swing over the boughs for them to play on, and maybe building them a little timber playhouse down the end of the garden, which she would paint in the softest shade of apple green. She had already visualised the nursery decorated in pale greys with a delicate canopy draped over the cot, but it had never transpired.

Helena put her key in the lock and let herself into her empty house which was now the shell of her broken dreams. How had her life come to this? She and James had never been more distant and now she had been deemed unfit to do the job that she adored. She pushed the door closed behind her and slid down along it with her back until she reached the floor. She stayed sitting on the black and white chequered tiles of her hallway until she lost all sense of time and when the doorbell rang suddenly, she jolted.

She picked herself back up again and through the stained-glass panes of the door, she could see the outline of a dark-clothed man.

'Hello?' she said, pulling the door back and quickly composing herself. It took her a few moments to register that he was dressed in a Garda uniform and a white squad car with blue lights on the roof was parked behind hers in the driveway. Her mind felt as though it was trudging through concrete as she tried to work out what was going on. Perhaps he had followed her home – maybe she had broken the speed limit, or run a red light... She barely remembered the drive, her head had been in a spin and her eyes blurred with tears. Immediately her heart was racing and blood filled her ears.

'Are you Helena O'Herlihy? Married to James O'Herlihy?' he began.

'Y-yes, I am.'

'I'm Garda Lorcan Murray from Donnybrook Garda Station.'

'Uh-huh,' she said, wishing he would just hurry up and tell her what this was about.

'I'm very sorry to tell you that your husband James has been involved in a serious road traffic accident on the Coast Road earlier.'

'James?' she repeated, buying her brain time to process what he was telling her, even though she had heard what he said.

'He's been taken to Dublin City Hospital by ambulance,' the Garda continued.

'Is he okay?' The voice that came out didn't sound like her own.

'Unfortunately I don't have that information, Mrs O'Herlihy, but you need to get to the hospital urgently.'

2

AIDAN

Aidan sat in the boardroom of Mason Fidelity Investments and looked at his watch. It was just after eleven a.m. He wondered how much longer this presentation was going to go on for. Joe, the guy who was standing at the top of the boardroom, had recently been recruited on their graduate programme and was keen to make an impression on the company directors, but Aidan didn't have time for his long, drawn-out style. He needed to leave early that evening because his fourteen-year-old son Callum had a rugby match after school. Aidan had a lot of work to get through that day and if Joe didn't wrap it up soon, he might not make it. He had missed the last match because he had got delayed in a meeting and Callum still hadn't forgiven him for it, so he had promised that no matter what happened, he'd be there today.

He looked beyond the boardroom glass out across Dublin's International Financial Services Centre skyline, where the graceful arc of the Samuel Beckett bridge spanned the broad mouth of the River Liffey just before it entered Dublin Bay. He could see other workers scurrying behind glass-fronted offices just like his. Everyone busy and time-pressed and wrapped up in their own pressures and deadlines.

'Aidan?' a voice was calling, jolting him out of his thoughts.

He swung his head around from the window and the strangest sight greeted him. A young female Garda, accompanied by Brenda, the company's receptionist, was now standing in the boardroom. Her inky-blue utilitarian Garda uniform with its blouson jacket and loose-fitting cargo trousers was in contrast with the sharp-cut suits sitting around the boardroom table. She looked young, probably in her mid-twenties. He was always remarking to Rowan that the Gardaí were getting younger and she usually teased him that it was he who was getting older. For some reason, all the eyes around the boardroom table were fixed on him, as if waiting for him to explain what was going on, but he was as nonplussed as they were.

'Aidan... eh... this is Garda Rachel Sullivan... sh-she would like to talk to you,' Brenda explained eventually. She seemed nervous, on edge. She was sliding the circular pendant of her necklace over and back across its chain.

'To me?' Aidan asked dumbfounded.

'I was wondering if we could go somewhere private?' Garda Sullivan was saying now.

'I have a meeting room free down the hall,' Brenda said to the Garda, flashing Aidan an anxious look.

'Take as long as you need,' Richard, their chairman, said with a wave of his hand.

Aidan followed Brenda and Garda Sullivan down the corridor to the meeting room wondering what the hell was going on. He felt mildly irritated at the Garda; he had so much to get through before he left that day and this was going to set him back even further. Who did she think she was, coming here in front of his colleagues and making a scene like this? He couldn't think of any misdemeanours he had committed; in fact he'd never been on the wrong side of the law. It could only be a parking offence or something equally minor. He hoped they weren't causing all this drama for parking on a double-yellow line; wasting taxpayers' money for something so insignificant.

'Can I get you a tea or coffee?' Brenda offered as she brought them inside the meeting room.

Aidan and Garda Sullivan shook their heads simultaneously, both waiting for Brenda to leave so they could get on with the reason for this visit.

'Just to confirm, you are Aidan Whelan?' Garda Sullivan began once Brenda had closed the door behind them.

Aidan nodded. 'Look, can you tell me what this is about? I'm in the middle of a meeting.' He just wanted her to get to the point.

'Are you the husband of Rowan Whelan?' Garda Sullivan continued, unperturbed by his self-importance. She had clear green eyes and her auburn hair was tied back in a neat ponytail.

'Yes,' he replied impatiently. 'Can you please tell me what's going on here?'

'I'm afraid I have some bad news for you, Mr Whelan, your wife and daughter were involved in a serious road traffic accident on the Coast Road shortly after nine a.m. this morning.'

Aidan felt as though he was hearing her from one end of a tunnel. The words felt all wrong. What was she saying about an accident? He shook his head, trying to reorder everything.

'Rowan and Milly?' he gasped. 'Are you sure?' They wouldn't be on the Coast Road. That wasn't the route they would have taken. They would have dropped the boys to school for nine and went on to the playschool afterwards, like they usually did. He felt a flicker of hope turn on like a switch inside him. Maybe Garda Sullivan had got this wrong, made a mistake...

'The car was registered in your wife's name and she was carrying identification. I'm so sorry, Mr Whelan, it is definitely them,' she stated solemnly, leaving him no room for doubt. No hope.

'Are they... are they okay?' the words tumbled from his mouth.

'I'm afraid they were both taken from the scene by ambulance. You need to get to the Dublin City Hospital quickly,' she advised. 'I can take you there.'

The room around him seemed to shift and swirl. His ears were ringing with the words. 'She should have been taking her to playschool,' was all he could think of to say.

Garda Sullivan nodded sympathetically. 'I'm sorry, Mr Whelan, we should go to the hospital now.' She was kind but firm.

He pushed back his chair and stood up. 'I'll just tell Richard and the board where I'm going...'

'You don't have time, you need to go now, Aidan,' she urged and Aidan saw by the crease of her forehead that this was serious.

The thrust of her words suddenly plunged into him. He thought of his daughter with her glossy hair and rounded, sweet face, giggling when he had caught her in the act of hiding a chocolate bar in her Peppa Pig lunch bag that morning. He thought of Rowan with her dark, wavy hair bouncing around her shoulders as she had danced with the kids in the kitchen. Had he even kissed her goodbye as he had hurried out the door? He couldn't remember. He had kissed the children, he always kissed them, but he hadn't kissed his wife. *Oh, God, no.*

'You have to tell me, will they be okay?' he begged.

'I'm very sorry but I don't have an update on their condition.' She shook her head. 'The hospital will be able to give you more details. We should go now.'

As he followed Garda Sullivan out of the meeting room, Aidan's legs felt like those of the Action Men he had played with as a child with stiff joints that worked independently of one another; it was as if he couldn't get them to move properly. The open-plan office was now eerily quiet and he was aware of the eyes of his colleagues surveying the scene as they wondered what was going on.

Surely this wasn't happening? It couldn't be happening. Things like this didn't happen to him. They happened to other people. But as he walked past Brenda at the reception desk, her eyes two pools of worry as he left in the company of a Garda, he knew somehow it was real. How he longed to go back to before; before when he was stuck in a tedious presentation, when Rowan was taking their daughter to playschool and everything was okay in his world.

This was all going to be all right, he told himself. His wife and his daughter would be fine because they had to be. There was no other option.

3

HELENA

Helena sat in the back seat of the squad car, blue lights wailing through the city towards Dublin City Hospital. Tears wound their way down her face as she looked out through the window, where the streets sped past in a blur of grey. As bright autumn sunshine streamed in through the glass, her mind whirred with regrets. How she wished she could turn back the clock. Why had she shut James out? They had been living like strangers for the last three weeks. She should have talked to him, explained just how hurt she was feeling by his contact with the surrogacy clinic instead of letting her anger speak for her. Why hadn't she listened to him on the many times he had tried to explain himself over the last few weeks? Why had she stayed late in work to avoid seeing him? He might have handled things differently to her, but he was suffering too.

With sudden clarity, she now realised he had just wanted to solve the problem. By nature, James was a fixer and he had thought he could do that by rushing straight into surrogacy; it wasn't his fault that she wasn't ready to consider that option. He wanted to wave a magic wand over their problems and produce a baby like a magician pulls a rabbit from a hat. *Abracadabra, one, two, three.* He clearly hadn't realised what a huge step it would be for her – or if she would ever be ready – to go down that route. She had to go through a grieving process first as she came to terms with the fact that she would never carry her own child.

Now she wished more than anything that she could turn back the hands of time, because no matter how much pain she was experiencing, the thought that she might never see him again was so much worse than anything they had been through together. Why hadn't she been able to see all the good things she had, instead of mourning what could have been?

Helena wasn't religious, but even so, she found herself pleading with God to give her another chance to put things right between them. She made a bargain with him that if he would spare her husband, she would never take his love for granted again.

When the squad car reached the hospital, Helena flung open the door and ran towards the Emergency Department before the Garda had even turned off the engine. She had spent a rotation working here, so she knew what direction to go in.

'I'm the wife of James O'Herlihy,' she announced breathlessly when she reached the reception desk.

She watched the woman's face change as she nodded knowingly. Her eyebrows pinched together in sudden recognition and Helena was sure she could see sympathy in the woman's eyes. It felt as though she had a brick sitting in her stomach. She knew that bad news was coming.

'Mrs O'Herlihy, if you want to follow me,' the woman said, removing her reading glasses and getting up from her seat.

Helena's heart was racing and her legs felt as wobbly as a new-born foal's as she followed the woman down the corridor. Her breath snagged with every inhale; she knew where she was being taken. They were going to the room they used whenever they had to deliver bad news. The one with the red door. She remembered it from her time working here. She shivered as she recalled the families to whom she had had to deliver awful news to once upon a time, the pain and anguish on their faces would never leave her.

They reached the door and her ears were buzzing as if a cloud of flies were swarming around her. She didn't want to go inside where she knew her life would never be the same again. She didn't want to hear what they were going to tell her. How she wished she could pause life right here. If she could just stay right here in the corridor, plant her two feet on the floor and not move, then everything could still be okay. However, when the woman kept walking down the corridor, passing the red door by, Helena was confused.

'You mean, he's not—?' Helena couldn't bring herself to use the word as she hurried to keep up with the woman.

'He's in theatre, Mrs O'Herlihy. I'm taking you to the waiting area for family members. One of the medical team will speak with you to give you an update on his condition as soon as they are finished in surgery.'

A sob choked in Helena's throat. *He's alive.* Relief flooded through her. Although she knew he wasn't out of the woods yet; she would take this one step at a time and right now he was still here and that was all that mattered.

She followed the woman to a room at the end of the corridor, where several blue plastic chairs ran around the walls. She was the only one in there. The woman asked her if she could get her a tea or coffee, but Helena shook her head. She knew she would probably just vomit it straight back up again.

She was pacing up and down reading the health posters absent-mindedly when eventually a doctor with black wavy hair, clad in scrubs entered the room.

'Are you Mrs O'Herlihy?' he began.

'Please, just tell me how he is?' she said quickly, not wanting to waste time with formalities.

'I'm Doctor Choudhary. Your husband is doing

well, all things considered. He sustained a fracture to his left femur which required emergency stabilisation surgery. Thankfully, that seems to be the extent of his injuries. He doesn't appear to have any internal bleeding, although we will be keeping a close eye just in case. He's not out of the woods yet, but he is doing as well as can be expected given the circumstances.'

Helena exhaled and felt the warmth of relief flooding through her body. She knew those injuries were serious – a broken femur could be life-threatening – but she was so grateful to get another chance with him. Bones could heal. They could be fixed.

'He should be counting his lucky stars,' Doctor Choudhary went on, 'to be a front-seat passenger in a crash like that... He is lucky to be alive.' He shook his head.

'Passenger?' Helena repeated the word. A seemingly small detail, but it threw up so many questions in her mind. She had assumed he had been knocked off his bike. Whose car had he been in? James usually cycled to the GreenCoffee offices in the Grand Canal basin – he hated sitting in traffic. He had set up the chain of environmentally friendly coffee shops seven years ago and they were rapidly expanding across Dublin. Then her mind caught up; maybe he was a passenger in a taxi or perhaps he was going to a meeting with a colleague and they had decided to travel together. There were lots of reasons why he would have been a passenger.

'Yes, Mr O'Herlihy was travelling in the passenger seat. He is stable now if you want to see him? Bear in mind, he's still quite drowsy after the anaesthetic, so don't be alarmed if he seems disorientated or confused.'

'What about the driver?' Helena pressed. 'Are they okay?'

'I'm afraid I'm not at liberty to say until the next of kin have been informed.'

Helena felt a chill wash through her. 'Of course.' She nodded. She knew the protocol.

'Now, if you'd like to follow me, Mrs O'Herlihy, I will take you to see your husband.'

4

AIDAN

Aidan took a deep breath as he followed Garda Sullivan through the sliding doors into the hospital building. He was glad that she knew where to go because his brain couldn't process what was happening. Everything seemed surreal; from the doctors and nurses hurrying past him, to the bright yellow sunlight streaming in through the glass atrium, making the reception area seem impossibly hot. He waited while she spoke to a member of staff and then they were led down a corridor until they came to a stop outside a red door. They were ushered into a small, windowless room, which was empty, save for a box of tissues standing on the table.

'I'll get one of the medical team,' the receptionist said before closing the door behind them again.

Aidan began to pace around the room.

'Why don't you take a seat, Aidan,' Garda Sullivan suggested after a moment.

He shook his head. 'I'm good thanks,' he said as he continued to walk in circles around the tiny room, like a hamster on a wheel.

The more Aidan looked at the Garda, the younger she seemed – far too young to be tasked with something like this.

Finally, the door opened, and a doctor entered and introduced himself, but Aidan's mind was too full of terror to catch his name.

'Please tell me, are my wife and daughter okay?' Aidan asked straight away.

The man's eyes darted away from his. 'Mr Whelan...' He paused for a breath, 'I'm so sorry to have to tell you this, but your wife didn't make it. My team and I tried everything we could to save her, but she sustained a massive head injury as well as catastrophic internal bleeding. I'm so sorry.'

Somewhere on the periphery, Aidan could hear this man's words, he could see the doctor's face studying his, waiting for a reaction to the news he had just delivered to him, but Aidan couldn't process it. Was the doctor saying that Rowan was dead? His beautiful wife, so full of fun and life, how could that be possible? He wanted to open the door, walk out of this claustrophobic little room, run out of the hospital and back to their house, where, just a few hours ago, they had all been sitting eating breakfast together.

'B-but she can't be,' he cried out, knowing how feeble it must sound. He placed his palm against the wall, afraid that he would fall to the floor if he didn't steady himself.

'I know this is a lot for you to take in,' the doctor said. His face was creased in sympathy and somehow Aidan knew, he knew, what he was saying was true.

'So-so, she's... dead?' he asked, finding the word seemed to stick and clot in his throat. His wife was dead. Rowan was gone. This was all wrong. Thoughts floated past him, but he was unable to grasp them. His brain felt as though it was congealed with sludge.

'I'm so sorry,' the doctor said.

Aidan thought he was going to be sick, as icy

sweat broke out across his body. He made his way down into a chair and bent forward so that his head was cradled in his hands. He suddenly remembered Milly and slowly he straightened up again. 'My daughter – Milly – is she okay?' Aidan braced himself, if they told him that Milly was gone too, he'd never survive.

'Your daughter is in a serious but stable condition,' the doctor answered. 'I can take you to her,' he was suggesting now.

Aidan nodded, trying to process it all.

Garda Sullivan stood up. 'Here are my details, Aidan,' she said, handing him a business card. 'I'll be your Family Liaison Officer from here on, so if you need anything please don't hesitate to get in touch. Once again, on behalf of An Garda Síochána, I wish to express my sincere condolences to you and your family.' Then she shook his hand and left.

Aidan began following the doctor but it felt as though his feet weren't connected with the ground. They went into the lift and ascended to the next floor. His shoes squeaked along the rubber floors as he walked until, finally, they went through the flap of a set of double doors signposted 'Intensive Care Unit'.

Aidan gasped when he saw Milly looking impossibly small lying on the huge white bed. Her china doll face was swollen and bruised and her left arm was in a cast. Machines beeped and a tangle of wires and tubes trailed her tiny body. This was all wrong. It was so at odds with her toddler bed at home, with its fairy lights that Rowan had entwined around the frame.

Aidan felt himself land in the present with a smack. He had just been told that his wife was *dead* and now his beautiful baby girl lay here all broken and bruised. How could this be happening? How had they all been sitting around the table together as a family that morning and then their world had been ripped apart so savagely just hours later?

'Milly,' Aidan whispered, moving closer towards her, desperately wanting to touch her but terrified in case he hurt her.

'She is in a coma, Mr Whelan, and has some abdominal internal bleeding. We have stabilised her blood pressure with IV fluids, but it may be necessary to operate or do a blood transfusion at a later point. We will monitor her closely over the next while,' the doctor explained.

'But will she be okay?' Aidan begged.

'I'm afraid I can't promise anything yet, Mr Whelan. It's a waiting game until she wakes up and we see how she responds. I'll leave you alone for a few minutes with her.'

Suddenly Aidan felt his legs might give way and he fell into the chair beside her bed. She looked like an angel, with her dark, shiny hair fanned out against the white pillow behind her. He gingerly reached for her tiny hand, its knuckles softened by baby fat, and took it within his own.

'Daddy's here, baby girl,' he whispered and at the same time he felt his heart twist because Milly hated when he called her baby girl. 'Me big girl now, Daddy,' she would correct him. The reality of what had just happened slammed into him. 'Please hang on, Milly, I can't bear to lose you,' he sobbed.

* * *

The lift descended into the basement and stopped with a shudder. The doors parted and when Aidan saw a sign for the mortuary, he felt the breath hitch in his chest. Aidan had asked if he could see his wife; a part of him was still hoping this was just an awful mistake.

They had sent a lady from the bereavement team called Marion to accompany him. She was a softly-spoken woman with close-cut, grey hair. She was wearing soft-soled shoes and a black trouser suit and Aidan guessed she was in her sixties. Marion led him inside a darkened room and introduced him to the assistant, a neat, balding man called Wayne.

'Are you ready, Mr Whelan?' Wayne asked.

Aidan swallowed back a lump in his throat and nodded. It still felt like a nightmare that he hoped he might wake up from.

Marion remained outside while Wayne showed him into another room. The air was sucked from Aidan's lungs when he saw the trolley cloaked in a white sheet that was standing in the centre of the room. He held his breath as the sheet covering the body was pulled back, praying that by some miracle it wasn't his wife underneath it and he could run out of that room, relieved that they had made a mistake and his life could go back to the way it was that morning before everything had gone wrong.

It was her swollen face he saw first; bruised and battered. Her lips were a horrible shade of mauve. Blood matted her curly hair, and her right eye socket was so puffy that the structure of her face was barely recognisable on that side.

Aidan moved closer and lifted the sheet so that his eyes landed on her engagement ring and wedding band and he knew it was her. This was real. Life as he knew it would never be the same again. His beautiful wife was dead. He tried to breathe in deeply, but there was no air in the tiny room.

'Is this your wife, Rowan Whelan?' Wayne asked.

Aidan swallowed a lump in his throat and nodded to confirm.

'I'm so sorry for your loss, Mr Whelan. I'll give you a few minutes alone with her.'

He left the room, closing the door softy behind him.

'Oh, Rowan,' Aidan whispered as he stroked her wounded face. He was startled by how cold it was. It suddenly hit him. She was gone.

Fudgy thoughts formed in his mind of the things

he needed to do – what was he supposed to tell Callum and Jack? They were still in school, oblivious to how much their world had been turned upside down. He had a couple of hours yet before they needed to be collected and he would have to tell them, but how was he meant to do such a thing? It would shatter their whole world – their life would never be the same again. Life without her was unimaginable. How did you explain that the woman who had kissed them goodbye at the school drop-off that morning was now dead? At fourteen and ten, they were far too young to have to endure such heartache.

God, he'd have to tell Rowan's family – and his own too – how was he supposed to deliver that kind of news? He suddenly felt overwhelmed and thought he was going to suffocate.

He kissed his wife on her cool forehead and walked straight past Marion and Wayne, who were waiting outside for him. 'Mr Whelan?' they called after him. 'Are you okay, Mr Whelan?' but he walked fast before they had a chance to catch up with him and took the lift back up to the ground floor. He waited for the doors to separate and then he headed straight across the foyer and outside through the sliding doors of the hospital that it felt as though he had only entered minutes ago. Beads of sweat were sticky beneath the cotton of his work shirt and the collar was choking him. He undid the knot of his tie and tossed it onto the ground and opened the top button of his shirt. He tried to pull the air deeply into his lungs, but it was as though he couldn't search it out. *In, out,* he told himself, *just keep breathing*.

He took his phone out of his jacket pocket and with trembling hands dialled her father's number. Rowan's parents, Philip and Sheila, were in their late sixties and had recently sold the furniture company they had set up almost forty years ago and now split their time between Dublin and their house in the Algarve, where they currently were.

It was devastating listening to Philip's anguished cries down the phone as Aidan told him about the crash that had taken their only child. Philip asked him straight out if she was dead and when tears overcame Aidan, Philip knew his daughter hadn't made it. He told Aidan they would be on the next available flight back to Dublin.

When he was finished talking to Philip, Aidan

had had to call his own parents, Bill and Agnes to deliver the same devastating blow to them. Then he had a horrible thought: what if Milly didn't make it either? Or was left with life-altering injuries. He shook his head, as if trying to rid his brain of its horror. Milly had to get through this – the alternative was unthinkable. He needed to see her. He needed to keep her here with him. He needed to be close to her when everything was so broken in his world. He needed to feel her warm skin beneath his fingertips – he had lost so much today. He would not let her leave him too, no way.

As he made his way back inside the hospital building, Aidan felt hollow as though the very essence had been carved out of him. He was just heading down the corridor back towards the Intensive Care Unit when he heard a voice call, 'Aidan?'

He turned around and saw a woman he vaguely recognised but couldn't place. She was dressed in a scarlet red, tailored dress with a matching jacket over it. She was very slim with honey-blonde highlights.

'You might not remember me – it's Helena – James O'Herlihy's wife?' the woman was saying now.

It suddenly clicked into to place: James was an

old college friend of Rowan's. They had been at their wedding a few years ago. Somewhere on the periphery of his mind, he wondered what she was doing here. Then he remembered that she was a doctor, so he guessed she was working there.

'James was involved in a car crash this morning...' she continued, chattering anxiously. 'His parents have just arrived, so I said I'd step out and give them a few minutes on their own with him...' Her words all tumbled out on top of one another, and Aidan was having a hard time following what she was saying. She shook her head. 'I still can't believe it,' she choked as tears filled her eyes.

'What?' Aidan asked, wondering what the hell she was talking about. His brain was trying to piece it all together, but it was as though the cogs weren't working properly – he was trying to add two and two, but he just couldn't get the figures to sum up.

'James was involved a crash this morning,' she repeated, her brows knitting together in puzzlement.

'James?' It was Aidan's turn to be bewildered now. 'Rowan and our daughter Milly were in a car accident this morning too —'

'Oh, Aidan, no!' Helena gasped. 'Oh my God, I'm

so sorry… I can't believe they were in an accident too… Are they okay?'

'Milly is in a coma and well… Rowan… Rowan didn't make it.' The words seemed to claw in his throat. He still couldn't believe he was saying them. Saying it out loud felt surreal.

'Aidan, I'm so sorry—' Helena's hands flew to her mouth. He could see her features crease as her mind tried to process it all. Her hands reached out to embrace him, but he quickly stepped to the side.

'I have to go,' he said. 'I need to get back to Milly.'

5

HELENA

Helena continued down the corridor towards the room where James was recovering, wondering what had just happened. She was still reeling from what Aidan had said. Had she misunderstood? Picked him up wrong? But, no... the pain that haunted his face told her that this was real – Rowan was *dead,* and their little daughter, Milly, was in a critical condition? How on earth could that be? Aidan was in an awful state – dazed and faraway – she knew it was shock. She didn't know him well, she had only met him a handful of times, but the man was a shell of his former self. It almost hurt to look at him, seeing the weight of grief cloaked upon him. How ironic it was that on the same day she had learned her husband had very nearly lost his own life in a road traffic accident, Rowan and Milly had been involved in a crash too. What were the chances? It certainly put her own problems into perspective; she realised once again just how grateful she was that James was alive and she was getting another chance to put things right between them.

She rounded the room door and saw James's parents sitting at his bedside, suddenly looking every one of their seventy-plus years. She herself felt she had aged at least ten years with the fright of having a Garda call to her door with that awful news. When Breda and Kevin had arrived at the hospital earlier, they had taken her in their arms and gripped her tightly. Her in-laws had always made her feel like part of the family, like the daughter they had never had. They didn't know about their struggles to have a child and she didn't want to worry them by admitting how strained things had been between James and her in recent months. Even though they had a lot to work through, she would never take her husband's love for granted again.

'I just met Aidan Whelan in the corridor,' Helena

blurted to Kevin and Breda as soon as she came into the room. She needed to talk to someone about it because the interaction seemed dreamlike and she was starting to wonder if she had imagined it. She of all people knew that shock could do funny things to people.

They both looked at her quizzically.

'Remember James's friend Rowan from UCD?' she prompted. 'Well, he's her husband.'

'Ah yes,' Kevin said as it clicked into place for him. 'I remember her well. She was at his twenty-first, remember, Breda?'

'Are Rowan and Aidan here to see James? How did they hear about the crash so soon?' Breda asked in bewilderment.

Helena shook her head. 'No, Rowan and their daughter Milly were involved in a crash this morning too...' She paused. 'He said Rowan didn't make it...'

'Oh my goodness, Helena, are you sure?' Breda stood up and walked over towards her, gripping her arm fiercely, bringing her back to the present.

'I-I think so... I mean, that's what he said...' She was starting to doubt herself. It all seemed such a weird coincidence to think that her husband and his old college friend had both been involved in separate crashes on the same morning.

'My God... what are the chances of our family and Rowan's being involved in two serious accidents on the same day?' Kevin shook his head.

Helena nodded, although she was having the same thoughts herself. Her head was still spinning from the news as she tried to make sense of it all.

'*There by the grace of God go I*,' Breda mumbled as she made the sign of the cross. 'It makes me realise just how lucky we were today.' She nodded towards James. 'God love poor Aidan; it just doesn't bear thinking about.' Her voice quivered.

'Did anyone tell you any more about whose car James was travelling in?' Kevin asked suddenly.

Helena had forgotten what the doctor had told her about James being a passenger in the car. She had wracked her brain to think whose car he might have been in but had come up with nothing. She had told Breda and Kevin when they had arrived at the hospital, and they seemed as surprised as she was. 'But he cycles everywhere!' they had said.

'I haven't heard anything more,' she replied,

shaking her head. 'They won't release any details until all the next of kin have been informed.'

'He was probably in a taxi,' Breda reasoned.

'Yeah,' Helena agreed. But if he had been travelling in a taxi, would he really have been sitting in the front passenger seat? He must have been travelling with a colleague, she thought, that was the most logical explanation. Guilt crawled its way inside her; if she hadn't been giving him the silent treatment, she would have known his plans for the day, but now she didn't have a clue what her husband was doing in the moments before he had very nearly lost his life.

'I'll go get you a coffee, love,' Kevin suggested, standing up. 'You look like you could do with one.'

'I'll go with you,' Breda said. 'I need to get some air.'

'Thank you,' Helena said, sitting into the chair Kevin had just vacated, as her in-laws left the room.

She reached for James's hand. He looked so vulnerable lying there and she wondered how she had ever been mad with him. Well, she promised, as soon as he was feeling stronger, they would talk it through properly. She would tell him that she was sorry for how she had handled things. She would never fly off the handle with him again. She was beyond grateful that she had been given a second chance with him.

She felt flooded with shame when she thought about poor Aidan Whelan and all he had lost today. She vaguely recollected that they had three children. Here she was celebrating at being given another chance with her husband, but poor Aidan was living her worst nightmare. He would never again get to tell Rowan that he loved her and now their children would have to endure life without their mother. Her heart tore thinking of the pain that they were now experiencing and would be for the rest of their lives.

She stroked her finger along the creases in James's forehead. She ran it down the vertical line near his left temple from sleeping on the same side every night. 'I'm here, darling, whenever you're ready to wake up, I'm right here waiting for you,' she whispered.

His eyelids began twitching, and Helena held her breath.

'It's me, James,' she encouraged. 'I'm right here.'

She watched as his eyes opened and tried to focus on his surroundings.

'Hey, how are you doing?' she said, tenderly

stroking his hand across the starched white sheets. She felt tears of relief pool at the corners of her eyes.

His lids fell closed again before opening once more and his pupils began to dart around the room. She guessed he was panicked by his surroundings.

'Hey, it's okay, darling,' she soothed, as she gripped his hand firmly to reassure him. 'You're in the hospital. You were in a bad car crash, but I'm here now and I'm not going anywhere.'

His lips began twitching and she knew he was trying to say something.

'Do you remember anything?' she prompted.

His reply came out as a choking sound as he began to cough and splutter.

'It's okay, take your time.' She reached for the water jug and poured him a glass and held it up to his lips for him to take a sip.

When he was finished, she put the glass down and watched as he began moving his lips once more. She knew that whatever it was that he was trying to say was important to him.

'What is it? What are you trying to say, James?' she encouraged.

'Ro—' The sound was propelled from his lips

with great effort, and she wondered if she could have heard him right.

'What was that, love?' she tried again.

'Rowan.' The word came out clearer this time and Helena knew there was no mistaking what she had heard.

'Rowan?' she repeated, feeling cold beads of sweat break out all along her neck.

It seemed just saying the word had exerted him and his eyelids fell closed once more as he drifted off to sleep again.

As Helena stroked her husband's tanned forearm with its dark black hairs, she couldn't shake the feeling of unease. Why was Rowan's name the first word he had mentioned after waking up? For both him and Rowan to have life-altering car accidents in the same city, on the same day, on the same morning, seemed almost too coincidental to be true. It was as if he had a sixth sense and had known she had passed away. But he couldn't possibly have... She couldn't even begin to get her head around it. Unless... No... it had to be the medication messing with his brain.

The door opened and Kevin and Breda came

back into the room. 'Here, you go, Helena dear,' Kevin said, handing her a takeaway coffee. 'I took the liberty of adding a little bit of sugar, you know, to help with the shock. I hope that's okay?'

She could do with something a lot stronger right now, but a sugary coffee was better than nothing. 'That's very kind of you, thank you, Kevin,' she said, taking it from him. 'I... eh... I have some good news – James woke up for a few minutes.'

'Oh my goodness,' Breda squealed as tears filled her eyes. 'Thank God.' She hugged her husband.

'Did he say anything?' Kevin asked hopefully.

'Not really... I mean, he tried... but it wasn't very coherent,' she lied.

'Well, that's to be expected after everything he's been through,' Breda said. 'We need to take it one step at a time.'

'I know it's early days, but at least he's on the road to recovery,' Kevin agreed, putting his arm around his wife's shoulders.

How Helena wished she could share their exuberance, but she couldn't help feeling off-kilter. She was obviously relieved that he had woken, but why had Rowan been the first person he had thought about? Suddenly it hit her that perhaps somewhere in his consciousness he had heard them talking about Rowan's death just before he woke, so naturally it was the first word he had spoken. The brain was a very powerful organ. This explanation sat better with her, and she felt herself relax again.

'What is it, love?' Is everything okay?' Breda asked, pinching her eyebrows together. Helena knew they were surprised by her muted reaction.

'Of course, I'm just feeling a little overwhelmed, I think it's all just hit me...' she sighed.

'I know, love, we're all still in shock to be honest,' Kevin said kindly as he patted her arm.

'When I think about poor Aidan and what he must be going through,' Breda shook her head. 'We're the lucky ones here today, isn't that right, Helena?'

'We really are,' Helena agreed. She stood up and forced a smile on her face. 'I should probably go and report the good news to the nurses' station.'

6

AIDAN

Aidan pulled up in the school car park and silenced the engine. In the distance on the pitch, he watched the rugby team as they gulped back water or some just squirted their bottles straight over their heads to cool off. The match was already over.

He had left his parents at Milly's bedside while he drove to the school. He hadn't wanted to leave her, still lost in the depths of her coma, but he knew he needed to be the one to tell the boys. His parents had promised to phone him if there was any change in her condition.

Aidan stayed in the car while the coach spoke

with the team for a few minutes before they began to disperse and head over to the sidelines, where other parents had been watching. He took a deep breath, got out of the car and made his way over towards them.

Callum's eyes narrowed as he spotted his father coming towards him in the distance. 'Why did you say you'd come if you weren't going to bother?' he shouted. His face was red and his hair damp and sweaty.

Aidan reached for his son's arm, but he brushed him off and stormed past him towards the car. Jack, his younger son, was following in the distance. Jack attended the junior school adjacent to the senior school that Callum went to, and Rowan had told Jack she would meet him there at the playing field that the schools shared and they would watch the match together.

'Callum, wait—' he called after him.

'Hi, Dad,' Jack said as he reached them. His eyes were looking around the car park and Aidan knew he was wondering where Rowan was.

'Hi, Jack,' Aidan said, before turning back to Callum. 'Look, I'm really sorry, Callum. I wanted to be here.' He thought back to that morning sitting in the boardroom, his only trouble back then had been worrying about making it to the match on time, but everything had changed beyond recognition since then.

'Yeah, you got delayed in a meeting,' Callum said sarcastically. 'We get it.'

'Where's Mam and Milly?' Jack asked, his nose wrinkled in concern. 'Mam told me she would meet me here. She said she was going to come watch it?'

'Come on, son,' Aidan put an arm around his youngest son's shoulders and steered him towards the car. 'I'll explain everything when we get home.'

The boys exchanged glances with one another as they threw their sports gear into the boot. As usual, they jostled to get the front seat; Jack was victorious, leaving Callum to climb into the back seat, which just served to darken his mood even more.

'What's going on, Dad?' Jack asked as Aidan started the engine and began to drive out of the car park. 'You're acting really weird.'

He didn't reply and the boys, picking up on his

mood, fell quiet too. How on earth was he supposed to handle this? He was going to shatter their whole world. He just wanted to continue driving the car through the suburbs, going around and around the same streets surrounding their home, where they could stay protected from the awfulness that was hurtling down the tracks towards them.

Finally, he pulled up outside their house on Ledbury Road. His sister Gemma's car was already there. She was four years older than him and lived across the city with her husband and three teenage sons. He had asked her to meet him at the house to help him face the mammoth task that was ahead of him.

'Why is Auntie G here?' Jack asked as he climbed out of the car, taking his school bag from the boot.

'I asked her to come,' was all Aidan managed to say.

He looked up at the biscuit-coloured, three-story over-basement Georgian house and all it represented. All the arguments it had caused. It was huge – even with three children, it was still too big for them. They would never have afforded a large family home like this in the affluent area of Ballsbridge without a nice helping hand from Rowan's parents. They had argued a lot about it at the time, Aidan had wanted to pay his own way and buy a house in a less salubrious part of Dublin that was within their budget. He always felt that Rowan was too quick to run to her dad for money and it undermined him and his ability to provide for his family. Aidan had never felt good enough for Philip's only child. It used to bother Aidan a lot; he had gone out of his way to impress his father-in-law over the years, he had even learned how to play golf and paid an extortionate membership to join the same golf club where Philip was a member, hoping they might bond that way, but he had learnt the hard way that he would never win Philip's approval so there was no point even trying. Now, it all seemed so trivial. Aidan felt a pang of regret at how he had let his pride get in the way. Rowan had only wanted to have a beautiful home for their family.

Getting out of the car, Aidan climbed the granite steps, worn in the centre by generations of feet, and put the key into the lock of the door that Rowan had painted sunshine yellow the summer before. He could still see her standing there with the paintbrush in her hand wearing her cut-off denim shorts and one of his old hoodies, her hair kept back with a bandana folded as a headband. He felt himself choke back a sob at the memory.

He let the boys into the house, where sunlight streamed across the honey blonde floorboards that were partly covered in Persian rugs in rich jewel shades of sapphire and ruby. Rowan's touches were all around this house; she had a great eye for interiors and could pull fabrics and textures together that ordinarily might clash, but somehow, she always made them work. She hated bland, minimalist, overstylised houses; theirs was colourful and lived in and she took pride that anyone who walked through their door would know that it was a relaxed and welcoming family home.

As they made their way through to the kitchen at the back of the house, his ear automatically waited for Rowan's sing-song voice calling out, 'hey, I'm in the kitchen,' and his heart stumbled as her loss hit him fresh again.

Gemma was standing beside the island waiting for them.

'Hi, G,' the boys chorused, walking past her and heading straight for the fridge.

'Where's Mam?' Callum asked as he opened a smoothie bottle and flopped down onto the sofa that sat at one end of their open-plan kitchen.

'Callum, Jack—' Aidan began. 'I need to talk to you both for a minute.'

'What is it?' Jack called over his shoulder as he searched the fridge.

Aidan looked anxiously at Gemma, who nodded at him. 'Come over here, boys,' he said. He saw worry flit across their young eyes as they came over and joined him at the island. 'Sit down,' he said, pulling out two stools for them to sit up on. Their faces searched his and he knew the time had come to tell them.

Aidan took a deep breath and braced himself. Once he had delivered this news, there was no turning back; a lifetime of pain stretched ahead of them. 'I have some bad news...' he began. 'Your mother and Milly were involved in a car crash this morning... her car crashed into the back of a lorry.' He recounted the details like he had been told by the Gardaí.

'Is Mam okay?' Jack asked, his eyes wide with fear.

He couldn't get the words out to tell them. They felt stubborn and misshapen in his mouth.

'Dad!' Callum demanded. 'Is she okay?'

Aidan shook his head. 'Sh-she didn't make it,' he blurted as sobs overtook him. He walked over and pulled the boys in close to him; his wife was dead, his daughter was in a coma in the hospital, the boys were the only things that hadn't been taken away from him today.

'Are you saying she's dead?' Callum asked, his eyes were blazing with anger as if this was somehow Aidan's fault.

Aidan nodded as Gemma came over and put her arms around all their shoulders.

'No, Dad, that can't be right,' he shouted, pulling away from him. 'You've got it wrong!'

'I'm sorry, son, I saw her in the hospital, it's definitely her.'

'What about Milly?' Jack asked, biting down on his bottom lip with trepidation.

'She still hasn't woken up yet...' he heard a crack

in his voice as he thought about her tiny body lying in that bed.

'No,' Jack said, shaking his head, his lips were trembling, and his eyes were blinking rapidly. 'This can't be happening...'

Aidan felt so helpless as he watched his sons crumple before his eyes, looking so young and dazed. What was he supposed to do or say to make this any better? Even though he knew that was impossible because this would never get better; this grief would be a shadow over them all for the rest of their lives. It would haunt them during every waking moment.

This is where he would turn to Rowan for advice; she always knew the right thing to say or how to comfort the kids whenever something was troubling them, and if she didn't have the answers, she would read up online about how to approach things or ask her friends that also had children of a similar age. Guiltily, Aidan realised he had left most of that stuff up to her, but she had been good at it – she was always far more tuned into the kids' feelings than he was. Yet now, the one person he needed to guide him through this awful landscape was no longer here. She was gone. In just a few hours, their whole world had been mangled, wiped out. She would never sit at their kitchen island, leafing through a cookery book as she searched for inspiration for their dinner, trying to keep everyone happy – nothing spicy for Jack, no tomatoes for Callum. She knew all their likes and dislikes intimately. She would never again stand baking with Milly in their matching 'Mummy' and 'Daughter' aprons. She would never shake her head good-naturedly as she reminded the boys once again to put down the lid on the toilet seat. All these tiny inconsequential details, that somehow were everything to him. They were the fabric of their home. He wanted to shout and rage and roar, throw something at the injustice of it all. How was any of this real?

'But what will we do without Mam?' Jack asked. 'You're always in work, who will take us to school? Who will make our dinner?' His simple questions summed up everything.

'I don't know,' Aidan choked, because that was the truth. What would they do without her?

* * *

The next few hours were a blur of shock, disbelief and awful, gut-wrenching sobs as the tidal wave of what had happened smacked into them again and again, whilst images of Rowan's crumpled body, lying over the steering wheel, broken and bruised, haunted Aidan.

His phone was ringing and buzzing constantly with messages as word about the crash started to filter out. Her friends arrived at the door looking shaken and stunned, asking him questions about what had happened, even though he didn't have any answers. His head was spinning. He was grateful to Gemma, who poured them tea, while he sat with the boys as they cried themselves to sleep. It broke his heart not being able to fix their pain.

When they were sound asleep, he left Gemma to stay with them, while he made his way back into the hospital. This was the way it was going to be from now on, he realised with sudden clarity – he would be doing it all on his own. He would have nobody to tag-team with or share the load with on the days when it all felt like too much. He felt torn, but as much as the boys needed him, he was aware of Milly, who was perilously close to slipping away from him too. He couldn't bear to lose her as well; he had to do everything in his power to keep her here. He needed to be at her bedside, holding her small hand in his own, begging her to hold on. He needed to protect what was left of his family at all costs.

7

HELENA

Helena had always preferred hospitals at night-time. When she had been training as a junior doctor, she was one of the few that looked forward to working the night shift. The dimmed lights, the sleeping patients, people talking in hushed voices, it was always a welcome calm after a hectic day. She had just said goodbye to Breda and Kevin, telling them to get some sleep and promising that she would call them if anything changed. Her own parents had travelled up from Connemara as soon as they got the news and James's brother, Brian, and his sister, Lisa, had been in earlier too, and maybe it was because she was a doctor, but everyone seemed to be seeking reassurance from her that James was going to be okay. She was exhausted from putting on a brave face when all she really wanted to do was fall apart herself. She was glad to be left alone when they all finally left, to give her head a chance to get to grips with everything that had taken place.

James had spent most of the day asleep. His eyes would open periodically and look around, but he hadn't said anything else, and Helena was now quite sure that his mention of Rowan's name earlier had been nothing more than the drugs talking. She had reviewed his chart and he was on a lot of heavy medication. She still hadn't been able to ask him about the circumstances of the accident, so she had no idea who the mystery driver was. She wasn't even sure where exactly the accident had taken place – all she knew was that it had happened on the Coast Road. She had decided to call the Gardaí in the morning to see if she could find out anything else.

She kept thinking about poor Aidan. She had asked one of the ICU doctors how Milly was doing, but he had said she was still in a coma. Helena was praying that she would pull through – it was horrendous to think of the alternative.

As she sat at her husband's bedside, her meeting with Ken that morning seemed like a lifetime ago. She still smarted with humiliation as she thought about how she had effectively been told that she wasn't up to doing her job, but now it seemed so inconsequential given what had happened since then.

Her eyes were burning with tiredness and a tension headache was pulsing in her skull. Knowing that she had a long night ahead, she decided to go downstairs to the vending machine that spewed out lukewarm coffee.

She had just fed the machine with coins and selected a black coffee from the pictures on the panel, when she saw Aidan coming across the hospital foyer towards her. She noticed his wavy hair was tousled and unkempt, and he was still wearing his work suit, which was now badly creased. She left the machine spurting out watery coffee and hurried over to him.

'Aidan,' she began, 'I've been thinking of you all day. How's Milly doing?'

'She's still in the coma, I'm just heading back up to her now... I had to go home to tell the boys...'

She watched as his whole face crumpled as he

started to break down into heaving sobs. Just a few hours ago, Helena had thought she had lost her husband and for those few minutes she had caught a glimpse of that terror, so her heart ached for the loss Aidan and his children were now enduring.

'Oh, Aidan... I'm so sorry...' She reached out to hug him. 'I can't even begin to imagine how awful that was.' She shook her head at the injustice of it all. It was desperate seeing him in so much pain and to not be able to help him. She shivered to think of the grief those poor children were experiencing at an age where they should never have to know that such agony existed. 'Look, James in on St Mary's ward and I'm going to be here all night and probably for the next few days too, so take my number and if you need someone to talk to... or anything at all... just come and get me or call me or text me and I'll come to you, okay?'

'Thanks, Helena.' He took out his phone and they exchanged numbers. 'How is James by the way – sorry... I've been so wrapped up in what's happened I never asked how he was?' he asked sheepishly, which just broke Helena's heart even more. Aidan was going through enough without feeling bad for not asking about her situation.

'We won't know for sure until he wakes up properly. He has a broken femur and has a long recovery ahead of him, but right now I'm counting my blessings.' Her eyes darted to the floor as once again guilt wracked her, because her husband was still alive, but Aidan's wife was not.

Aidan nodded. 'Tell him that I'm thinking of him.'

'I will, Aidan. Look after yourself.'

She went back to the machine, which was now finished, and took her coffee upstairs to James's bedside. As she sat by her husband, watching the hours change, she couldn't get the image of Aidan's devastated face out of her head. The man was broken. She remembered him at their wedding, playing air guitar with her brother when the DJ had played 'Satisfaction' by the Rolling Stones.

She and James had met almost four years ago; he had proposed after just two months, and they had wed a few months later. It had been a wonderful whirlwind, but they had both been thirty-nine and neither of them had wanted to hang around. They had both had relationships before, but they knew as soon as they met that this was different. She had once overheard James telling his father that he knew he had met 'the one' so he wasn't going to delay in making her his wife.

They had started trying for a baby even before their wedding. She had sought a referral for a fertility clinic when nothing had happened after six months. She hadn't waited because she knew that her age was against her. She hadn't been upset when it was suggested they would need to do IVF. She had seen so many of her patients in the same boat, but she had never thought she would have to endure six heart-breaking miscarriages on their journey to become parents.

As soon as the second blue line had appeared on that first pregnancy test, she had started to imagine what their baby would look like, would they have James's nose or her pointy chin? Even though the books said they were a mere collection of cells at that stage of pregnancy, she already had a whole life planned out for her baby. She couldn't help it. But then the bleeding had started and the hospital confirmed that all her hopes and dreams had left her body. She had picked herself up again after a few months and they had tried another round of IVF but little did she know that they would go on to endure that same pain a further five times and she still wouldn't have a baby to hold at the end of it all. The losses had never left her; Helena still remembered all her babies' due dates and often thought about what age they would be now if they had lived.

To be turned away from the clinic and given no hope of carrying a child of her own at that last consultation had been the straw that broke them. The awful finality of those words had crushed her. How do you accept that the one thing, the one thing your heart desired most in the world, no matter how much you yearned for it, would never happen?

Tears fell down her face and landed onto the sheets as she gently stroked James's bruised face. 'I love you,' she whispered. 'I'll never leave your side again.'

His eyelids began to flicker.

'Helena, you're here,' he croaked.

'Of course I am,' she cried, as she was overcome by tears. Relief, warm and joyous flooded through her. He remembered her. He hadn't said her name earlier. This was a really good sign. Although the team had said his brain scans had all looked good, they couldn't be sure there was no damage to his brain until he woke up.

She pressed the bell beside his bed to call a nurse.

'I was so scared,' she sobbed. 'I thought I was going to lose you. I'm sorry – for everything, I want you to know that.'

'I'm... sorry,' he managed to say as he tried to sit up straighter in the bed but winced as pain shot through him.

'Take your time,' she cautioned as she helped prop him up with pillows. 'You've had pretty major surgery.'

The door opened and a nurse entered the room.

'He's awake!' Helena called out.

'That's good news; how are you feeling, James?' she asked as she began checking him over.

'Everything hurts,' he moaned. 'I feel like I've bruised every bone in my body.'

'Well, that's because you practically have.' The nurse smiled.

'How is he doing?' Helena asked the nurse eagerly.

'Everything looks good to me. We'll keep an eye on his pain levels, but if you need anything else just ring the bell.'

'Your mam and dad were here earlier and Brian and Lisa too,' Helena continued as soon as they were alone again. 'You gave us all a fright. Do you remember anything about the crash?'

'I remember the car... and the sunlight...' he rasped. 'I can remember that, but then it's a total blank... What about the others? Are they okay?'

She knew she had to ask the question that had been plaguing her. 'Whose car were you in, darling?'

'Rowan's car... and her daughter,' he paused for a breath, 'Milly... was there too...'

Rowan and Milly. Her ears began ringing and her hearing went fuzzy. Her mind began whirring with questions. She knew they had been good friends in college, but as far as she was aware, they hadn't seen each other since their wedding almost three years ago, bar the odd text here and there. Why was he in the car with Rowan? Then the rational part of her brain told her to calm down, there was probably a perfectly good reason for it. Perhaps his bike had had a puncture and she had been passing by and had given him a lift. There were lots of possible explanations, she couldn't jump to conclusions.

'Is she okay?' he croaked.

Helena shook her head. 'She passed away, James. Milly is in the ICU.'

She watched his face crease in pain and his eyes grew watery. 'No – she can't be,' he cried.

Helena felt panicked as the peaks on his heart rate monitor became increasingly tachycardic and the bleeps on the machine became louder.

'Take a deep breath,' she ordered and was relieved when his heart rate began to slow once more. Once it had stabilised, she asked the question that she knew she had to ask no matter how much she wished she could run from it. 'Why were you in the car together, James?' She didn't want to ask, but she knew she had no choice but to follow this through, even though she was terrified of what was waiting on the other side for her.

'I... don't know...' he choked. 'She said... she wanted to... to meet me... I said we could go to one... of the coffee shops...' He stopped to catch his breath, which was heavy and laboured. 'But she wanted to go somewhere where... we wouldn't bump... into anyone.'

'I don't understand,' Helena said. Her brain felt like it was filing through all this information but couldn't make sense of it. She was unsure what he was trying to tell her. 'So you haven't been in contact for ages and then she gets in touch out of the blue wanting to meet up? Why would she do that?'

'I'm... not... sure,' he admitted. His eyelids were growing heavy, and she knew he was getting tired. She was on borrowed time, but she needed to get to the bottom of this.

'Do you think it was something to do with UCD – I don't know – maybe she was thinking of organising a reunion or something like that?' She was grappling for reasons here, anything at all that would explain why her husband was travelling in a car with his old college friend and her young daughter.

His gaze dropped to the bed linen, and something told her that there was more going on here.

She felt as though she was unpicking a tapestry, stitch by stitch, but she was going to get to the bottom of this if it killed her. 'What is it?' she demanded. 'What's going on here, James?'

'Well… Rowan and I… had history…'

'What's that supposed to mean?'

'In college, well… we had a thing… we slept together… a few times.'

She had often wondered if anything had ever happened between them back then but had never asked James, feeling it was all so long ago. They were practically kids, and besides, it was none of her business anyway. 'Okay, look that was over twenty years ago. We've all had college flings and, to be honest, I kind of suspected that was the case, but I don't understand why you're telling me this now?'

'There's more…' he said cagily as he closed his eyes again. She knew the effort was exerting him, but she needed to discover the truth.

'Please just tell me, James,' she begged. She was holding her breath, bracing herself for the impact of whatever James was about to say next, knowing it could change everything between them.

James exhaled heavily. 'Rowan and I… we slept together again… a few years ago… before I met you,' he added quickly.

'But she's married to Aidan!' Helena was horrified.

'It never... should have... happened.' His voice was weak and his breathing came ragged.

'I can't believe she did that to her husband!' Helena was reeling from this revelation. She couldn't help but think of poor Aidan's devastated face when she had met him in the corridor earlier. Had he ever found out that his wife was unfaithful? And why had Rowan contacted James after all this time? Had she been hoping that something might rekindle between them? She felt fury warm her veins.

'I'm sorry, Hel...' he mumbled. She could see that the effort to tell this story had exhausted him. His breathing slowed to a shallow beat as he fell back asleep once more.

8

AIDAN

Aidan woke up with a start. He had dreamed of Rowan with her pretty heart-shaped face and those bright green eyes, always so full of fun and mischief. She had been lying slumped over the steering wheel in a crumpled mess, calling to him. Her hair was covering her face and when he brushed it back, he saw that she was smiling at him, but when he looked at her eyes, he realised she was dead.

He had a crick in his neck and pain shot through his muscles as he tried to stretch it out. His forehead was sweating even though the air in the room was chilly. He cursed himself for falling asleep, but as he looked at his daughter in the bed beside him, surrounded by high-tech machines which beeped incessantly, he could see there was no change in her condition. He had brought Mousey, her favourite teddy from home, and had tucked it in beside her. It was a mouse dressed like a ballerina that she had slept with every night since she was born. The doctors had told him that the sooner she woke, the better her prognosis would be, and it was now coming up to almost twenty-four hours since the crash. He gripped her hand and squeezed it, as if, somehow, his touch might be able to pull her out of the depths of her coma, but she lay there motionless.

He unplugged his phone from the charger the nurses had loaned him during the night and saw he had several missed calls and texts and WhatsApp messages of sympathy from shocked friends and relatives. He had silenced his phone as message after message had arrived as word about the crash continued to filter out. He listened to his voicemail and, as well as many messages of condolences, there was a message from Garda Rachel Sullivan to say she would be dropping by the hospital that morning to talk to him. He had been too stunned the previous day to properly process what had happened, but now he hoped she could answer the questions he had. There was also a message from Rowan's father, Philip, to say their flight had landed in Dublin and they would be coming straight to the hospital. The direct Aer Lingus and Ryanair flights from Faro to Dublin were full by the time they had got to the airport the day before and, in the end, they had had to take a connecting flight via London with a six-hour layover.

Aidan didn't reply to anyone and instead called Gemma to see how the boys were doing. She told him that they had just woken and were really upset. She had already informed the schools and Milly's playschool of what had happened. He asked her to put the boys onto him for a few minutes and it was as if their voices had changed overnight and were now laden with grief. Jack asked him how Milly was doing and he lied and said she was good, because he couldn't bear to tell him the truth. He ran his hands down over his face, feeling the prickle of fresh stubble along his palms. Aidan's heart broke when the call was finished because he should be there with them. He felt so torn; he should be the one holding them and soothing them, but he also needed to be with Milly. He was afraid that if he left her side, she might just slip off on him too and he'd never survive that.

The door opened and Rowan's parents, Philip and Sheila, entered the room. They looked exhausted and wan, despite their suntans. They were both dressed in bright summer clothes too cool for the autumnal air outside and Aidan guessed they hadn't even taken the time to change when they got the call the day before. He imagined them lying by the pool, basking in the glorious Algarve sunshine just moments before their lives would change forever.

'I'm so sorry,' Aidan said, getting up from his chair as they came into the room. He shook Philip's hand and Sheila put her arms around him and dissolved into tears.

'I just can't believe any of this is real… we saw her laid out in the Chapel of Peace; she doesn't even look like our daughter…' she sobbed.

Aidan felt his eyes sting as he blinked back another hot surge of tears as grief pummelled him all over again. He still couldn't get his head around how much his world had altered in twenty-four hours.

Philip moved up to his granddaughter's bedside and stroked her pale face. 'How is she?' he asked, nodding towards Milly.

'We're still waiting on her to wake up. I've been here all night.'

'Sheila dabbed at her eyes with a tissue. 'When you called us yesterday, I still hoped you might have made a mistake, but now that we're here, I know it's all true – Rowan's gone – my daughter is gone.' She shook her head with disbelief. 'And my poor little Milly,' she choked, as tears overcame her once more.

Philip walked back over, took his wife in his arms and pulled her in close as she sobbed into his shoulder.

After Sheila had gathered herself, she took the seat Aidan had just vacated beside Milly's bed and reached for her hand. 'She has to pull through, I can't bear to think she won't—'

Philip began pacing around the room. 'I keep wondering how it happened – the weather was good, I checked the conditions online – it wasn't raining, the roads weren't wet or icy. Do you know what happened, Aidan?'

Aidan shook his head. 'Garda Sullivan is dropping by today and I was hoping I'd find out more then.'

'When did you last have the car serviced?' Philip asked. 'Were the tyres okay?' He was firing questions at Aidan like missiles.

Aidan knew he was getting a dig in about the age of the car; it was a twelve-year-old people carrier, but it had never given them an ounce of trouble. It had been on his mind to replace it with a newer model at some stage, but, like everything, it had fallen down the priority list. With three children, there always seemed to be other things that had to be bought. There were school fees, swimming lessons, ballet classes; there was always something to be paid.

Aidan ran his hands down along his face. 'It passed the NCT last month, Philip.'

'It just doesn't make any sense...' Philip continued, 'maybe if she had been in something newer... something with better impact protection or a more modern braking system... she might still be here.'

'Look, this isn't helping, Philip,' Sheila said, becoming emotional once more as she dabbed at her eyes with the balled-up tissue. 'We're all finding this tough.'

Sheila's distress seemed to shake Philip, and Aidan watched as he swallowed back his angry words and calmed down again. They had just lost their precious only daughter, Aidan realised tempers were bound to be frayed, but he had lost his wife and was perilously close to losing his daughter too.

Aidan thought he might suffocate if he spent a minute longer in this room and even though he hated to leave Milly's bedside, he needed to get out of there before he said something he might regret. 'Look, I could do with a coffee,' he sighed. 'Can I get you both anything?'

'No thank you.' Sheila and Philip shook their heads wearily.

'You'll call me if she wakes up, won't you?' Aidan asked as he left the room.

'Of course,' Philip said.

Once outside in the corridor, Aidan took a few deep breaths to slow his heart rate. Why did Rowan's father have this effect on him? Philip always managed to rile him up. Even at a time like this, the man couldn't resist getting a gibe in.

Aidan took the stairs down to the ground floor and continued along the corridor until he reached the coffee shop. He went inside and ordered an Americano. Some people laughed and chatted with one another at the surrounding tables, whilst others sat alone with tired eyes and unwashed hair, looking dishevelled, like him. It was surreal to watch normal life unfold all around him. Everything still continued on even though his world had ended.

The smell of bacon aroused his stomach, and he had a vague sense of being hungry, but yet when he looked at the sandwiches and cakes displayed behind the glass screen of the counter, he couldn't summon the appetite to eat anything.

He was just paying for his coffee when a newspaper headline on the stand below the till caught his eye: 'Woman Killed in Horror Crash'. He lifted the paper and read on.

> A woman was killed in a fatal collision on the Coast Road in Dublin yesterday morning and two passengers are said to be in a serious condition – one, believed to be a child, is critical. The dead woman, who was the driver of the car, has been named as Rowan Whelan (42). It is believed her car crashed into a sta-

tionary queue of traffic. Weather conditions were said to be good at the time and Garda Forensic Collision Investigators are continuing their investigations into the circumstances surrounding the fatal crash.

As he read his wife's name inked on the paper, Aidan had to shake his head to make sense of it. Why did it mention two passengers? Milly had been the only other person in the car.

'Do you want the paper too?' the woman at the till was asking him, pulling him out of his thoughts.

'Sorry,' he mumbled, handing her the money and walking away clutching the newspaper in one hand and the coffee in the other before she could give him the change.

Once outside the coffee shop, he stopped in the corridor and read the article again, thinking that perhaps his tiredness was affecting his vision, but no, it definitely said 'two passengers'. Garda Sullivan hadn't said anything about there being two passengers in the car, had she? But maybe she had, and he hadn't been listening properly… or maybe the journalist who wrote the story had made a mistake…

His heart was racing, and thoughts careered wildly around inside his head. He stepped outside the hospital doors to breathe in the fresh morning air, sweetened by the trill of birdsong. After a few minutes, he decided he had better head back up to Milly just in case she woke.

He was making his way back down the corridor towards the ICU when he heard commotion coming from inside her room. Panic seized him. He began to run.

'What is it? What's wrong?' he cried as he hurried inside. He noticed there was a nurse in there with them.

Sheila and Philip were grinning at him with tears in their eyes.

'She woke up, Aidan!' Sheila gushed. 'We were sitting here with her and suddenly she just started blinking, so we called her name and she opened her eyes and looked at us.' Her diamond-studded fingers were fluttering around her throat.

'She recognised our voices,' Philip added, and Aidan couldn't help but wonder if he was imagining a smugness in his smile.

'Why didn't you call me?' Aidan shouted, rushing

up to his daughter's bedside. He couldn't help feeling aggrieved that he had missed it. He would have come straight back instead of taking a breather outside. Then he felt guilty; she had woken up, wasn't that all that mattered? 'Did she say anything?' Aidan continued, feeling contrite.

Sheila shook her head.

Her eyes remained closed, and she looked just like she had looked before he had left. Aidan reached for her hand. 'Milly?' he called. 'Milly, it's Daddy,' he tried again, but there was no reaction.

'Don't expect too much too soon,' the nurse cautioned. 'She's been through a huge trauma, but it's a really good sign that she's starting to come out of her coma.'

Aidan nodded, knowing she was right. After everything Milly had been through, he needed to be patient.

* * *

When Sheila and Philip, both wall-fallen with tiredness and weary with grief, decided to head back to their Foxrock house to get some sleep a while later, Aidan was relieved to be left alone with his daughter once more and away from Philip's overbearing presence.

'Milly, it's daddy,' he tried again as soon as he was alone with her and, this time, he saw her eyelids begin to twitch. She recognised his voice; he was sure of it. 'Come on, love,' he encouraged. He gently squeezed her hand inside his own.

Aidan hardly dared to breathe as she opened her eyes, two huge pools of blue, and looked around the room, taking it all in. He could tell she was confused by where she was.

'You're in the hospital, sweetie,' he explained.

'Mama,' she said after a few moments. 'Me want, Mama.'

Aidan's heart twisted as though somebody had ripped it clean from his chest and put it between the jaws of a vice grip. He felt panicked and out of his depth. The trauma nurses had told him to wait until she was stronger before telling her the news. So what was he supposed to say now? How could he tell her the truth? She was still so weak, would the news of her mother's death set her recovery back? Did a three-year-old even understand the concept of death? This was another instance of where he could use Rowan's advice – she would have known how to handle this, what to say or what not to say. She would know how to distract Milly or explain it in an age-appropriate way.

'Mama will be back soon, sweetie,' he lied, hating himself with every word that left his mouth. He knew he would have to face telling her eventually, but right now he needed his precious daughter to hang on.

9

HELENA

The seal of the door made a prolonged squeak as it swept over the rubber flooring while Helena entered the room. Aidan didn't bother to turn around to see who it was, probably assuming it was one of the medical team doing their checks.

'Thought you could use this,' she said, holding out the cardboard coffee cup and a brown paper bag containing a croissant and banana that she had bought in the shop downstairs.

Aidan swung around and she knew he was surprised to see her standing there. Dark circles hung beneath his eyes, and he looked shattered, but she guessed she didn't exactly look too great right now either. Like her, he was still wearing the same clothes as he had been wearing the previous day.

'Thanks,' Aidan said, taking it from her gratefully. She guessed caffeine was probably the only thing keeping him going right now.

'I heard the good news.' She nodded towards Milly, who was asleep once more. 'I trained with one of the registrars on duty today and he filled me in,' she explained. 'You must be so relieved to be moved from ICU to High Dependency. I know she's not out of the woods yet, but it's a step in the right direction. So, how's she doing?'

'She was asking for Rowan,' Aidan said, looking crestfallen.

'Oh, Aidan, that's awful. What did you say?'

'I didn't tell her yet – I just didn't think it was the right time.' He shook his head. 'I don't think it'll ever be the right time,' he sighed.

Helena nodded. 'I think that's a good call, wait until she's feeling a bit stronger. And what about you? How've you been?'

'I still can't believe any of this is real to be honest,' he admitted. 'I've been so focused on Milly and making sure she pulls through and then worrying about how the boys are doing at home that I keep forgetting. Then I'll go to tell Rowan something or ask her for advice and I remember.' He shook his head as if trying to shake off the horror. 'It keeps sneaking up on me like a big mallet and whacking me all over again.'

She remembered that awful stage of grieving after her brother had passed away from cancer a few years ago. Even now, after all these years, she still picked up the phone to call him before she would remember. 'Grief is sneaky,' Helena agreed. 'People say time is a healer, but that's a lie, it never gets any easier, you just get better at dealing with the pain.'

'How's James doing?' he asked, stroking the pudgy skin on Milly's arm.

She felt heat warm through her face. She was still trying to come to terms with his revelation about his one-night stand with Rowan. She was trying to process what he had told her, but it was as though the words couldn't penetrate her brain. How could he do something like that? How could Rowan have done that to Aidan?

'It was before I met you and it was only one time,' he had tried to justify it since, as if that automatically excused everything. 'We bumped into one another on a night out and one thing led to another... Rowan was feeling lonely, James was travelling so much with work... she was on her own with the two boys all the time and it just sort of happened.' Although he swore that he had never been unfaithful during their marriage, she still hadn't thought that her husband would be capable of doing that to another man. She had been torn between wanting to rage and scream at him but also conscious of the fact that he was in an extremely fragile and vulnerable state, and she didn't want to set back his recovery. Nonetheless, alarm bells had fired in her brain. Why had Rowan made contact with James again after all this time? Why couldn't they have met in one of his coffee shops like James had suggested? Had she wanted to reignite the flames of passion once again? Or maybe they had already ignited, and James wasn't being honest with her? To think Rowan had sat in the church at their wedding with Aidan sitting loyally in the pew beside in her, blissfully unaware that she had betrayed him with the man standing on the altar. As Rowan had watched James exchange his vows,

Helena wondered if she had felt any remorse for what she had done to Aidan?

Helena paused for a breath to gather herself. 'He's doing okay; he's lucid now.'

She wondered if Aidan had figured it out yet? Surely, he had pieced it together by now? It was all over the news. She had read about it on her phone. Although James's name hadn't been mentioned in the newspaper articles she had read, the fact that there had been two passengers in Rowan's car must have triggered alarm bells in Aidan's head. But perhaps he hadn't seen the news with everything that was going on... Then she spotted the folded newspaper on Milly's tray table, the ink on the front page screaming up at her. *He has seen it*, she thought. But wouldn't he have said something about it? He certainly wasn't acting off with her. Perhaps he was in shock...

'I see you got the paper,' she said to test the waters.

'Yeah, front-page news.' He shook his head bitterly. 'Usually you read about these things but they're always people you don't know, and you think how tragic, but then you forget all about it and go on with your day.'

Judging by his reaction, Helena realised that he hadn't pieced it together. 'Do you know who the other passenger was?' she ventured, feeling as though she was taking steps across a sheet of ice.

'Well, I assumed they made a mistake…' Aidan admitted, suddenly sounding doubtful. 'Garda Sullivan is due to call in and I was going to ask her about it actually.'

'Aidan…' she began. There was no easy way to tell him this. She knew she was about to shake up his world once more, but she had no choice, because he was going to discover the truth soon anyway. Once he spoke with the Gardaí, they would tell him the full details of the crash and she hated to think of him being humiliated in front of a stranger like that. It was better coming from her. She took a deep breath. 'James was the other passenger in the car.'

She watched as Aidan's face changed through several expressions as he tried to process what he had just been told.

'James, as in your husband?' Aidan knitted his

brows together in incredulity. 'But why would he be in the car with them?'

'I'm not sure to be honest, Aidan. Rowan had contacted him and asked to meet up.' She lowered her gaze. 'She never got to tell him what she wanted to say.'

She could see Aidan trying to process this new revelation, as it threw up more questions inside his head. He was going through the exact same shock and disbelief as she was.

'Was it some sort of college meet-up? I didn't think they were really in touch any more.'

She shook her head. 'I'm not sure, but I reckon that's what it was.' She forced a smile on her face to reassure him. It was kinder to leave it this way. It was for Aidan's own good, because the truth would destroy him. She wanted to spare him the knowledge of his wife's betrayal – what did it matter now anyway? Rowan was no longer here, and Aidan didn't need to have her memory tainted like that. The damage was done and there was no point dredging it back up again.

'Maybe James could tell me what happened?'

Aidan asked hopefully. 'Does he remember anything?'

Helena felt her heart rate quicken. 'That's all he can remember unfortunately. He's still quite weak, Aidan,' she lied, feeling fear flood through her. Aidan wasn't letting this go and she knew it would only be a matter of time before he came searching for answers.

10

AIDAN

Aidan's head had been spinning with questions after Helena had gone. It was only when he was alone that he had had time to really process it all. Garda Sullivan had arrived not long after Helena had left and his heart had sunk as she had confirmed what Helena had told him – that James O'Herlihy was the other passenger travelling in the car with his wife and daughter. He had so many questions that he needed answered, but Garda Sullivan was only able to help with circumstances surrounding the crash. She told him that forensic crash investigators had examined the scene and their findings would be made known in the inquest in a few months' time but that several witnesses had come forward claiming that the lorry in front of Rowan was stationary in a queue of traffic at the time and her car hadn't braked early enough. They said she had tried to swerve at the last minute, but the driver's side of the car had ploughed into the lorry. Garda Sullivan had told him that the car was written off and had been taken to a dismantlers' yard. As she was leaving, she had handed him a clear plastic bag with belongings retrieved from the wreckage. Amongst other items, Aidan saw Rowan's phone with its screen smashed, her handbag, a pair of sunglasses, a bottle of sun cream, a hoodie belonging to Callum, two footballs and Milly's lunch bag. All evidence of happy family life, nothing that had foretold of the carnage that was coming down the tracks for them and nothing that explained why James had been travelling in the car with them.

He watched Milly as she slept peacefully beside him. He wondered if she remembered anything from the crash. She hadn't mentioned it during the brief periods she had woken and now that she was just starting on the road to recovery, Aidan didn't want to risk upsetting her by triggering any memories she might have, but he longed to ask her about James and whether she remembered what had been going on in the moments before the crash.

He had always known that James and Rowan had had a 'thing' back in college. Rowan had once told him that their friendship sometimes transcended into sex, but they had never officially been a couple. As far as he knew, they kept in touch sporadically, a text message here and there. James had invited them to his wedding, along with all the old college gang. Rowan used to have nights out with her college friends, but they had died off in recent years. They were all married now, most of them had young children and it had become harder to organise a night that suited everyone. He was sure Rowan hadn't seen James since his wedding day. Until now. So why on earth was James in her car? Had something rekindled between them... But no... they were both married – Rowan had children. She wouldn't do that to them – to him.

Aidan and Rowan had always been something of an odd couple, everyone knew that. Even Aidan knew that. She was so creative and vivacious, he was so steady – so *safe* – but she told him that that was what she liked about him. When Rowan had first introduced him to her friends, they had all regarded him as something of a curiosity.

They had met at the party of a mutual friend when they were in their early twenties. Aidan had noticed her as soon as she had walked into the room; she had glossy dark hair and her green eyes had been accentuated by the emerald shade of her dress. She had picked up a guitar that was standing in the corner and Aidan had been transfixed as she started to play. Aidan hadn't thought she would even cast him a second look. Safe, dependable Aidan, with his work suits, a mortgage and a pension plan before he had even turned twenty-three.

Somehow that night they had got talking and had got on well. He had offered to walk her home and as they had laughed together as the sun was rising over the Irish Sea, Aidan knew something had started between them. They had quickly become inseparable. Aidan had felt a bit unsure of himself at the start, but she said she liked his sensible clothes and the way he always called when he said he would. She liked the way he took care of her. Once, she had told him that he reminded her of her father and at the time Aidan had taken that as a compliment, but now he wasn't so sure.

Aidan had been raised in a working-class family; his father was a line manager in a factory that bottled soft drinks and his mother had worked in the canteen there, so it had been drilled into him from a young age that he had to work hard and get a solid education or he would end up working in the bottling factory too. He was determined to have a better life than they had had, so he got his degree in finance (first class honours) and landed a good job in an investment bank straight out of college. He had worked his way up the ladder rung by rung and was proud that he was a director now. Rowan had studied art history in UCD and although she sometimes helped out in her friend Annabelle's gallery, she earned a pittance from her work there, but Aidan was pretty sure Philip kept her account topped up.

He always thought it was the difference in their upbringings that gave them such diametrically opposing attitudes towards money; Aidan always took a cautious approach when it came to their finances, whereas Rowan could be frivolous and if Aidan ever dared to say anything, her reply was always 'it's only money'. *It's only money* – like he hadn't had to spend his whole life grafting to make sure his family had enough of the stuff! He never could get his head around that, but Rowan's family had never had to worry about money and he guessed that bought freedom. She was always complaining about the crazy hours he worked; yes, he did work long hours, but it was all for them. There was no way they could keep up with the lifestyle Rowan was accustomed to without his job and his annual bonus, and even then it was a struggle.

Money had been tight after Christmas last year and when the invoice for Callum's school fees had arrived in January, Aidan had pushed it out for a while to give himself a breather, but when he went to pay it a few weeks later, he found it had already been magically paid. It appeared Philip had saved the day yet again. Rowan had shrugged when he had asked her about it. She knew he didn't agree with her readiness to take handouts from her father, but what could he say without appearing ungrateful, and so it had slipped away unspoken, like everything else between them. Now it seemed so silly. Why had he spent so much time worrying about that stuff?

Things like pensions and mortgages and having college funds set up for the kids. He should have relaxed more; loosened up, instead of being boring, dependable Aidan.

Rowan definitely would never fit into the mould of suburban stay-at-home-mum and if he was being really honest, he sometimes had found her unconventional ways a bit tiring over the years. Not long after they had first met, she had spent five nights sleeping rough on the steps of Leinster House to highlight the growing numbers of the city's homeless population. While watching his girlfriend outside government buildings on the nine o'clock news every night, Aidan had been torn between pride and mild embarrassment in case his work colleagues recognised her on their TV screens, as the news cameras reported live from the scene of the protest.

Then there was the time a few years later when she had befriended a young homeless girl called Magda and had moved her into their house for three months. Aidan was proud of his wife's strong sense of social justice, but the boys had only been small at the time and he didn't think it was right to have a stranger living with them. She had argued that she owed it to share their privileged life with others, but it was easy to be a social justice warrior when you had never worried about money a day in your life. Things had come to a head when he had arrived home from work one day to find Magda sitting at their kitchen table entertaining a group of her friends with Rowan nowhere to be seen. That day, Aidan had given Rowan an ultimatum – it was either Magda or him. In the end Rowan had got Magda a job as a live-in house-keeper for a friend of hers and so she had finally moved out.

There had been many times he had wished she could just try to fit in a bit more, just *try* to live a more normal life. However, these thoughts were usually followed by a rush of guilt – he had fallen in love with Rowan purely because she *was* different, he loved her free spirit and flair for anything creative. He couldn't expect her to change who she was just so he would feel more comfortable. She was like a tree that you tried to shape but it just grew whatever way it wanted to anyway, no matter how much you tried to prune it. Now he couldn't help but wonder why had he wanted her to change? Why hadn't he appreciated her for the way she was?

* * *

Sheila and Philip arrived again that evening, looking a lot more refreshed than they had when they had come in earlier that morning. They had changed into clothes more suitable for the Irish weather. Aidan asked them to sit with Milly while he returned home to see the boys for a few hours. It was so difficult being apart from them at a time like this, when they needed him more than ever. He knew the hospital wouldn't let them in to visit Milly yet and besides, she was still in and out of sleep and he was worried it would upset the boys to see her like this instead of their livewire little sister who was always tearing around the house. Gemma was keeping him updated on how they were, but he longed to be with them. He also knew he could use a shower and change of clothes himself.

'The boys are in a bad way,' Philip began. 'We called in on our way here.'

As usual, Philip didn't beat around the bush.

Aidan felt a flood of guilt. While Aidan was desperate to see his sons, he was equally dreading seeing their raw grief.

'They've lost the best mother in the world, of course they are,' Sheila said, her voice dancing on tears once more.

'Did you manage to find out who the other passenger was?' Philip continued, lifting the newspaper that Aidan had bought in the coffee shop that morning and studying it again. Aidan could see it in Philip's eyes that his lack of awareness about such a key detail in the crash was yet another sign of his failure as a husband. Sheila and Philip had read the newspaper earlier on and had asked Aidan who the third person was. Aidan had explained that he was just as mystified as they were and that he assumed it was a journalistic error but now he knew differently.

'Actually I did,' Aidan admitted.

'Well go on,' Philip said.

'It was James.'

'James who?' Philip asked impatiently.

'James O'Herlihy – you know, her friend from UCD?' Aidan prompted. He was sure that Philip and Sheila would have met him over the years.

Sheila paused in thought for a moment. 'I remember him – wasn't he the one who—' she broke off, leaving the sentence unfinished. 'But why would he have been in the car with Rowan?' She was clearly bewildered.

'I'm not sure, but I think she might have been giving him a lift,' Aidan lied, thinking on the spot. He knew that if he told Philip and Sheila the truth, that Rowan had wanted to talk to James about something, it would open a whole new chasm of questions that he was still searching for answers for himself. 'His bike had a puncture and she happened to be driving by.'

Sheila shook her head sadly. 'She was always helping other people right up until her dying moment. How is James doing?'

'He has a broken femur apparently, but he'll be all right.' Helena had said that James didn't know why Rowan had called him out of the blue wanting to meet, but Aidan was sure she wasn't telling him the full story. There had been something she was holding back; he could tell. He decided that once Rowan's parents were gone, he would go down that corridor to St Mary's ward and ask James himself. He would ask all the questions that were tormenting him.

'He had a lucky escape then,' Philip said, shaking

his head. 'I was talking to the mortuary director a little while ago... The body will be released tomorrow.'

'I see,' Aidan said, feeling like he had been punched. Why had nobody informed him? Surely as Rowan's husband and next of kin, they should have told him; but knowing his father-in-law, he had probably instructed them to call him first. Philip had to be in control of everything.

'We'll have to organise the funeral,' Philip continued.

Here he goes, thought Aidan sourly, Philip was already starting to take charge of the arrangements. Aidan nodded, it was one of those things that was looming on the horizon, but he didn't have the strength to think about it right now. The thought of his wife lying in a wooden box, being lowered into the ground, was terrifying.

'We were thinking of St. Xavier's church for the mass,' Philip went on.

St. Xavier's was the parish church where Rowan had grown up, but their church now was St Brigid's, beside the kids' school. They weren't very religious, but they traipsed to mass there every Christmas morning and it was where their children had been baptised and made their communions. This was where the kids would expect it to be.

'But St. Brigid's church is in our parish,' Aidan said. 'It's the church that the kids know best.'

'Well, my little girl made all her sacraments in St Xavier's and you both got married there in case you have forgotten,' Philip said pointedly.

'It's what Rowan would have wanted, Aidan,' Sheila backed up her husband, knowing there was no comeback from that.

'Okay,' Aidan agreed, clenching the bar at the end of Milly's bed tightly. He didn't have the energy to fight them on it. If it meant that much to them, he would go with it. Aidan knew from years of dealing with his in-laws that it was wiser to pick your battles.

'I'll contact Father Waldron,' Philip said, satisfied that he had won the battle.

11

HELENA

Since her husband's confession, Helena's mind was whirling with questions. James had had a steady stream of family members visiting and as she had put on the face of the loving and devoted wife waiting patiently at his bedside, nobody would have ever guessed at her inner turmoil. She was still reeling from the news of James's one-night stand with his old college flame. Although James hadn't betrayed her, she thought it was crass of him to sleep with a married woman.

She was also still trying to come to terms with her forced leave of absence from her job. She hadn't told anyone that Ken had requested she take a month off; she felt ashamed and was worried what people would think of her. If she opened up to them, she would end up having to tell them the whole sorry tale about their infertility journey and she couldn't face that right then. Everyone, including James, just assumed she had taken leave to be at his bedside in the aftermath of the crash and that was the way she wanted it.

While James snoozed, she was attempting to read a magazine that she had bought in the shop downstairs, although she kept having to reread paragraphs as her mind wandered. He still spent a lot of time in and out of sleep, as his body tried to recover from the accident and she was keenly aware that even when he was awake, he was under the influence of heavy medication.

She suddenly felt a presence in the room and she looked up to see Aidan standing there. 'Aidan,' she said, closing her magazine. 'I didn't hear you come in...' She sat up straight and her heart suddenly began pounding. 'How are you?'

She had been expecting him; she knew that once he had had time to get his head around the fact that James was in the car with his wife and daughter, it was only natural that he would want answers, but what if he began asking awkward questions? She really didn't want to have to tell him about James and Rowan's one-night stand. The man was going through enough right now, but she knew that she could only fob him off for so long before he would grow suspicious.

She saw James's eyes open at the sound of another voice in the room and her chest tightened. What if Aidan questioned James directly? James was still quite weak and something like this could set back his recovery.

'How are you doing?' Aidan asked, looking directly at James.

'I-I'm good, thanks, I'm feeling a bit better today.' He hoisted himself up against the pillows, his face grimacing in pain from the movement.

Helena gestured to the free seat beside her. 'Sit down.'

Aidan sat down on the chair but remained quite rigid. 'I hope you don't mind me coming in like this, but I just wanted to ask you a few things. As you can imagine, my head is all over the place...'

Helena's heart began to ratchet. 'Of course it is.' She nodded sympathetically.

'I'm so sorry for you loss,' James said. His voice sounded scratchy. 'I can't imagine what you're going through.'

'Thanks...' Aidan mumbled. There was a flash of pain in his eyes and Helena felt as though she was looking right into the depths of his grief. 'When I discovered you were travelling in the car with Rowan and Milly, well I was shocked – you were the last person to see her alive and I just feel I need some answers... it might help me to make sense of what happened, y'know?'

Helena held her breath. She knew they couldn't avoid telling Aidan the truth no matter how much she had hoped they could.

James took a deep breath. 'Of course,' he began. 'Well, we were driving along, it was a really sunny morning... the sun was glaring through the windscreen... and I'm sorry but I don't really remember anything after that...'

Aidan's brow creased in a V in the centre. 'But why were you in the car in the first place? She should have been dropping Milly to playschool... I just don't get it.' He shook his head.

'To be honest, I don't really know myself...' James admitted, looking like a rabbit caught in headlights.

'Come on, James,' Aidan demanded, his voice climbing higher. 'You were hardly put in the car at gunpoint, are you honestly telling me that you don't know why you were with her that morning?'

'I'm telling you, Aidan,' he pleaded, 'Rowan called me up out of the blue, she said she wanted to talk. I did think it was a bit odd, but I just assumed she was organising a college reunion or something... I suggested we go to one of my shops, but she said no, she wanted to go somewhere more private, so she suggested a walk along the beach, which I did think was strange... I guess she seemed a little... distracted maybe... like she had something on her mind. She never got to tell me what she wanted...' he broke off.

'Look, Aidan, I don't think this is–' Helena tried to intervene.

'So let me get this straight,' Aidan cut across her before she could finish, 'You haven't seen each other since your wedding day and then she contacts you out of the blue?'

'Well, yeah...' James replied.

Aidan squeezed his eyes shut for a moment to get his head together. 'So you're there in the car with my wife and daughter, you're driving to the beach,' a sardonic note laced Aidan's voice as he spoke, 'and you're shooting the breeze... catching up on old times... and you didn't even think to ask her why she wanted to meet you after all this time? Do you know how ridiculous that sounds?'

'Aidan, calm down,' Helena instructed, 'Or I'm going to have to ask you to leave.' She knew that Aidan needed answers but she was concerned that he was putting too much stress on James.

'Of course I asked her!' James said defensively. 'As soon as I got into the car, I tried to figure out what was going on, but she said she wanted to wait until we got there before telling me.'

Aidan pinched the bridge of his nose between his thumb and index finger. 'You see, this just doesn't make sense to me...'

'I swear that was what happened,' James said, sounding panicked.

'There's something more – I know there's something you're not telling me,' Aidan pushed.

Helena felt her heart rate quicken. James shot her a look and she could tell that he didn't know what to he was supposed to do or say. They were skating dangerously close to thin ice here; they both knew it.

'What is it?' Aidan demanded, catching the exchange between them. 'What is going on here?'

'Aidan, I think you should go now,' Helena suggested. She needed to end this conversation now before it went any further. 'James needs to rest.'

'No way, I'm not going anywhere until he tells me what the hell is going on,' Aidan replied doggedly.

Helena nodded at her husband, a look that implicitly told him that it was time to come clean. They had no choice.

James took a deep breath before beginning. 'Rowan and I used to have a... a... thing back when we were in college...'

'I already know that,' Aidan said impatiently. 'But that was over twenty years ago.'

'There's more...'

'Go on,' Aidan urged.

'Well, we were on a night out a few years back and one thing led to another...'

'And?' Aidan demanded.

'We slept together.' James visibly winced. 'I'm so sorry, Aidan,' he added.

Aidan shook his head as he tried to process what he had just been told. 'You're saying that Rowan was unfaithful to me?'

Helena flinched. Even though it was difficult to break this news to Aidan, she knew James had no choice now but to keep going and answer Aidan's questions.

'It was one time, I swear. I'm not trying to excuse it, but we had both had a lot to drink and it just sort of happened.'

'It "just sort of happened"?' Aidan repeated in disbelief. 'Do you know how pathetic that sounds?'

'I'm really sorry,' James pleaded. 'I never meant to hurt you. I can't imagine how awful it feels to learn this now, when you've just lost your wife. It never should have happened.'

'When was it? Did you do it in my house? Did you sleep in our bed? Were the kids there?' Aidan goaded.

'No, of course not!' James was horrified. 'The kids were at home with your nanny and we checked into a hotel in town. It was around four years ago maybe, I think she was a bit... well... a bit vulnerable... She said you were travelling a lot with work... I think you might have been in the States at the time and I guess she was lonely...'

Helena watched the revelation hit Aidan like a slap. 'Rowan was vulnerable? She was lonely?' he repeated. 'So why did you sleep with her then if she was vulnerable? You took advantage of her!' he roared.

'I never meant to hurt anyone – you have to believe that,' James said. 'We both regretted it the next morning – she was really upset by what she had done to you. I'm really sorry, Aidan.'

'Well it's a bit too late for that now,' Aidan spat, his whole face contorted with anger. 'So now we're a bit closer to the truth... Is that why you were in the car together? Were you heading off for a quick shag for old times' sake?'

James and Helena flinched. 'I swear on my life – on Helena's life – I don't know why she contacted me. I've told you everything I know, you have to believe me.'

'How do I know you're being truthful? You could

be making all of this up and Rowan isn't even here to defend herself,' he blasted.

'My phone – you can check my phone…' James's face contorted in pain as he moved to pick it up off his locker and attempted to hand it to Aidan. 'You can check my call log; you'll see she called me last week. There are no texts or WhatsApp messages or anything – it was just one call out of nowhere.'

'You're pathetic,' Aidan snapped, as he pushed back the chair and stood up to go. 'I need to get back to Milly.' He stormed out of the room.

'Fuck,' James sighed heavily after Aidan had left, as he fell back against the pillows. 'I feel like the biggest prick that ever walked the planet.'

'Look, that conversation was never going to go well,' Helena sighed. Poor Aidan, he was going through hell and now her husband's actions had made an awful situation even worse. She was exhausted, the culmination of her worry about James, the lack of sleep the night before and now seeing Aidan hit with this revelation was unbearable. Had they done the right thing by telling him? Maybe if her mind had been clearer and they hadn't been caught off guard, they could have fabricated a reason why James was in the car with his wife and saved him so much pain and torment, but as the saying went, 'the truth will out' and she knew he probably would have found out eventually anyway. 'I'm going to head home too,' Helena said, gathering up her things. 'I need to get some sleep.' She gave him a kiss on the forehead and headed on. She felt bad for leaving him alone after everything that had happened but she needed some space to process it all.

As Helena drove home from the hospital that evening, darkness had started to fall. The early autumn evenings were already starting to close in. Light rain misted the windscreen, and the wipers screeched to clear it. She came up to a set of traffic lights near the street where she knew Aidan and Rowan lived. She thought about Aidan and everything that he must be going through, what a hammer blow it must have been for him to realise his wife and her old college friend had slept together and she wasn't even here to get angry with.

As she drove on, she suddenly remembered the first time she had met Rowan when they had gone out together with some of James's college friends to celebrate their engagement. She and James had been sitting opposite Rowan and Aidan at the table. The four of them laughing away together, her and Rowan exchanging 'annoying partner' anecdotes with one another when the men were out of earshot – she had *liked* her, thought she was good fun. There had been a few 'in' jokes between Rowan and James and a lot of reminiscing about the 'good old college days', but she hadn't minded, in fact she had enjoyed hearing their stories and getting to know the man her fiancé was in his younger days before he had met her. Rowan and James had always seemed to get on well, but now she was wondering had there been an underlying current of flirtation all along? She was examining every detail in a new light, looking for clues, for something that would explain the awful mess they now found themselves in. All this new information was sloshing around inside her head like murky water being swirled inside a basin. Her whole world had been altered by the crash and a deep feeling of foreboding seemed to be shadowing her, hunting her down, telling her that life was forever going to be different from here on in.

12

AIDAN

The next day, Aidan pulled into the hospital car park and silenced the engine. He didn't get out of the car straight away, instead he remained sitting there, taking a minute to breathe. In some ways, it was a relief to be back in the hospital. He had gone home that morning for a couple of hours to see the boys and he hadn't realised how tough it would be. They weren't coping well. Callum was so angry. Aidan had sat at the side of his bed, but he just roared at him to 'get lost' every time he tried to talk to him. He didn't know what he was supposed to do in this situation. Eventually, he had decided to give the child space if that was what he needed and he'd left the bedroom feeling utterly useless.

Jack wasn't faring much better; the boy had retreated into himself completely, it was like someone had hollowed out his son and switched off the light in his eyes. He seemed to wander around the house in a daze. Aidan had felt wretched seeing the boys' grief displayed so viscerally. Never had he felt so out of his depth as a father.

'I don't know what to do,' Aidan had admitted, coming into the kitchen where his mother was sitting at the island in the kitchen. She and his sister Gemma were taking turns to stay with the boys. 'I feel so useless.'

'It's only been two days, Aidan,' Agnes had said, standing up and coming over to him. She'd rubbed his arm and shook her head sadly. 'They're still in shock, the poor kids.'

Aidan had nodded. She was right. Their world had been torn apart, of course they were going to react like this. It was just hard knowing there was nothing he could do to fix it.

He was also still grappling with what James had

told him about his wife's betrayal. He had been pulled between utter disbelief, thinking that what he had said couldn't possibly be true but knowing in the darkest corner of his mind that it was. Why had Rowan done it? What James had said about her being vulnerable and lonely had come as a shock to him.

Aidan had wracked his brains, thinking about that period of their lives. He had been travelling back and forth to the US because his company had taken on a new client there. She had complained at the time about how hard it was with the boys on her own, so they had hired a nanny to help her out for a few hours every day. Clearly that hadn't been enough.

How had he missed the signs? Sure, their marriage had been under stress, but that's what happened in marriages, wasn't it? They had their ups and downs. Had they not been as happy as he had thought? Had he not been enough for her? What was so lacking in their marriage that she needed to seek it out with her old flame?

He was grieving his wife, but now his grief was replaced with newer feelings of anger and betrayal and they were much harder to reconcile. He felt guilty for his anger towards her and he didn't know how to deal with it – how could you grieve for someone you were angry at? He loved her so much and he missed her, yet he was so hurt by James's revelations.

The cruellest part was that he couldn't even ask Rowan. They only had James's version of events and perhaps Rowan would have had a completely different story to tell.

* * *

'Did she wake up at all?' was the first thing Aidan asked Sheila and Philip as soon as he returned to Milly's bedside. He was praying for good news, he needed something positive to cling to when everything seemed to be going wrong.

'No, the poor mite is still exhausted,' Sheila said as they gathered up their things to return home.

The amount of time that Milly seemed to be asleep was worrying him. He would have expected her to be spending longer periods awake at this stage, but maybe this was normal for coma patients – maybe some people just took longer to recover?

However, he knew by the way the medical team had started asking how long she had been sleeping for, that they were growing concerned.

'How were the boys?' Sheila asked.

'They're devastated,' Aidan said. 'Callum won't talk to me and Jack is still in shock.'

'It would break your heart to think of the pain they're in.' Tears filled Sheila's eyes. 'I'll call over to them tomorrow. They might open up to their granny.'

Aidan doubted it, but anything that helped the boys through this awfulness was welcome. 'Thanks, Sheila, I'd appreciate that.'

'I've spoken with Father Waldron about the funeral mass,' Philip interjected sombrely. 'It's this Friday at eleven a.m. You might start thinking about the eulogy.'

Aidan sucked in sharply. How was he meant to stand up there in front of the mourners and say good things about his wife after everything that he had learnt about her duplicity? People would see straight through him. The thought of standing in a packed church was overwhelming; people coming up to shake his hand and offer their condolences, while inside he was seething, felt all wrong. How was he supposed to act like the devastated husband when his feelings flitted between desperately missing his wife and mother of his children to fury at her betrayal?

And what about the kids? Milly would hardly be well enough to attend and he would need to prepare the boys for such an ordeal. It was going to be so difficult for them to feel the eyes of the congregation upon them while they grieved for their mother. They were only children; Aidan was dreading it and he was a grown man.

'Actually, Philip, maybe you could do it,' Aidan suggested. 'I was never any good at public speaking…'

Sheila gasped. 'But Rowan was your wife, Aidan. It has to come from you.'

Philip's eyes were boring into him, brimming with anger. 'You were married for fifteen years, she was the mother of your children. It's the least you can do for her.'

Aidan sighed. 'Okay, I'll try to put some words together…' he agreed in a bid to keep the peace.

* * *

'Hey,' a voice said a while later as he held his head in his hands and thought about everything. He had just seen Philip and Sheila off and had taken back the seat at the head of Milly's bed. He looked up and saw Helena standing inside the door looking concerned. 'I just wanted to see how you're doing?'

He lifted his head quickly. 'I'm okay,' he lied. 'Exhausted but no point complaining.'

'How's she doing?' She nodded to Milly.

'Still asleep,' Aidan sighed. He paused for a breath. 'The funeral is this Friday.'

'Aidan, I'm sorry.' Helena shook her head. 'That must be so hard to think about right now.'

'I've no choice but to get through it. Philip has asked me to write the eulogy, *Hey did you know my wife had cheated on me?*' Aidan began in a mocking voice. 'I'm going to feel like such a liar standing up there in front of everyone.'

'You and Rowan had a good marriage, Aidan – I know I didn't know her well, but on the few occasions I met you both, I saw that. Maybe try to remember the happy times, like when you first got married or the kids were born,' she suggested.

Aidan nodded. 'Yeah, you're right... Anyway, how are you doing?'

Helena sighed as she flopped into the other chair and placed her handbag at her feet. 'Do you know something... I don't really know. Doesn't that sound crazy? I just don't know how I feel to be honest – or how I'm supposed to feel. When I heard about the crash, I was so grateful that my husband was still alive, but then I learnt about what they did... I don't know what way I'm supposed to feel.' She gave a hollow laugh before falling silent for a moment. 'Even before the crash, I wasn't exactly in the best place. That morning, the practice owner in the surgery where I work had suggested that I take some leave,' she confessed sheepishly.

'Why would he do that?' Aidan asked, aghast.

She took a breath. 'Well, I broke down in front of a patient,' she admitted. 'The patient had recently miscarried a much-wanted pregnancy and I couldn't help but see my struggles mirrored in her and... I... eh... guess you could say I lost it...'

'You and James are trying for a baby?' he asked.

'Well, we were until the clinic recently told us that I'd never be able to carry a child of my own.'

'I'm really sorry to hear that,' Aidan said.

Helena shrugged. 'That's life.'

Although she was trying to pull off nonchalance, Aidan could tell that this cut far deeper than she was letting on. 'And then the crash happened and that can't have helped,' Aidan added.

Helena nodded. 'I'm so mixed up. I'm sad, I'm angry, I'm relieved, but I'm scared, and that's just for starters. I feel like I'm stuck on a roller coaster that I can't get off. And now I feel guilty for offloading all of this on you because your wife died, your daughter is just coming out of a coma and your boys have lost their mother, while my husband is still alive and I know I should be grateful...' her voice danced with tears. 'But it's so hard.' She began rooting in her handbag and took out a packet of tissues.

'Hey, it's okay,' Aidan soothed as she removed a tissue and dabbed her eyes with it. 'I don't think there is a right way to feel. I'm the exact same; one moment I'm crying for all I've lost, and the kids have lost their wonderful mother, but then I think of what she did to me and I'm consumed with rage so strong that if she was still alive, I'd kill her myself. I know that sounds awful.'

Just then, Dr Humphreys, a member of the medical team looking after Milly, entered the room.

'Ah, Mr Whelan, I missed you on my rounds earlier. I wanted to have a word with you.'

'I should leave,' Helena said, quickly composing herself and turning to go.

'No, please stay.' Aidan wanted to continue this conversation. It felt so good to have someone to talk to about everything. Someone with whom he could be brutally honest – she was the only person who knew about the one-night stand. He couldn't confide in anyone else. 'You don't mind, do you?' he turned to Dr Humphreys.

'Very well. I've asked the lab to run some more tests on your daughter and it would appear that her red blood cell count and haemoglobin levels are quite low, probably as a result of her blood loss following the accident. I believe this is one of the reasons why she is tiring so easily and is still sleeping so much. With your consent, I would recommend we carry out a blood transfusion.'

'Of course, whatever she needs to get better,'

Aidan said. 'What type is she? I'm O so I'm happy to donate if I can. It's probably better coming from a relative.'

'Ah… I see… well… em…' Dr Humphreys fumbled for words. 'Although Milly has the rare AB blood type… she can receive O negative which is a universal donor. However, we strongly discourage directed blood donations from relatives, Mr Whelan. We have blood stocks ready to go, whereas we'd have to screen yours before we could give it to her, which would delay everything by several days. There is also an increased risk of reactions with blood donated by close relatives, so for this reason we don't accept donations from parents except in extraordinary circumstances. I have an information leaflet here and a consent form.' He handed them to him. 'I'll leave you to read through it and if you're happy, you can sign it and I'll put a request in with the lab.'

'Let's hope this works…' Aidan sighed as Dr Humphreys left the room. He picked up the information leaflet and quickly scanned through it. Helena was staring at him but she seemed to be miles away and Aidan knew she hadn't heard a word he had said. 'Helena?' he tried again.

'Sorry, Aidan… what was that?' she said coming to.

'I said let's hope this works,' he repeated once more.

'Of course it will,' Helena said, patting his arm. 'She has a great team looking after her. She'll be right as rain in no time…' She pushed her chair back and stood up abruptly.

'You're going?' Aidan asked.

'Yeah, I'd best be getting back.' She seemed to be in a daze as she fumbled around the floor for her handbag. She had left the room before he had even said goodbye to her.

13

HELENA

Helena left Aidan and walked back along the corridor towards her husband's room. The conversation she had just witnessed with the doctor had left her head spinning and goosebumps prickled along her arms. She could feel her heart racing and she took a few deep breaths inwards.

Calm down, she told herself, *stop jumping to conclusions.*

Aidan hadn't realised the significance of what he had said, but she had, and she knew by the way Dr Humphreys had raised his brows and been momentarily stuck for words, that he had too. It was a fact that had stuck in her head from all those years ago. But maybe she was getting mixed up or recalling it incorrectly. She knew her brain wasn't as sharp as it usually was with everything going on at the moment.

She took out her phone and typed 'O parent AB child' into Google and was filled with sickening dread as what she remembered from medical school was confirmed. An O blood type couldn't possibly have an AB child. She clicked onto another link that showed a blood type table and she saw once again that an AB child could only have parents with either A, B or AB blood types, and so if Aidan really was blood type O, then he couldn't possibly have fathered Milly. She read on that there were very rare instances in medical literature where it had happened in Asia, due to a certain mutation of a gene found there, but even still, it was statistically tiny. So if both Dr Humphreys and Aidan were each one hundred per cent correct in what they were saying, it was unlikely that he was Milly's biological father.

Aidan had made a mistake, the more rational part of her brain said. It was the most logical explanation. She was forever seeing patients in the practice that swore they were a particular blood type when in fact a blood test revealed they weren't. Normally she would just brush something like this off as an error and not give it a second thought, but after the revelations of the last few days, she couldn't help but worry. What was really concreting the fears in her mind, however, was the fact that James also had an AB blood type and when you linked this key piece of information with his revelation about his one-night stand with Rowan four years ago, it was hard not to let her mind run away with the possibility that maybe her husband was Milly's father...

But, no, she talked herself down, she was being ridiculous. The most obvious explanation for this situation was that Aidan had simply got his blood type wrong.

She entered the room and found her husband sitting up in his bed, reading something on his phone. He was still heavily encased in plaster and the bruising around his face had now turned from blue-black to a dirty greenish yellow. The doctors had said he might be allowed go home early next week as long as he had someone to take care of him. He couldn't walk unaided and she knew his care would fall to her. She had hoped that once they were away from this hospital and together again in their own home that they could start taking the steps to work on their marriage but now the shockwaves from Rowan's secrets were reverberating around them and shaking them once more.

James had shown her his messages and call log on his phone and he appeared to be telling the truth about Rowan's phone call coming out of the blue. It seemed he was as much in the dark about the reason he was in the car that morning as she was. If James was Milly's father, she couldn't help but wonder, had Rowan planned on telling him that day? Was that why she had wanted to meet up with him? But no, she shook the thoughts away as quickly as they had entered her head, she was being ridiculous. Of course James wasn't Milly's father. There was most likely a perfectly innocent explanation for why Rowan had asked to meet him that day.

James placed his phone down as soon as she appeared at the end of his bed. 'I wondered where you had got to,' he said. 'I'm trying to catch up on emails.'

Colm, his second-in-command, had taken up the reins of GreenCoffee in his absence, but she knew

James found it difficult to switch off and was trying to stay on top of everything from his hospital bed.

She pulled out the chair beside him and sat down. 'I was checking in on Aidan and Milly.'

'How are they?' he asked anxiously.

'Pretty much the same.' She paused. 'Rowan's funeral is on Friday.' She was studying his face for a reaction.

'I see.' His eyes darted away from her and she could see a watery sheen to them. She knew that at some level he must be grieving for her, despite everything that had happened, they had been good friends – even more than that – at one period of their lives.

'Obviously you won't be able to attend,' Helena continued. 'But that's probably for the best under the circumstances.'

James nodded. 'I don't think it would be fair to Aidan,' he agreed sheepishly. 'How is Milly doing?'

'She's still tiring easily... The team have recommended that she get a blood transfusion.'

'The poor kid, she's really been through the mill.'

Helena took a deep breath. She needed to clarify some things in her mind, maybe the dates wouldn't match up and she could breathe a sigh of relief that she was wrong in her suspicions. 'James – I need to ask you something…' she began. 'Before we met… when exactly did you and Rowan sleep together?' She was gripping tightly to the arm of the chair, bracing herself for his answer.

James sighed. 'Well, I can't remember exactly when it happened,' he shrugged. 'It was a few months before I met you and I remember it was around Christmastime because I was out for my work party when I bumped into her in the pub.'

Helena did a quick mental calculation. She knew Milly had just turned three and she and James had met over three and a half years ago so he was talking about the Christmas before that, which would have been around the time when Milly was conceived. Her heart began pounding. There were too many coincidences for her liking: he had slept with Rowan around the same time that Milly would have been conceived, both he and Milly had a rare blood type and then when you threw in the fact that Aidan claimed to have the blood type O…

'What's wrong?' James asked. 'You're looking very pale.'

'I'm just tired,' she lied. Her head was spinning. She didn't want to tell him her suspicions. Judging by his reaction, James had clearly never even realised that he might be Milly's father. How would she find out for sure? She knew she could check the chart at the end of Milly's bed for her date of birth, but it still wouldn't confirm anything. It wasn't as if she could ask Rowan, and Aidan had been through enough without her telling him this too and crushing him completely. She didn't want to cause the man any more pain. 'I think I'm going to head home,' she said, standing up. 'It's been a long day.'

'Will you be here in the morning?' he asked hopefully.

'I'll see you tomorrow,' she said as she left the room without leaning in to kiss him like she usually would.

'I love you,' he called after her, but she didn't reply.

Tears of anger and pain brimmed in her eyes, turning the shapes in the corridor into blurry outlines. *Why did you do it?* She wondered for the millionth time as she walked down the hospital corridor. They could have been working on their marriage now and looking forward to the future together and even if that was a childless future, she was sure they could have been happy again, but instead James's confession had left her questioning everything. Her husband had opened up a festering can of worms and he didn't even know it.

14

AIDAN

Aidan swallowed a lump in his throat as the imposing stonework of St Xavier's Church came into view. Beyond the glass, he could see boys from both Callum and Jack's schools standing in a guard of honour shaped liked the wings of a swallow. He inhaled sharply.

'Are you okay?' Aidan asked the boys as the tyres of the funeral car crunched over the churchyard gravel. Philip had organised two funeral cars; one for Aidan and the boys, and he and Sheila were following behind in the second one.

'I don't want to go in there,' Callum said from beside him in the back seat as he looked through the window.

'It's okay,' Aidan coaxed. 'I'll be by your side the whole time. Granny Aggie and Grandad Bill and Sheila and Philip will be with you too.' They had waked Rowan at home in Ledbury Road the evening before, and although Philip and Sheila had wanted to open the house to allow people to express their condolences, Aidan had been adamant that the house be strictly private for family members and Rowan's close friends only. He knew the boys would find it too difficult dealing with strangers coming up to shake their hand or standing around crying in their home. Callum and Jack were anxious about the funeral and he had considered leaving them at home with a relative, but Sheila had been horrified at the suggestion and insisted that they needed to say goodbye to their mother.

'Everyone is going to be looking at us, like we're a freak show,' his eldest son spat.

'That's not how it's going to be, Callum, people are here because they care. They just want to show their support and say goodbye to your mam, that's what people do.'

Callum was still expressing his grief angrily, whereas Aidan wasn't sure if it had even hit Jack yet. Sometimes he seemed to be doing okay, and then other times, he would be really subdued, with his shoulders sunken downwards, looking so small and lost in the world. He was too young to comprehend the magnitude of his loss.

The driver silenced the engine and he came around and opened the car door for them. Aidan's heart began thumping as the three of them stepped out into the sunlight. He stood in between both boys, put an arm around each of their shoulders and led them over towards Sheila and Philip.

Sheila was wearing a matching two-piece black bouclé suit and dark sunglasses covered her eyes. She even managed to be glamorous at her own daughter's funeral, Aidan thought bitterly. They greeted one another, then Sheila led the boys up the limestone steps of the church, while Aidan made his way over to the hearse, where Philip, his own father and some other family members were gathered to help carry the coffin. He felt the weight burn his shoulders as they hoisted it up.

The soaring voices of the choir singing 'Be Not

Afraid' filled his ears as he entered the church and Aidan felt his breath snag in his chest. He just needed to get through this. Colourful shadows danced along the walls as sunlight shone through the stained-glass windows. St Xavier's, although not small by any stretch, was almost full. So many people were here, far more than he had expected, but he knew that when a young mother in the prime of her life was taken away so suddenly, people were shocked and he guessed they wanted to show him support.

As they made their way down the aisle, he felt hundreds of eyes upon him. He spotted some of his work colleagues; Richard and Brenda and even the new guy Joe had turned up. Joe with the boring presentation. Aidan couldn't help thinking back to how much simpler life had been right at that moment sitting in the boardroom listening to Joe before everything had changed. He had spoken to Richard the day after the crash and he had told him that they were all thinking of him and to take as much time off as he needed.

He recognised friends of Rowan too; other mothers from the school and people he vaguely recognised from the gallery where she sometimes helped out. There was a woman she had met at a mother and toddler group; she had had a baby around the same time as Rowan had had Jack, but he had forgotten her name. He kept his head bowed because he didn't trust himself not to fall apart if he made eye contact with anyone.

They placed the coffin in front of the altar and then took their seats. He and Philip climbed into the pew where the boys were already sitting with Sheila. His own family were in the row behind. Callum was tugging at the stiff collar of his shirt. Sheila had gone out and spent a small fortune judging from the labels, buying the boys matching trousers, shirts and woollen blazers for the funeral. Although, admittedly they looked very smart, it was strange to see them dressed formally – they didn't look like the same boys who lived in football jerseys day in day out. He sat in between his sons and reached for their hands. He gave them a squeeze, for his sake as much as theirs, and for once Callum didn't pull away from him.

'Look there's teacher,' Jack said, turning around and pointing.

Aidan turned and followed Jack's line of sight to where his teacher had just entered. People were still flooding into the church and were now standing along the back and in the aisles. He saw Rowan's college friends sitting a few rows behind him. James, who was still in the hospital, was the only one missing from the gang. He wondered if they knew about the one-night stand; had Rowan ever confided in them? They would all know by now that James had been in the car with Rowan that morning. What did they think was going on? Had they made their own assumptions given their past history? Or maybe they believed the more palatable version of events that Sheila and Philip and his own parents did, that Rowan happened to be giving James a lift that morning because 'his bike had a puncture', Aidan thought wryly.

As Aidan had taken a few minutes alone to say goodbye to Rowan that morning before the coffin was closed for the last time, he had sobbed at the unjustness of it all. As he'd looked down at her bruised face, which no amount of make-up was going to conceal, he had cried, his tears falling upon her cold skin. His head was full of so many conflicting emotions and he just couldn't begin to process them. He wanted to remember her as the fun-loving wife, the adoring mother, the free-spirited woman that she was, but all that was left was a sour taste in his mouth where there once was love. The undertaker had asked if he wanted to take her wedding band, but he had decided to leave it on, no matter what he had learnt in recent days, she was still his wife and she always would be.

Then he had helped the boys in the unthinkable task of saying goodbye to their mother. They had each placed a white rose and a letter they had written inside the coffin. They had put in a third rose from Milly too and Aidan had thought his heart might break. Milly wasn't well enough to leave the hospital and Aidan was glad she wasn't here to witness this; no child, especially one so young, should have to attend their mother's funeral. Time was marching forward and he knew he would soon need to tell her about her mother's death. He wanted to wait until she had built herself up a little more. She had had the blood transfusion the day before and seemed to be benefiting from it already. He had been in to see her briefly that morning and she had spent a bit longer awake and had even eaten a small piece of toast. He prayed she was turning a corner. Aidan was grateful when Helena had offered to sit with her while they were all at the funeral and he knew she was in good hands.

'We are gathered here today to celebrate the life of our dearly departed sister, Rowan Whelan…'

Aidan sucked in sharply as the priest began the funeral mass. Aidan had been to many funerals before, but when it was someone you loved, it seemed surreal to be sitting in the front bench with everyone staring at you like you were some kind of weird celebrity.

Aidan's mind drifted off to the last time he had been in this church, on their wedding day. Rowan had broken from tradition by wearing a blue dress and she had surprised him by writing her own vows. He had felt like the luckiest man in the world that day, standing in front of all their friends and family with his beautiful bride. How had it gone so wrong for them?

Why did you do it, Rowan? he wondered for the millionth time.

In many ways, he wished he had never known

about the one-night stand and then he could have been blissfully unaware of her betrayal. She could have been the woman he adored forever in his mind and he could look back on their marriage together with only fond memories, but he couldn't do that any more. That version of his wife was gone and he would never be able to bring her back. He was split between intense grief for his wife and now anger for the betrayal by this woman he had loved like no other.

'Aidan...' He felt Philip nudge him with his elbow. 'Father Waldron is asking for you to go up to do the eulogy,' he hissed.

Aidan startled. He had tried several times to put some words down on paper, only to ball up his attempts and fire them angrily into the wastepaper bin. He picked himself up and squeezed past Jack, and when Philip and Sheila didn't stand to let him out of the seat, he had to awkwardly squeeze past them too.

The aisle leading towards the altar had never felt so long. Hundreds of eyes bored into his back as he climbed the steps and made his way over to the lectern. He had no idea what he was going to say in front of all these people; he just hoped he could hold it together. Philip would be expecting him to go a good job.

He adjusted the microphone and there was a screech of feedback before it settled again. He just needed to get through this. He cleared his throat and began. 'I'm sorry – I... eh... tried putting some words down, but...' he broke off. 'As you all know... eh... Rowan was my wife for fifteen years and the mother of our three wonderful children. 'We... had some good times together.' Inwardly, he cringed, how lame was that?

'She was a great mother,' he went on. His eyes met Philip's and he could feel the pressure building, but his mind just seemed to be blank. 'I know the boys, Milly and me will miss her desperately.' He needed to get it together here, but the more stressed he became, the more the words just wouldn't come to him. 'And her parents, Sheila and Philip, too,' he added. 'I loved her very much...' Tears choked in his throat and he knew he was about to unravel. He needed to get off this altar right now before he made a show of himself. 'I'm sorry—' he broke off. He left the stand and made his way down to his seat. As he climbed back into the bench, Philip and Sheila had faces on them that would stop a clock.

'Ashes to ashes, dust to dust,' Father Waldron was saying as he began sprinkling her coffin with holy water and the pungent smell of incense being burned in the thurible wafted around the church. It scratched and cloyed at Aidan's throat until he thought he might not be able to breathe. Beside him, Callum started coughing. He felt his fingers entwine around the boys' hands as he gripped them desperately, trying not to break.

When the mass ended, Aidan and the other pallbearers assembled once more at the altar and carried Rowan on her last journey out of the church. He didn't know if Rowan would have preferred to be buried or cremated; it wasn't a conversation they had ever really had. They had tended to avoid the topic any time it had come up, feeling it was too morbid, but Aidan thought it might help the children to have a headstone to visit when they were older and so they had all agreed that a burial was the best option but as he carried his wife's coffin out of the church, he just wanted to get this part over with.

He stood in the churchyard as the undertakers

loaded the coffin into the funeral car before the procession would travel the short distance to the graveyard. He felt a pair of arms encircle him and saw it was Rowan's friend Annabelle. 'It's just so awful, Aidan,' she sobbed in his arms. 'She was only in the gallery last week, she popped in for a coffee and we were having a right laugh about things. I just can't believe she isn't here any more,' she choked.

'I can't believe it myself,' Aidan said. He saw more of her friends coming towards him in the distance and he wasn't able to deal with their grief. 'I'd better go.' He excused himself and went over to where Philip, Sheila and the boys were standing. The hearse set-off towards the graveyard and they began walking together behind it.

'That was it?' Philip began as they fell into step together. The boys were a few paces behind, walking with Sheila. 'That was the best you could do up there? I've heard more sentiment from the fella in the McDonald's Drive-Thru,' he spat.

'I'm sorry.' Aidan shook his head. 'I'm just all over the place.' How could he explain to Philip how he was feeling? He wasn't just a grieving husband, he had been betrayed in the very worst way possible and now, he somehow had to marry those feelings together.

'We're all finding this tough, Aidan, but come on, you were married for fifteen years for God's sake, that was your opportunity to tell the world what a great person she was... I knew I should have done it myself... Sheila told me I had to let you do it, but I shouldn't have listened to her.' He shook his head.

'You just never know when to stop, do you?' Aidan snapped. He couldn't help it. Philip was forever needling him and he had had enough. In his eyes, Rowan was still this angelic little girl, but he didn't have a clue of the deceit his daughter was capable of.

Philip glared at him. A vein bulged angrily in his forehead. 'Excuse me?'

'I just mean, I'm doing my best,' Aidan said, calming down again. This wasn't the time or the place for a showdown.

Aidan stepped back into line with the boys. Their eyes were red, and tears had left salty trails on their young faces. Aidan was worried how they would cope with the starkness of seeing their mother's coffin being lowered into the sticky brown soil.

They reached the graveyard gate and went inside. The sickly smell of freshly dug earth filled his nostrils. His eyes sharpened into focus as the hole into which his wife's body was about to be lowered came into view.

He clutched his sons' hands tightly in his own as the priest gave his wife her final blessings. As her coffin was lowered into the dark earth, he said a last goodbye to the woman he loved, wondering how many other secrets she was taking to her grave with her.

15

HELENA

'Again! Again!' Milly cried out.

'Okay then... *Itsy bitsy spider climbed up the water spout...*' Helena sang as she walked her fingers up the child's pudgy arm pretending to be the spider. She had come in earlier to sit with her while Aidan attended the funeral. James was resting in his room on the floor below; he was exhausted after a gruelling rehabilitation session with the physiotherapist that morning. '*Down came the rain and washed the spider out. Out came the sun and dried up all the rain and the itsy bitsy spider climbed up the spout again.*' When she reached the top of her arm, she tickled Milly beneath her armpit and she convulsed into a fit of giggles. It was the sweetest sound. After everything that had happened over the last few days, Helena couldn't help but be buoyed up by it.

The blood transfusion seemed to have worked. She had taken Milly's chart from the holder at the end of her bed and had a look over it. She saw that her blood counts had normalised and it was evident by the longer periods she was spending awake that her playful energy was starting to return.

'Lena?' Milly asked in her lispy voice. 'Did you know that baby spiders are called spiderlings?'

Helena laughed. 'I'll tell you a secret, I'm a doctor and people think we are very clever, but I didn't know that.'

'Mama says I'm the smartest girl in the whole world.'

'Well, she's right,' Helena agreed, feeling her heart twist at the mention of her mother. Aidan still hadn't told her that she was dead. Although she had done a module in medical school on how to approach breaking bad news to people, she still couldn't imagine how Aidan would ever find the words that would crush this little girl's world.

Milly grinned back at her and used a chubby hand to push her fringe out of her eyes.

This child was so smart and joyous, *so precious*. It was hard not to look at her and wonder if she and James had had a daughter, if this was what she might have been like. She had assumed that Milly took after Rowan, with her sallow-skin and dark glossy hair, but James was dark too. As she had played with the child, she had noticed that Milly's eyes were the same cornflower blue shade as James's too.

Stop it, she warned herself. Lots of people had blue eyes. Was she seeing a resemblance because that was what she wanted to see?

Had Rowan known? she wondered. Had she suspected that there was a chance, even a small one, that Milly was not Aidan's child? Or had the thought not crossed her mind at all? Was that why she had contacted James out of the blue, was that what she had wanted to tell him that morning? Perhaps she knew that there was a possibility but had chosen not to dwell on it. Some people could bury their head in the sand and block out things like that, but not Helena, something like this was an itch she had to scratch. She knew she thought about things far more deeply than most people; it was a personality trait that sometimes drove James mad, but that was just the way she was, which is why she had to know if Milly was James's daughter.

'Be the spider, Lena,' Milly begged again, so she pretended to be the spider once more until Milly was breathless with laughter at the end of it.

'Do you need a sip of water, sweetheart?' Helena asked. She didn't want to tire her out. She was conscious that Milly was still quite weak. She had been awake for over two hours now; Helena knew it was the longest period she had spent awake since she had been in the hospital and she didn't want her overdoing it.

'Yes, pease, Lena.'

Helena guided the plastic cup and straw towards her mouth and Milly took a sip.

'When is my daddy coming back?' she asked.

Helena looked at her watch. She guessed the mass was probably over at this stage and the burial would be taking place round about now. 'He'll be back very soon,' she promised.

'Mama never comes to see me,' she said sadly. 'I don't know where she went. When I was in the car, I was calling her, but she didn't come.' Her whole face was screwed up with confusion.

Helena froze. 'You were calling her in the car, sweetheart?' she prompted gently. She didn't want any traumatic memories that the child might have from the crash to resurface.

Milly nodded her head solemnly. 'After the big scary bang. I was really scare-ded and my arm was really owwee and I was crying for my mama, but nobody could hear me.'

Helena felt a huge pang of emotion. How scared must she have been? This poor little mite had witnessed horrors that nobody should ever have to. She suddenly felt a rush of protectiveness towards this small girl and everything that she had been through. 'It's okay, sweetheart, you're safe now,' she said, stroking her hand. She imagined that this must be what it was like to be a parent and feel a primal instinct to protect your child from the world's pain.

Milly sighed and fell back against the pillows. 'Me tired, Lena.'

'Well you get some rest, you've had a busy day today.' She brushed the child's hair back off her face and Milly closed her eyes, where a network of tiny blue veins ran along just underneath the surface. She stroked the smooth skin of her forehead that felt like silk beneath her fingertips. Helena watched as her breathing began to slow as her body relaxed. Was this how it felt to stroke your child's skin ever so gently in feather-light, tracing movements until they finally gave into sleep, Helena wondered, or to watch the shallow rise and fall of your child's chest as they drew breath into those ever so tiny lungs? All these intimate moments of parenthood that she would never get to experience.

Helena closed her own eyes. She allowed herself to imagine what it would be like if Milly was her child – just for a second – just to know how it would feel. She silenced the part of her brain that told her this was wrong. She just wanted to know the true depths of all she was missing out on. She had been through a lot as well. She may not have lost as much as Aidan, but she was also grieving – she was grieving for her lost dreams and her chance to be a mother. Was it really so bad if she briefly indulged herself and tried to forget all the heartache?

Suddenly she felt another presence in the room and she quickly opened her eyes, feeling guilt flood through her. What the hell was she playing at? She shouldn't be doing things like this, especially after everything that had happened over the last few days and her realisation that her husband might be this darling girl's biological father. It wasn't fair to Aidan. She took her hand away from Milly's face and sat back in her chair as if she had been slapped.

'She's out for the count again,' the nurse, who Helena knew was called Sandra, said nodding in Milly's direction.

'She was awake for two hours, so that's progress,' Helena said, sitting up straight.

'I didn't see her daddy here today?' the nurse enquired, lifting her chart and flicking through it.

'He was in earlier, he's at the funeral now.'

'Ah, I see... It's just desperate,' Sandra said as she replaced the chart and began to carry out her checks. 'I see that poor man sitting here day after day, your heart would break looking at him. His whole life turned upside-down like that in a split second.' She shook her head. 'It's terrible. It makes you appreciate everything you have. You get one chance to live your life with no regrets.'

When she was finished, she retreated out of the

room and left Helena alone with Milly once more. Sandra's words were ringing in her ears. *You get one chance to live your life with no regrets.* If the crash had taught her anything it was that life was too short – it could all change on a sixpence. She felt like a failure for being the reason she and James couldn't have a child, but maybe he already had one and he didn't even know it? If Milly was his biological child, was it fair to deny him that? Perhaps they had a chance – a slim shot – at parenthood... well James anyway. It felt agonisingly close. It was in touching distance if she was brave enough to discover more. She had even thought about contacting Aidan's GP to see if they would allow her access to his medical records so she could confirm his blood type, but she knew if she was caught violating data protection laws, it would have serious consequences for her career. Her head was in a spin. She felt tormented by the knowledge. At least if Milly wasn't James's daughter, she could put this out of her head and forget all about it, but at the moment, the secret was there, teasing her, tantalising her mind with silly fantasies.

It was then that she saw it: Milly's toothbrush was sitting in a glass on her bedside table. She could take the toothbrush, nobody would notice it was gone and if they did, they would just assume it had gone walkabout somewhere. She could do a DNA test. Nobody would ever need to know. She was probably way off the mark about James being Milly's father, but at least then, if the results showed that he wasn't, she could put her mind at ease and forget all about this craziness. The way her mind was right now wasn't healthy for anyone.

She stood up and walked over to the glove dispenser and snapped on a pair of latex gloves. She felt grubby for what she was about to do, but she needed to know the truth. She removed the toothbrush from the glass and took another glove from the dispenser and wrapped it around the brush-head to protect it, before putting it into her handbag.

16

AIDAN

Aidan crept into the room to see Helena tenderly stroking the hair back off Milly's sleeping face. She hadn't heard him come in and so he stood where he was and watched the scene before him. Helena was brilliant with Milly, she had such an easy way with children. She was kind, patient and caring and would have made a brilliant mother. He was grateful to her for staying with Milly especially when he knew it might have been difficult for her. From the bits she had told him of their fertility struggles, it was such a shame to think that she would never have a child of her own.

'Hi there, how was she?' Aidan asked as he took the other seat beside Milly's bed.

Helena startled. 'Oh hi, sorry I never heard you come in.' She straightened up quickly. 'She was in good form, Aidan, I think the blood transfusion seems to have done its job. She was awake for over two hours.'

Aidan exhaled loudly. 'That's such a relief.' Although he hated that he had missed out on seeing her awake, he knew it was a positive step forward in her recovery.

'We had a great time playing games and singing songs together. I really think she has turned a corner.'

'Thank you for staying with her, Helena, it's been such peace of mind to know you were here.'

'It was my pleasure, she's an amazing little girl. So, how was it?' she ventured.

'It was awful.' He sighed and closed his eyes as he remembered the crushing finality of seeing Rowan's coffin being lowered into the freshly dug earth as the boys stood looking on. In many ways, it still seemed surreal. He kept waiting to wake up from this nightmare, but it never happened.

After the burial, a long line of mourners had queued to shake their hands and express their sympathies and Aidan had gone through the motions, shaking hand after hand, thanking people for coming, while the boys stood beside him, their faces sticky with tears. He had longed to take them out of there, away from all those people and their whispered condolences.

Sheila and Philip had organised a meal at their golf club after the funeral, and they had taken the boys with them, while Aidan had returned to the hospital. He was glad to avoid it to be honest. He didn't think he could shake another hand or listen to one more well-meant platitude about how 'heaven needed another angel' or something equally banal. He hated having to leave the boys so soon after they had laid their mother to rest, but he needed to see Milly.

Helena reached across the bed linen and gave his hand a squeeze. 'I can only imagine.'

'I made a mess of the eulogy,' he continued. 'I just went blank when I was standing up there with all those faces watching me. I couldn't get it together. Philip nearly hauled me down off the altar.'

'Don't beat yourself up. It's not like you ever get to practise writing a eulogy for your wife's funeral. Emotions can run high at these things,' she soothed. 'How are the boys doing?'

'They're so lost, they're in so much pain and the worst part is I can't even help them.'

'It's going to be rough, I won't lie, but time will help you. And this little girl would lift anyone's spirits.' She nodded towards Milly. 'She will light up your home.'

Aidan couldn't help but smile with pride. 'She's pretty amazing, isn't she?'

'She is,' Helena agreed and Aidan was sure he could detect a wistfulness in her tone. He guessed Helena was still coming to terms with the fact that she would never have a child of her own. 'She was asking for Rowan,' she continued.

Aidan drew his hands down along his face and groaned. 'I know, she's been asking me too – I don't know what to say to her. She thinks Rowan is at home and hasn't come to visit her,' he admitted. He had already spoken to the hospital grief counsellor about what was the best way to approach it and they had told him that he had to be honest and speak in clear, simple terms, but he still hadn't been able to face doing it yet. He kept waiting for the right time, but would there ever be a right moment to tell a three-year-old that their mother was dead?

'I think she might remember the crash,' Helena said anxiously.

'Really?' Aidan asked.

'She told me that after the big scary bang, her arm was sore and she was calling for her mama.'

Aidan's heart sank. It was awful to think of her being scared and helpless while trapped in the wreckage of the car with her dead mother. 'Oh God,' he said.

'I think the time has come to tell her,' Helena suggested kindly. 'I know it's awful to think about shattering her world like that, especially when she's been so poorly, but the longer this goes on, the harder it will be to break the news to her. I'd imagine her doctors will allow her to go home soon if she keeps going the way she is and you don't want her to run through that door and expect her mother to be waiting for her.'

'You think it might be soon?' What a relief it

would be to see the back of this hospital. At least he would be around more for the boys too.

'I don't want to speak for her medical team, but I can't see why she wouldn't be, everything is going in the right direction.'

Aidan nodded. 'I guess I need to do it soon then. But what am I supposed to say? She's three years old! She won't even understand.'

'I think you just have to be honest and explain it in really simple terms. There's no easy way through it unfortunately. I can help you if you want?'

Aidan shook his head. 'Thanks, but it's probably something I need to do on my own.'

They both fell silent before Helena spoke again, 'James is being released tomorrow. They're very happy with his progress. It seems his fitness before the crash has really helped him and his rehabilitation is going well so far.'

Aidan's eyes darted to the floor. He could feel the anger rise within him; his heart beat a little faster, and the blood warmed his veins as it always did whenever he heard James being mentioned. 'So you won't be around the hospital any more?'

Helena nodded.

Aidan felt a wave of sadness flow through him. His bedside chats with Helena would be over. They had been the only good thing in such a dark period. She had become a confidante and good friend to him over the last few days. She was always there with a listening ear and a word of advice. She was the only person who knew the full story. He could be completely honest with her; if he wanted to offload about Rowan's betrayal or tell her that Philip was being an arsehole or to share his worries about the children, he could and she would listen without judgement.

'I'll miss your company,' Aidan said. 'You've been a rock for me over the last few days. I know it hasn't been easy for you either. You're the only one who understands what I'm going through. I wouldn't have got through it without you.'

Helena's eyes darted away from his. 'Well… you've helped me through as well, Aidan…' she mumbled as she stood up. She hurriedly picked up her handbag and slotted her arm through the strap, keeping it close to her. 'I should go—'

'Sure…' Aidan said awkwardly as he stood up too. 'Sorry, I've taken up enough of your day. You've probably lots of things to be doing to get ready for James coming home…' He wondered if he had said something wrong? It was like he had flicked a switch and the atmosphere had completely changed. She seemed to be embarrassed by the compliment. Maybe he had been too gushing and she had felt uncomfortable?

'I'm sorry, Aidan, I really am,' she blurted.

He opened his mouth to reply but before he could say anything else she had turned and left the room.

17

HELENA

Helena turned the car on to Abbeville Road and continued along the tree-lined road until she reached their house. Her tyres crunched over their biscuit-coloured gravelled driveway and she silenced the engine. She climbed out and went around to the passenger side to assist James.

'Take it easy now, watch that step,' she warned as she aided him up the chequered tiled step that led to their front door. She made sure he was steady on his crutches before putting her key in the lock and helping him inside. Not for the first time, she felt daunted by the recovery that James had ahead of him. His physiotherapist in the hospital was pleased with how quickly he was regaining his strength, but James still had a long road ahead to get back to the man he once was.

She helped him into the living room. Gone was the sofa and the coffee table and in their place now stood a bed. Breda and Kevin had come over the evening before and helped her to set it up, so that he wouldn't have to use the stairs.

'You're amazing, Helena, I just wanted to tell you that,' James said, surveying the room. 'I can't tell you how good it feels to be back home with you.' She knew by the way he held her gaze that he wasn't just referring to his hospital stay but to their marital difficulties before the crash too.

Although James was excited to be home, she was more reticent. She had no problem nursing him back to health, that was what she was trained to do after all, but it wasn't just James's bones that were broken, their marriage was too and now they would have to face the issues which had torn them apart in the first place – the heart-breaking losses, the gruelling rounds of IVF, the pain of knowing that she would never carry her own baby. They had reached a point where they hadn't been able to look at each other without seeing the grief mirrored in the other's eyes so it was easier to avoid one another. On her darker days, Helena had even questioned whether James might be better off without her.

Her eyes landed on the collage of wedding photos that hung on the wall. Suddenly their smiling faces beaming from the pictures seemed mocking. She moved closer to take a better look at what had been the happiest day of her life. She could still feel the excitement that had radiated from her that day, still disbelieving that, after spending so long waiting to meet the love of her life, within six months she had met and married him. As she and James had recited their wedding vows, she felt like the luckiest girl in the world. Her fairy tale had had its happy-ever-after ending. Her eyes moved along the photographs and they landed on a shot of her and James having their first dance. She leaned in closer and she could make out Rowan's beguiling smile in the background. Milly had only been a couple of months old when she and James had married; had Rowan stood at the side of the dance floor on their wedding day as James had twirled her around to Frank Sinatra's 'I've Got You Under My Skin', wondering if her small baby could have been James's? Had she even felt an ounce of guilt that day for betraying Aidan? Helena wondered bitterly.

She couldn't help but think about the last time she and James had been together under this roof. She had been in a world of pain, having had the clinic snatch her dreams away from her. She had thought that life couldn't get any worse that day, but it had; since then she had been forced to take leave from her job and had very nearly lost her husband too. Her life of old now seemed so simple by comparison – yes, her heart had been broken in their fruitless struggles to have a baby, but back then she hadn't had to deal with her suspicions about Milly's paternity.

She had tried telling herself over and over again that of course Aidan was Milly's father and he had just been confused about his blood type, but a louder voice would always drown her out and ask *what if*? What if James was her father?

Something had happened in the hospital the day

before as she had sat at the little girl's bedside. It was as though Milly had cast her under a spell. The time they had spent together felt magical. As they had played and sang together, her voice so joyous and sweet, Helena had felt something change inside her. Milly was such a special child, to think there might be a part of her husband in that little girl was intoxicating. A dream that was so beautiful, it teased her. That darling, smiley little girl. When Aidan had returned, the spell had been broken and Helena knew she was fooling herself. She was playing a game in her imagination but she needed to stop because Aidan was Milly's father, no matter what happened. His friendship had come to mean so much to her. They had bonded over their shared shock and pain, but as she'd left, she couldn't look him in the eye, knowing that she had Milly's toothbrush in her handbag. She still hadn't removed it. Now that she had it, she wasn't sure what she was going to do with it. Could she really go through with the paternity test? It seemed so deceitful. So shady. Like a story you would read about in the pages of a gossip magazine. And if it transpired that James really was Milly's father, what then? What would she do with that knowledge? Would she tell James? Would she ever be able to tell Aidan, knowing that this would shatter the only piece of him that remained intact? Something like that could crush him entirely; he might not survive it. What would she do with such an earth-shattering piece of information? Aidan had been through so much, she could hardly storm in and throw that at him as well? But was it fair to James to have what might be his only opportunity to have a child of his own – his own flesh and blood – taken away from him? Despite his role in betraying Aidan, she knew she couldn't stand by and let him be robbed of a chance at fatherhood because of Rowan's deceit. Morally he had a right to know the truth, but she didn't know what was right or wrong, fair or unfair any more.

If she wanted to go ahead and do the test, then she would need a DNA sample from James; that was the easy part, she could take his toothbrush too, or some of his hair. The only thing that was stopping her was the knowledge that once she did this and found out the truth – whatever that might be – there would be no turning back. For better or for worse, she would need to be prepared to deal with whatever the test told her. Once she opened the lid of Pandora's box, she couldn't close it again and she knew she needed to be ready for that.

She hated herself for what she was doing to Aidan who had already suffered enough. She was nearly as bad as Rowan with the secrets she was carrying. But what else could she do? She had to know the truth before she went round the twist. Her mind was too full of possibilities and it unsettled her. Helena couldn't deal with question marks in life, it was just the way she was. Now that the seed had been planted in her mind and taken root in there, she had no option but to climb the branches and explore.

'Helena?' James was saying, pulling her out of her thoughts. 'You're miles away.'

'Sorry,' she said, moving away from the photographs and snapping back to reality. She began to guide him into the bed and took off the trainer that he was wearing on his supporting foot.

'I was just saying that I know we have a long road ahead to get back to where we were. I can deal with our being childless, but I can't live my life without you.'

'Let's take it one day at time, yeah?' she replied as

she plumped his pillows to help make him more comfortable. *No promises.* He was forever apologising for contacting the surrogacy clinic, she knew he regretted what he had done, but now it all seemed so insignificant given everything that had happened since then.

She handed him the TV remote and went out to the car to get his small suitcase from the boot. Lifting it out, she took it into the kitchen. She flicked the switch on the kettle to make herself a camomile tea. She was exhausted, the tiredness ached right down into her bones. While the kettle boiled, she pulled the case over towards her and began taking out the belongings that she had packed for him after he had been hospitalised. She removed his robe and slippers, his tablet and phone charger and tossed the dirty laundry into a pile on the floor. Finally she came to his washbag. She held it in her hands for a moment. The truth was terrifyingly close. Just one more step and she could put herself out of her misery, she could have all the answers to the questions that were tormenting her. Before she could talk herself out of it, she rooted in the cupboard where she kept the first-aid box. She opened it up, removed a pair of latex gloves and put them on, then she unzipped the washbag and lifted out his toothbrush. She twirled the handle around between her thumb and index finger. To hell with the consequences, it was time to untangle Rowan's web of lies.

18

AIDAN

Aidan stood in the kitchen where sunlight warmed the honey-coloured floorboards and surveyed the place. Dirty dishes were piled in the sink and the room had a grubby feel about it. His mum and Gemma were great, cooking meals for them all and taking care of the boys while Aidan was with Milly in the hospital, but there was only so much they could do. Although Rowan was never a fan of housework, she would never have let it get into this state and he felt guilty for how he had let things slide. It was all going to fall to him now, he realised: the housework, the laundry, the meals, the parenting, on top of trying to hold down his job to keep a roof over all their heads. Never had he felt so daunted about what was ahead. It was only now he understood how much of the mundane day-to-day stuff Rowan had taken on while he had been at work every day. She kept all the balls in the air. Had she ever got fed up of the drudgery of domestic life? Maybe he needed to take a share of the blame for her turning to James. How many times had he put his work before his family? He wondered if he had shared the load a bit more, travelled less and spent more time at home, would things have been different? He had always thought he was doing it so he could provide a good lifestyle for them, but maybe what they really needed was to have him around more. Was that why Rowan had contacted James and asked to meet up with him – was she hoping to rekindle things between them because she needed some excitement in their dull, suburban life? Was he a means of escapism from the daily grind? But no, he had to stop thinking about that right now, he was driving himself mad. He needed to get these thoughts out of his head and concentrate on his family.

'I have some good news, boys,' Aidan said as he

set to work loading the dishwasher to try to restore a bit of order to the place.

They both turned and looked up at him from their screens, with disbelief written all over their faces. They had become so accustomed to bad news recently that it was hard to see how there ever could be good news again.

'The doctors are allowing Milly to come home today,' he continued. Aidan was sure that once he had his three children united again in their own home, things would be a little easier and he wouldn't feel as though he was being pulled in two different directions. Although the core had been ripped from their world, he hoped that the boys could begin to heal as they all helped each another through the dark days. But Aidan was disappointed by their muted reactions. He knew this was hard on them, but surely somewhere amongst all the pain, they had missed their little sister?

'Dad?' Jack said.

'Yes, son?'

'Does Milly know that Mam is dead?' he asked as worry creased his young brow.

Aidan shook his head, as guilt and dread poured

into his stomach. He had tried telling her, but the timing never seemed to be right. And Milly had been in such good form over the last few days that he was afraid that news like that might set back her recovery and she'd never get out of there. So, in the end, he had decided to wait until she was at home in her familiar surroundings.

'So you still haven't told her?' Callum asked, lowering his phone and shaking his head in disbelief. 'Mam has been dead for over a week and she doesn't know yet?'

'I was waiting for the right time,' Aidan mumbled, knowing it sounded lame even to his ears.

'Well I could make a banner saying "welcome home" and maybe we could put up some balloons for her too,' Jack suggested. 'That's what Mam would have done.'

Aidan's heart twisted. Jack was right, Rowan would have made a big fuss for something like this. Despite everything he had learnt recently, Rowan had been a great mother. It was all those touches and thoughts that his children would miss sorely as they grew up and tried to navigate life without her and now it would be solely up to him to remember all these little things that made a childhood special.

'I think there are some balloons in the drawer leftover from her birthday, why don't you blow them up, Jack, and Callum might give you a hand sticking them up,' Aidan said.

'Balloons?' Callum said in disgust. 'You really think they're going to help her when you tell her that her mother is dead?' he sneered.

'I know it's hard, Callum, we're all in pain here, but we have to try, for Milly's sake. She's your little sister.' Aidan reached out to put a hand on his son's shoulder, but Callum shrugged him off and walked out of the kitchen. He knew Callum's grief was manifesting itself as anger and teenage hormones didn't help matters, but Aidan was starting to lose patience with his son. Milly's discharge from hospital was a little chink of light after what had been a terrible few days, but Callum's outburst had taken the shine off it.

Jack stood there looking crestfallen.

'Never mind him,' Aidan reassured. 'I think it's a lovely idea, you know how much Milly loves balloons.'

'Okay, Dad,' he said anxiously, eager to please but with doubt written all over his young face.

* * *

'Are you ready to go home?' Aidan said with excitement dancing in his voice later that day as he took off Milly's pyjamas and dressed her in proper clothes. He had taken a pair of leggings, a sweatshirt and her trainers with the lights that she was so proud of, from her wardrobe.

Gemma had come to stay with the boys while Aidan returned to the hospital and as he'd walked through the revolving doors, he'd hoped it was the last time he would ever have to set foot in this place. It held nothing but bad memories for him now. He wondered how Helena and James were doing since he had been released from hospital. He hoped she was well – James on the other hand; he didn't care what happened to him.

'Me going home,' Milly cried as she bounced on the bed. The cast on her left arm was tucked inside the sweatshirt and the empty sleeve was swinging freely.

'Everyone is really excited to see you,' Aidan continued. 'The boys have a surprise for you.'

'And Mama,' she added.

Aidan winced.

'Take it easy, little lady,' the nurse who was releasing her laughed as she came into the room to do her final checks before signing off her paperwork. 'We don't want you coming back here again.'

The nurses and doctors all stood lining the corridor to wave her off and Aidan felt a lump in his throat as he led her out of the hospital. He held her hand tightly within his own as they made their way out into the bright autumn sunlight. This was the start of a new way of life for them all. It felt like the day they had left the maternity hospital when she had been a new-born. That same mixture of excitement and terror.

When they reached his car, he opened the door and lifted Milly to put her into her seat, but she began wriggling in his arms. 'No, Daddy!' she screamed. 'No car!'

His heart fell. *Damn it.* He should have known that travelling in the car could be a trigger for Milly. 'Hey, it's going to be all right, sweetie,' he soothed.

'Me scared, Daddy,' she started to cry. 'Please, Daddy,' she was clawing at his hands, trying to pull them away from the straps.

He bent and kissed her forehead. 'I'll drive really slowly, I promise I'll be careful. Okay?'

She nodded slowly, her eyes wide with fear, and Aidan felt his heart twist.

He went around and climbed into the driver's seat. He wondered how much she could remember from the accident? He didn't want to risk triggering bad memories by asking questions but clearly she recalled something.

He drove extra slowly through the suburban streets, checking and rechecking his mirrors, ensuring he had enough distance between him and the oncoming traffic before pulling out at the junctions, taking care not to brake suddenly in case it upset Milly. It was a relief when he eventually turned the nose of the car through their granite pillars.

He turned off the engine and went around to the back to unstrap her from her seat. He knew by the way she was still gripping the sides of her seat, even though the car had stopped, that the journey had been traumatic for her.

He held her hand as she climbed the steps with her right foot leading while her left one played catch-up, the rise still too large for her little legs. He put his key in the door and let them into the house.

Callum and Jack were standing with Gemma just inside the door waiting for them. Jack was holding out a banner made from a roll of old wallpaper saying "Welcome Home Milly" and balloons decorated the arch leading to the kitchen. They all rushed forward and hugged her tightly, but she wriggled away from them and ran down the hallway towards the kitchen, her trainers pounding over the wooden floors.

'Mama, me home!' she called with excitement lacing her voice as she ran underneath the balloon arch.

A wave of panic upended Aidan. 'Wait,' he called as he ran after her.

'She doesn't know yet?' Gemma turned to Aidan as she hurried after him. 'I thought you'd told her?'

Aidan shook his head sheepishly.

They watched Milly's face fall as she looked around the kitchen in confusion. Normally Rowan could be found there, perched on a stool at the island. She would jump up and say 'There you are, my darling girl,' and Milly would run into her arms and Rowan would swing her around and cover her silky hair with kisses.

'Where's Mama gone?' She turned around to face him. 'I want to see her.'

Aidan felt the crack in his heart separate even further. He risked a glance at Gemma and saw her eyes fill with tears. He lifted Milly up into his arms and sat down on the sofa with her, cradling her on his knee. He knew he couldn't hold it back forever. The dam was about to burst and he was going to be carried along by the flood.

'Milly, love,' he began, hearing the tremble in his voice. 'Your mama isn't here.'

'Yeah, she's dead,' Callum interrupted.

Aidan winced at the anger in his son's tone. He was too young to be experiencing such bitterness. Milly looked up at him in bewilderment and Aidan shot him a warning look. He knew Callum was angry, but it wasn't fair to do this to Milly.

Milly's bottom lip began to wobble and Aidan knew tears were coming. 'Me want my mama,' she began to cry.

'Come on, boys,' Gemma said, leading them out of the room. 'Let's give them some time alone, yeah?'

'Where is my mama?' Milly demanded again when they were on their own.

'Your mammy is gone to heaven, love,' Aidan said, feeling the words solidify like cement in his throat. All the advice that the grief counsellor had given, deserted him, and he didn't know what to say to her.

'No she's not,' she replied with all the confidence of a three-year-old. 'She's here waiting for me.' She jumped off the sofa and began searching around the kitchen. 'Mama?' she called, opening cupboard doors. 'Where are you, Mama?' She walked into the pantry. 'You in here, Mama? You playing hide-a-seek?'

Aidan followed her and turned her to face him. He bent down on his haunches so that he was at her level and gripped her tiny shoulders on either side. 'I'm so sorry, sweetie, your mammy died in the crash.' Aidan wondered when he would be able to say these words without choking up. He was still in disbelief that this had happened to them.

Milly began blinking rapidly as she tried to process what her dad was saying.

'Do you understand what that means, pet?' Aidan continued.

She shook her head, looking so small and lost.

'When a person dies, it's forever, they can't come back.'

'So my mama is never going to come back again?' Her blue eyes were two huge pools of worry. 'But where is she gone?'

'She's gone to heaven, do you know what that is?' He didn't really believe in the concept of an afterlife but he couldn't bear not to give the kids something to cling to – the reality was too harsh for a child to get their head around.

Milly shook her head.

'Well, when people die, they float up to the clouds and everything is really nice in heaven, the sun always shines and you can eat ice cream all day long.' God, he sounded pathetic.

'But I want her,' Milly began to sob, not caring how much he dressed it up.

'I know, pet.' He fell to his knees, hugged her tightly and stroked her hair. He was feeling the exact same way. No matter what he had learnt in recent days it would never change the fact that Rowan had been the only woman he had ever loved and he missed his wife desperately. His heart ached for her. 'I do too,' he cried into her hair.

19

HELENA

Helena stood in the kitchen and held the envelope in her hands. Although it was plain and deliberately unmarked, she knew by the thickness of the fold of paper inside what it contained. She had sent the samples off to be analysed over a week ago. Even though she knew what she was doing illegal, she had made up false identities and signatures for the consent form, pretending she was carrying out the test on behalf of a patient.

Her heart was racing and her palms felt clammy as she stuck her index finger under the gummed flap and pulled along the seal to open it. She removed the letter and just held it between her fingers. She needed to be certain that she really wanted to do this. She could bin it now, forget all about it and nobody would ever have to know.

James was still completely oblivious to the secret that she was keeping from him. He was recovering surprisingly well. He was doing the rehabilitation exercises that his physiotherapist had given him and was making good progress. Because he was laid up and she was still on leave of absence, they had no choice but to spend a lot of time in each other's company. She had finally told him about what had happened in the surgery. He had been shocked as she had recounted how she had broken down in front of Julie Carroll and how Ken had suggested she take a few weeks off.

As she had shared the true depths of her pain with him, she'd suddenly realised that she had never let him in. She had never let him see just how broken she really was in her fruitless journey to have a child because she was afraid that if she fell apart, then he would too and once the floodgates opened there would be no saving them from the torrents of their grief. Normally life was so busy that it was only now that Helena realised how little time they actually spent together. She guessed they had slipped away from one another over time. She knew she was guilty of filling her life with stuff; going for a run, meeting a friend for coffee, working late – anything to avoid the sadness that had been their struggle to have a baby. There were times when it had just been too painful to look at her husband and see the emptiness in their life where a baby should be. It had been easier to avoid him and run from the pain, but now she had had time to think, to process her feelings and gain clarity, and she was starting to see glimpses of the way they used to be before they got beaten down by the disappointments of infertility.

They had talked through a lot of the old hurts and pain and what the infertility had done to them as a couple. James had explained to her that when he had contacted the surrogacy clinic, he had thought he was helping. He had hated seeing her in so much pain and he just wanted to fix it; he had never meant to hurt her. She now understood that they dealt with their disappointments differently; Helena needed to process it and grieve first, whereas James just wanted to mend it via the fastest route possible.

They had stayed up late the night before

laughing and reminiscing too and it reminded Helena of the early days of their relationship. She always joked that James had wooed her with his coffee cups. He had opened the first branch of GreenCoffee just down the street from the surgery and she used to pick up a latte there most mornings on her way to work. She had noticed the good-looking barista working there but didn't think anything of it until one morning she sat down at her desk and realised he had written 'Will you go out with me?' along the side of the cup with a Sharpie. At first she thought it was meant for someone else, she guessed he probably tried it on with lots of women and so she put it out of her head. The next time she went in, he had written 'Please?' on her cup. She had flashed him a smile behind the counter and continued onto work.

The next morning, he had said, 'Well, what's your answer?' over the din of the coffee grinder. So they had gone on a date – a picnic in the park on her lunch break. It had been sweet and romantic and things had moved quickly after that. He had brought her to his friend's wedding two weeks later. She had done the macarena with the children, dragging him up with her until they were both creased in laughter.

They had stayed talking into the dawn until they were the last of the wedding guests still up. As sunlight rose on a new day, James had led her by the hand out into the garden. She had taken off her high heels, which had been burning her feet, and as she walked over the dewy grass, they had kissed and she knew there and then that she had met her soulmate. It had taken a while to find him but they had had a connection that she had never had with anybody else. It was the twinkle of his blue eyes and the way he held her gaze when he talked to her. The way she hated being apart from him and counted down the hours until they would see one another again. Despite everything that had happened in recent weeks, she was starting to fall in love with her husband all over again.

She stared at the envelope that she clasped in her hands. It felt like holding a bomb; whatever was inside it could destroy everything. She knew this was her last chance to stop this; to put this whole crazy charade out of her head and just forget about it. Aidan had texted her the week before to say that Milly had been released from hospital and she'd felt consumed by guilt as she'd replied to say how happy she was for him. He thought she was his confidante, an ally and friend through these difficult days, when the truth was that her deceit was worse than both Rowan and James's put together. But she needed to know – one way or the other – if she didn't discover the truth, it would haunt her forever.

She began to unfold the wad of paper in her hand. Her eyes scanned quickly across the words, unable to read them. She flipped the page and skipped straight to the Statement of Results towards the end of the letter. Then she saw it.

> The alleged father cannot be excluded as the biological father of the tested child. Based on our analysis, the probability of paternity is 99.99999999%.

Oh God. She felt her legs grow weak and she sank into a chair. There it was in black and white. Definitive. James was Milly's father.

Why had she done this? She now realised there was a huge difference between having suspicions and then actually having them confirmed. The burden of this knowledge was even worse than she had anticipated. What was she supposed to do now? So many lives would be torn apart by this.

'What is it?' James asked, entering the room on his crutches. 'You look like you've seen a ghost.'

'It's nothing,' she bluffed.

His eyes searched her face and she had to look down at the kitchen floorboards.

'Come on, I know you better than that,' he said, grinning at her.

'It's just work stuff.' She quickly folded the letter and put it inside her handbag. 'I don't know about you but I'm starving… I'd better start dinner.'

She opened the fridge and began taking out the ingredients to make a stir-fry. 'Would you prefer chicken or beef?' she called over her shoulder.

'I don't mind, maybe chicken?' James suggested, his question about the letter forgotten about.

As Helena took a knife and began chopping peppers, she was torn. She pictured Aidan, Milly, Callum and Jack sitting together on their sofa watching a family movie on the TV, oblivious to the heart-breaking secret she now kept. They were already fractured with the loss of Rowan and this would crush them completely. But how could she keep this from James? Having a child of his own was all he ever wanted. She had the chance to change his life forever. If the situation was reversed and she had had a child out there unbeknownst to her, it would have been a dream come true to discover it. And Milly was wonderful, so wonderful.

* * *

Helena slept fitfully that night, tossing and turning and wrestling with her mind about what she should do now that she knew the truth.

As the light in her bedroom changed from the inky shades of night to the primrose yellow dawn, her decision became clearer. Her mind was made up. Even though she felt guilty for denying James the chance to know that he had a child, it was for the best. It was too big, she needed to contain it and the only way to do that was to keep it to herself. The secret had to stay with her. She had decided she would take this knowledge to her grave; let everyone get on with their lives the way they should and nobody would get hurt. Secrets were dangerous. Once one person knew the truth, these things had a way of unravelling, like a ball of wool; once you tugged on the end a little, soon the whole thing would unfurl and it would only be a matter of time before everyone found out and she couldn't let that happen.

She tied her robe around her and descended the stairs. The smell of freshly brewed coffee woke her senses as she entered the kitchen. She knew James must already be up.

'Helena, what is this?' he asked as soon as she came in. She saw he was sitting at the table, holding the paternity test results in his hands.

Her heart stopped. She marched over and snatched the letter from him. 'Where did you get that?' She had never thought he would go near her handbag.

'Why have you got a paternity test result in your bag?' he asked.

'You shouldn't be looking through my things,' she snapped.

'I swear I wasn't. You left your phone in your bag and it was ringing, so I went to answer it and then the letter fell out.'

'It's confidential information concerning one of my patients,' she continued crossly.

'But why is our address on the letter? Why didn't you get it sent to the surgery?'

It was almost as if he could tell that she was trying to hide the truth.

'Because I knew I wasn't going to be able to get it in the practice, so I had it sent here,' she lied.

'Come on, Helena. You looked like you were going to faint when I came into the room last night and you were reading it. Are you going to tell me what's going on here?'

Icy cold sweat broke out across her neck as fear flooded through her. He wasn't going to forget about it. She had really hoped she could avoid this but he could see right through her lies. The whole thing was unravelling and she was terrified. It was only a matter of time until he worked it out for himself. She knew she had no choice but to tell him the truth. She took a deep breath.

'James, I think you should sit down,' she began as her heart began pounding.

His brow furrowed in concern. 'What is it? What's wrong?'

She pulled out a chair for him and waited until

he had manoeuvred himself down onto it before beginning.

'It's Milly—'

'Rowan's daughter? What's wrong? Is she okay?'

'Aidan is not her father...' The words sat in the air and she watched as he tried to grapple with them.

'W-what do you mean? Of course he is.'

'I did a paternity test.'

She watched as bewilderment knitted his brow. 'Helena, are you serious? Why on earth would you do that?'

'It's a long story...'

'But if Aidan's not the father then who i—'

She waited for the penny to drop as his mind processed what she was telling him.

'You think it's me?' He pointed at himself in disbelief.

Helena nodded to confirm.

'Oh my God, Helena... but...' His face was a sea of confusion and she knew he had never suspected anything himself. 'We only slept together once – I swear.'

She explained everything then, from Aidan's admission about the blood type in the hospital and how seeds of doubt had been planted in her mind to how so she had carried out a secret DNA test on him and Milly.

'But is that even legal without Aidan's consent?' James asked, holding his head in his hands.

'No it's not, but I had to know...' she said. 'I did it to put my mind at ease. I know it sounds stupid, but I never thought it would actually come back that you were Milly's father.' She was just as shocked as he was. What was she meant to do with this new information?

'Oh God, Helena, I don't know what to think... I mean, I've wanted a child of my own for so long, but not like this...' He looked up at her. 'What about Aidan? I mean the one-night stand was bad enough, but this...?'

Guilt as thick as sludge trickled slowly through her veins. Now that they knew the truth, she wished she could erase it from their minds and pretend it had never happened. 'I shouldn't have done it.' She shook her head. 'I don't know what I was thinking.'

'Do you think Rowan knew that I was Milly's father?' James continued, as his mind tried to process this information. 'Is that what she wanted to tell me that morning?'

'I'm not sure, I keep asking myself that. Maybe she was going to tell you the truth, but we'll never know now. For all we know it's possible that she didn't even realise Milly's true paternity herself; aren't we all guilty of sticking our heads in the sand and believing the truth we want to believe sometimes?'

'I can't believe she's my daughter...' he said, clearly still trying to get his head around this information. 'Wow.'

'It's a lot to take in all right,' Helena agreed.

'Imagine if we had known from the start? We could have been present in her life. Imagine what that would have been like, Helena? We've been robbed of so much. All those stages, her first steps, taking her to playschool for the first time, pushing her on a swing, movie nights snuggled up together, we've missed out on all of that and if it wasn't because of the crash and then thanks to you following your instinct I'd never have known. I would have gone to my grave not realising I was a father. This changes everything.'

'Does it?' Helena asked fearfully, as she realised the magnitude of what she had done. She hadn't expected him to react this way; she had expected shock yes, perhaps anger too but he almost seemed grateful for her deception. The repercussions were rippling out like shockwaves and it was unbearable to know it was all because of her.

'What should I do now?' James asked, running a hand through his wavy hair that was falling over his eyes.

Her breathing snagged. 'Well, do you have to do anything? I think you need to take some time to think about this properly.' Helena was already regretting her role in all of this.

'I can't just do nothing!' he spluttered. 'There's a part of me out there – I have a chance to be a father – I've already missed out on three years of being her dad, I don't want to miss any more.'

'Think of Aidan,' she pleaded. She hadn't expected such urgency from James. He seemed determined to plough ahead without thinking about what this would do to everyone.

'But you know how much I've yearned for a child – you too – we could have had one if Rowan hadn't filled everyone full of lies. There are no winners here. Don't you see, we're all victims – Aidan, me – even you. If Rowan had been honest from the start, could you imagine the pain it might have saved us?'

Having Milly in their life might have healed his pain but it wouldn't have stopped hers, how could it? Milly wasn't her child. 'What are you going to do?' she asked, her words danced with fear. She thought of Aidan at home trying to hold himself together for the kids' sake, just about picking himself up again after the blow that life had dealt him and then this happens. This would finish him off completely. It was cruel and it was all her fault.

'Well what else can we do? We have to tell Aidan.'

20

AIDAN

Aidan felt as though he had only just closed his eyes when he could hear crying. It was Rowan. She was calling him. Caught between sleep and wakefulness, he tried to answer her, but the words wouldn't come out. She was tugging his arm and he reached out to her, but there was just empty space where his wife should be.

He woke with a start and opened his eyes in panic. He saw Milly was standing at the side of his bed in her pink gingham pyjamas, her hair a wild tangle around her face and clutching Mousey to her chest with her working arm.

'What's happened?' he asked, quickly jumping out of the bed trying to work out what was going on.

She stood sobbing, trying to catch her breath. 'I had a dream.'

'Come here, little one,' he said, lifting her into his arms.

She threw her arm tightly around his neck and her small body softened against his.

He switched on the bedside lamp using one hand and saw that Milly was red in the face as fat tears fell.

'What's going on?' a sleepy Jack came into the room after them. 'Why is Milly crying?'

'It's all right, I think she just had another bad dream,' Aidan said. In the time since she had come home from hospital, Milly seemed to be plagued with bad dreams. He wasn't sure if it was memories of the crash or the grief of losing her mother that was causing them. The earliest appointment he could get with a play therapist wasn't until January; they all had crazy waiting lists. He hoped they would be able to guide him on what to do to help his daughter but until then he would have to navigate this path himself. Luckily, he had been able to get the boys a counselling session.

Well, Jack had gone in, Callum wouldn't get out of the car when it was his turn, so Aidan, seething with anger, had started the engine and turned for home. Callum had refused several more attempts to see the counsellor so Aidan had given up trying. Callum seemed to be consumed with fury since his mother's death and Aidan just didn't know how to help him.

Milly's small body was still trembling in his arms. 'I think you should sleep with me again tonight,' Aidan said as he stroked her face, gently pushing strands of hair back off her cheeks, which were sticky with tears. She had wandered into his bed every night since she had come home from the hospital.

'Can I sleep with you too, Dad?' Jack asked, climbing into the bed beside them. 'I don't like being on my own.'

'Yeah of course, son.' Aidan moved over to make room for Jack. At ten it had been a long time since Jack had crept into his parents' bed during the night, but it obviously helped him feel safe and Aidan was glad to be able to offer him that security when there was little else he could do to fix his pain.

Soon the three of them drifted off to sleep again wrapped in each other's warmth.

* * *

Aidan woke sometime later to find himself clinging to the edge of the king-size bed, caught in a tangle of limbs. He looked around the room with its high ceilings and ornate plasterwork running along the perimeter and central ceiling rose. Rowan had painted the walls a deep smoky green colour a few years back. Aidan had never really liked the shade, he found it too dark, too oppressive. As he lay there in the bed they had once shared, he found himself wondering when they had last made love. Shamefully, he couldn't remember. Had that been a sign that things weren't well in their marriage? he wondered. Or perhaps their relationship had been stale all along and he hadn't realised it.

He got up and quietly crept into the bathroom taking care not to wake the children. There were reminders of his wife everywhere. Her toothbrush still stood in the holder in the bathroom cabinet. Her make-up and glass bottles of perfume with notes of amber and bergamot stood cluttered on the shelf. Her floaty dresses still hung in the wardrobe. Would he just leave them all there forever, gathering dust, getting holey by moths? It seemed easier to let them sit there, until… well, he wasn't sure when he'd ever be able to face boxing them all up and putting them in the attic or maybe donating them to the charity shop. He knew he would need to tackle it eventually but that was a job for another day, right now he was just trying to concentrate on getting through each day.

He left Jack and Milly to sleep on, then descended the stairs. He entered the peaceful kitchen and made himself a strong coffee. In another life, he would rise early on a Saturday morning, leaving Rowan to sleep on in their bed. He would flick through the news on his phone, savouring the calm before the chaos that the children's activities would bring later. Dashing to and from rugby matches, guitar practice, swimming lessons, Milly's ballet class. He would use the time to catch up on some work too; how important he had once felt, staying on top of it all, being the person who replied to emails on the weekend. They used to argue about it; Rowan would call him a workaholic, she would say that the company wouldn't fall apart if he didn't reply to his emails out of hours and he would argue back, full of self-importance, that he was providing for his family – that if she wanted the nice house, the holidays, the private schools, then someone had to pay for it. He cringed now at the memory. Ironically, since the crash, he hadn't given his job a second thought; it was crazy now to think how much of his life his work had once taken up. How his priorities had changed.

Aidan took a sip of his coffee and stretched out his neck; it was stiff from the awkward angle he had slept at the night before. He saw the pile of condolence cards still sitting on the island. He hadn't been able to face opening them. He had had so many people sending messages of support; his freezer was full of casseroles and lasagnes that had been dropped off and he had numerous offers of help from well-meaning friends. Rowan's friend Annabelle had dropped over a canvas that Rowan had been working on in the gallery in the weeks before she died that she thought he might like to have. He knew people cared, but it felt as though there was an invisible force field between him and them and he now realised what a lonely place grief could be.

He looked at the collage of family photos Rowan had hung on the wall. His eyes landed on their wedding picture and the pain of her loss seared his heart once more. The photographer had taken it just before they said their vows and they were standing facing one another with big grins on their faces as they held hands before the altar. Aidan could still remember the pride he had felt that day as they shared their love with their friends and family.

He got up from his stool and lifted it down from the nail it was hanging on and held it in his hands. He traced his finger along the outline of her face. He still couldn't believe she was gone. He felt tears push into his eyes again – when would they ever stop? Every time he thought he was all out of tears, new ones would arrive. It hurt too much to look at her. He opened a drawer and put the photo inside.

It was after eight when Milly entered the kitchen.

'Me hungry, Daddy,' she said as Aidan pulled her up onto his knee.

'I can make pancakes?' he offered, remembering

happier mornings when Rowan would make pancakes for everyone as a Saturday treat.

'But you don't know how to make the Mickey Mouse ones that I like, only Mama knows.' Her small face crumpled and Aidan felt a lump in his throat.

'Well how about I try and you can help me?'

'Okay, Daddy. Mammy keeps the mould in here.' She tore off across the kitchen, happy once again, and pulled open a drawer filled with baking equipment.

Aidan was just mixing the batter when Callum came down and sat on the sofa at the end of the room, his head buried in his phone. He was pretty sure Rowan never allowed him that much screen time, but he didn't have the energy to face the battle. It was easier just to ignore it and say nothing. Whenever Callum wasn't out with his friends, he stayed holed up in his room. On the rare occasions when he did venture downstairs, it was usually to stir up trouble with Aidan, and Jack often bore the brunt of his moods too. He knew his son was in pain – he was like a wounded animal kicking out when you tried to help it – but Aidan was at a loss what to do with him. *Rowan would have known what to do*, a voice echoed in his head. *Yeah, well Rowan isn't here*, he snapped back at the imaginary voice.

'I'm making pancakes if you'd like one?' he tried, but he was stonewalled again.

Jack entered the kitchen next.

'Ah good morning, sleepyhead,' Aidan greeted him. 'Did you sleep well?' Aidan asked.

'I slept great,' Jack said. 'Your bed is so comfy.' He grinned at him. At ten years old, his adult teeth were still sitting with some of his baby teeth, giving his face a goofy appearance.

'Jack the big baby sleeping with Daddy,' Callum jeered from the sofa.

'Stop it, Callum,' Aidan warned. He was really testing his patience at the moment. He was constantly riling his younger brother, to the point that Aidan was worried it was turning into bullying. He was creating an unbearable atmosphere in the house for everyone. This behaviour was so out of character for him and it all fell squarely upon Aidan to fix it.

Aidan, Jack and Milly ate their misshapen pancakes in silence. Callum's mood seemed to have rubbed off on them all.

'How about we go for a cycle,' Aidan suggested,

trying to lift the tension a little. A bit of fresh air was probably what they needed. They were all getting cranky being cooped up in the house. 'It's a nice day out there.'

'Can me get a hot shocklat after?' Milly asked.

'Of course. Let's get this place tidied up a bit first and we'll go then.' The housework seemed like a never-ending battle he just wasn't able to get on top of.

Callum stood up and went into the utility room, before coming back into the kitchen again with his coat.

'Where are you going?' Aidan asked as Callum slid his arms down into its sleeves.

'Out.'

'But I thought we were all going for a cycle?' Aidan said.

'Stop trying to be Dad of the Year,' Callum roared at him suddenly. 'Just because Mam is gone, you can't start trying now. It's too late.' His whole face was turning puce with fury.

'Callum... I...' Aidan tried. He reached out and placed a hand on his arm.

'Get off me,' Callum shouted, pushing Aidan's arm away.

Milly put her two hands over her ears to block out the noise. 'Oppppp, Callum,' she screamed.

Callum walked past them all, his feet pounding over the floorboards in the hallway until they finally heard the slam of the front door.

'I don't like it when he shouts,' Milly sobbed. 'It makes my ears owee like the scary bang.'

Aidan's heart stopped. He bent down on his haunches so that he was on her level. 'Do you mean the crash, Milly?'

She nodded fearfully, biting down on her bottom lip. 'Me was scared.'

'Oh, Milly,' Aidan said. How he wished he could erase those memories from her brain. He pulled his daughter in tight against his chest. 'I'm sorry, sweetie, that must have been so horrible for you. Callum didn't mean to upset you.'

'He's very angry,' Jack agreed.

'I think he's missing your mam,' Aidan said. Even though Callum's words were the words of an angry child, they had stung. Aidan knew Callum was right, he had spent so much time working long hours, but he had done it all for them. Now, with the benefit of hindsight, he couldn't help question if he could have been present more. Would it have been so hard to collect them from school now and then? he wondered. He tried to make all their matches at the weekend but how many school plays and award ceremonies had he missed because he had a meeting he couldn't get out of or a looming deadline? Even when he did manage to make a match or concert, he would get distracted by emails pinging on his phone. It would be a while yet before he would be going back to the office, but things were going to change. Never again would his work come first.

'We all miss her,' Jack stated, 'but fighting with everyone isn't going to bring her back.'

Aidan's heart swelled with pride at his youngest son's maturity. 'You're right, Jack. I'll have a word with Callum later.' Callum was really testing him, but Aidan had lost his wife and he wasn't going to lose his son too. These kids were his world. He didn't know how he was going to do it, but he would find a way to get through to Callum, to get beneath his prickly layers of grief.

He pulled both kids into a tight hug, when suddenly the doorbell went. He guessed it was Callum returning with his tail between his legs, having forgotten his key in his temper. Maybe he had calmed down and regretted his behaviour. Aidan felt a glimmer of hope; maybe his son wasn't as far out of reach as he thought.

'I'll be right back,' he said to the kids as he left the kitchen.

He walked down the hallway where light flooded through the fanlight, throwing segmented shapes along the walls. He pulled back the door, but Callum wasn't standing there. It was Helena and James.

21

HELENA

Helena helped James up the steps to 14 Ledbury Road. When they reached the top, she pressed the bell and waited. She turned and looked around her at the neighbouring Georgian mansions. How had Rowan and Aidan afforded to live at this address? Sure, Aidan had a good job as a director, but even with generous bonuses there was no way he earned enough to buy a home on this street. Their neighbours were either tech millionaires, embassies or large-scale property developers that had made their money during the Celtic Tiger days; ordinary people didn't buy houses here.

Suddenly the door was being pulled back and

Helena was jolted out of her thoughts. This was a bad idea. She felt as though her stomach was spinning inside a washing machine. Aidan was standing there wearing a faded grey T-shirt, joggers and sliders, dressed casually like it was any other Saturday morning and not the day when they were about to deliver a sledgehammer to the last remaining pieces of his life.

James had insisted on going to see Aidan straight away. She had tried to persuade him to take some time to think about it all and the repercussions that telling the truth would bring, but there was no convincing James to wait. He was adamant that he needed to see Aidan and said he'd take a taxi if she wasn't willing to drive him, so in the end she had had no choice but to go with him.

Now, seeing Aidan standing in front of them like this, she wasn't sure if she could go through with it. She felt sick to the pit of her stomach. What on earth would they say to him? How could she even begin to explain what she had done? They could make up some silly reason for their visit – it wasn't too late – she could pretend that James had just come to apologise once again and then they could turn around and go home instead of dropping the bombshell that was weighing her down. Was honestly really the best policy? It was one thing thinking you were doing the right thing, but the truth also had a darker side. Helena knew that more than anyone. Perhaps in this situation it was kinder to lie. She didn't know what was right or wrong, good or bad any more.

'Aidan,' Helena began. 'How are you doing?'

'What do you want?' Aidan cut across her, his eyes were locked on James's. For a moment, she thought he might reach across the threshold and punch him.

'We're sorry for calling over like this...' Helena continued, trying to stay calm even though she was a mess on the inside, 'but...well... we wanted to talk to you about something.'

'Who's at the door, daddy?' Milly said, coming out beside him and wrapping her arm around one of his thighs. 'Oh it's Lena!' she cried as she spotted them.

Helena's heart sang. That precious child. She was everything Helena wanted but had been denied. She represented all of her hopes and dreams, the future that she had yearned for but couldn't have. She was wearing the cutest pink and white gingham pyjamas, the outline of her sling visible beneath the top. She grinned up at Helena with a mouthful of tiny teeth, her dark hair gleaming in the sunlight. Helena could definitely see it now – she had the same eyes as James. She risked a glance at her husband and she knew he could see it too.

'Hi, Milly,' Helena said, hearing how her voice danced with nerves.

Her face clouded as she spotted James. She pointed at him with her index finger. 'You were in mama's car when the scary bang appened.'

They all shifted awkwardly.

'Come on, Lena, me show you my new teddy. Daddy got it for me cos I was so brave in the opital.' Then she reached for Helena's hand and slotted her own small hand inside it. Milly had led her inside the house before Aidan could stop her, leaving James to hobble after them on his crutches. As they walked down the hallway together with the warm softness of the child's hand inside her own, Helena felt a longing inside herself, so ferocious that it frightened her.

They entered the large, open-plan area at the

back of the house where morning sunlight flooded in. There was a kitchen area with an island in the middle, a lounge area with a sofa and TV sat at one end of the room and on the opposite end a dining table, over which a gallery of family photos in mismatched frames were displayed. The colours were so dark, Helena thought. Being an old house, the room was dark anyway, but the navy blue cupboards and lead-coloured walls made it feel even darker.

Helena surveyed the messy kitchen; it looked as though a bomb had gone off in the place. Pots and pans were piled up in the sink and mugs and plates were scattered across the worktops, toys were strewn around and a pair of Nike trainers lay kicked off in the middle of the floor, but despite the chaos, it told the story of a relaxed family room and Helena knew she would gladly trade it for her own orderly kitchen at home.

A boy of around nine or ten was watching TV, lying on the mustard-coloured sofa with his chin resting on his hands. He too was still in his pyjamas even though it was nearly lunchtime.

'You must be Jack,' Helena greeted. 'Your dad told me lots about you. I'm Helena.'

'Hi,' he replied, barely looking up at them.

'Daddy maded Mickey Mouse pancakes,' Milly continued chatting, oblivious to the unease between the adults. 'They're not as good as Mama's ones, but they're okay if you put lots of marshmallows on them.'

'Milly and Jack, why don't you two go upstairs and get dressed and then we'll go on our cycle, yeah?' Aidan suggested.

Reluctantly, Jack picked himself up off the sofa. 'Come on, Milly, I'll help you to get changed.'

'Me going to show you my ballet costume, Lena,' Milly said, heading out of the kitchen with Jack. 'Stay there,' she ordered. 'I show you...' The warmth was suddenly gone as Milly's hand slipped out from inside her own and Helena felt emptiness fill her once more.

Aidan waited until the children had left the kitchen and they heard their footsteps on the stairs. 'To what do I owe the pleasure?' he asked sardonically, his eyes still fixed on James.

Helena looked at James, to see if he still wanted to do this. It wasn't too late to back out of it.

'Helena can explain it better than me,' James

said, nodding at her, telling her to begin. As the person who had carried out the test, she knew it had to come from her.

Although they had been through this, it felt as though the words had evaporated from her brain. Her hands were trembling. She took a deep breath, hating herself for what she was about to do. 'Back when Milly was in hospital,' Helena began, 'you mentioned that your blood type was O and the doctor said that Milly's was AB.'

'And?' Aidan asked. She knew by the expression on his face that he clearly didn't want them there but she had no choice but to continue.

'Well, a person with an O blood type cannot have an AB child... I mean, there are very rare instances of it in Asia where there is a genetic mutation, but on the whole it isn't scientifically possible.'

Aidan narrowed his eyes at her, clearly wishing she would spare him the medical lecture. 'What are you getting at?' he said impatiently.

Helena knew his world was about to come crashing down even further but she had gone too far to turn back now.

'Well, when I heard you say that and I had also

recently, like you, just found out about the one-night stand four years ago, I couldn't help put it all together in my head. I was so torn, Aidan...' she broke off.

'There has been enough damage done and it's time for honesty,' James was saying now. 'No more lies. I think we all have a right to know the truth.'

'For Christ's sake,' Aidan said with fury. 'What the hell are you saying?' The anger in his eyes couldn't disguise the fear that lurked there. 'You're both talking in riddles!'

'Helena did a paternity test on Milly,' James continued as Helena held her breath, 'I'm so sorry to tell you this, Aidan, but I'm Milly's biological father.'

Helena watched Aidan's features change through anger to disbelief and back to anger once more. She could see the pain deeply etched on his face and thought she might actually be sick. She knew there was never going to be an easy way to tell Aidan all of this, but seeing his face crumple in front of her, his whole body suddenly looking smaller, it was so much more awful in reality than she had imagined.

Aidan looked from James to Helena and back again in disbelief.

'Get out, the pair of you,' he roared. 'Haven't you caused enough trouble? How dare you!'

'I know you won't believe me, but I'm really sorry, Aidan. This is the last thing I want to do to you,' Helena said as they turned to leave the kitchen.

'GET OUT NOW!' he roared after them.

22

AIDAN

Aidan closed the door after James and Helena had gone. His head was spinning. He had initially thought their visit was some sort of pathetic attempt by James to apologise once again, but instead it had turned into something more – James and Helena were actually trying to lay claim to his daughter. They were like vultures, picking off what remained on the carcass of his family. If they hadn't left when they did, he was pretty sure he would have punched James's lying, cheating face. The smug head on him standing there, pretending that he was doing Aidan a favour by telling him what he claimed was the truth. Helena had been so supportive of him in the hospital; he had thought she was his friend, but she had her own personal agenda. Helena was worse than both Rowan and James put together. It seemed she would stop at nothing to have a child of her own and now she was trying to take his daughter from him? And if they had actually done a paternity test – which he very much doubted – how would they have got a sample from Milly? The audacity of the pair of them would almost be funny if it wasn't so serious.

He marched into the kitchen and looked around at the detritus of family life. He still couldn't believe that a month ago he had been living an ordinary existence, but it was like someone had come and swept the rug out from underneath him and everything was chaotic and falling down around him. He could hear the kids running about upstairs, playing a game together. He was glad they seemed to have got distracted from what they were supposed to be doing because he knew if he saw their sweet faces he would never be able to hold it together.

Suddenly he felt a presence behind him in the kitchen and he turned around to see his sister Gemma standing there.

'I was ringing the bell, but you didn't hear me so I

used my key. Here are your dinners for the next week,' she announced as she set an armful of foil containers down on the island. 'There are two lasagnes, a bolognaise and a curry – I didn't put much spice in because I know what Milly is like.'

'Thanks,' he mumbled.

Gemma had been a lifesaver over the last few weeks. Even though she was busy with her three sons and her part-time job as a primary school special needs assistant, she would drop off a lasagne or a hearty casserole or stick on the washing machine for him. He just never seemed to be able to get on top of everything. Whenever he thought he had everything done, he would remember something else that needed doing.

'Did I just see James and Helena coming out of here?' she continued.

Aidan nodded.

'I suppose he wanted to apologise?' Gemma went on. 'I hope you told him where to go.' She opened the freezer door and put in two sliced pans. 'He probably didn't even have the gumption to do it himself – I'd say it was Helena's idea,' she said wryly.

Aidan had told Gemma the truth about James

and Rowan being in the car together and what he had learnt about the one-night stand. He had felt ashamed telling her; it was embarrassing admitting that his wife had betrayed him in the worst way imaginable. Rowan's parents, and his own too, still believed that Rowan had just been giving James a lift to work that morning. So far, he had managed to shield them from the truth of Rowan's double life. Although he was so angry with his wife, he didn't want to taint her memory, that wouldn't be fair to her parents, especially when she wasn't here to defend herself and give her version of events.

'Are you okay, Aidan? You don't look too good,' Gemma asked in concern.

Aidan felt his legs grow weak and he made his way down onto a stool.

'They said some stuff.'

'Like what?' Gemma asked, closing the freezer door again and giving him her full attention.

'Helena said she carried out a DNA test on Milly and that James is her father.'

Suddenly, laughter spluttered from Gemma's lips. Of all the reactions Aidan had been expecting, it certainly wasn't laughter.

'Are you serious?' she said in disbelief. 'Oh my God, that pair have some neck.' She took a seat beside him at the island and he filled her in on the full conversation. 'I'm sorry, but you buried your wife just a few weeks ago, you nearly lost your three-year-old daughter too. You're trying to help your three young children come to terms with their mother's death and they call over to dump some more shit on your doorstep? Are they having a laugh?' She was even more outraged than he was.

Aidan felt his shoulders come down from his ears and his heart rate began to slow a little too. 'So you think they're making it up?' Aidan continued, feeling a little more sure of himself.

'C'mon, Aidan, what do you think? They must think you're really gullible.'

'I just don't get it; Helena was so good to me in the hospital – she was such a good friend. I don't know why she would do this to me now.'

'Well, what you said about them not being able to have a baby, maybe James is filling Helena with shit and he thinks that by telling her that there is a chance he could be Milly's father, it will keep her on side.'

Aidan felt reassured. That was one explanation for it. 'But it's so twisted. Helena is a clever woman, surely she wouldn't fall for that?'

'As the saying goes: *Love is blind*. Sometimes we see what we want to see. Milly is your daughter, Aidan.'

'She's a lot darker than the boys,' Aidan said, once again feeling upended by a wave of uncertainty.

'But Rowan was dark,' Gemma countered. 'I'm telling you, they're so desperate for a child – Helena told you that herself – so now they've set their sights on your daughter. They've hatched this bizarre plan together – it's actually crazy when you think about it.' She shook her head in disbelief once again.

'Yeah, you're right,' he agreed.

'If you were really worried, you could do your own test to put your mind at ease, that way you'd know for sure,' Gemma continued.

'But I know she is my daughter,' he said, feeling more sure of himself now.

'Well then, that's all that matters. You need to put those crazy lowlifes out of your head and forget about it. Where are the kids anyway?'

'Jack and Milly are getting dressed, I was going to take them out for a cycle.'

'And Callum?'

Aidan sighed. 'He's gone out, I don't know where or who with. He won't answer his phone if I try to ring him. He's being really difficult.'

'Have you got a GPS tracking app installed on his phone?' Gemma asked.

'No,' Aidan said, feeling even more useless. 'Should I?'

'Well, I have one on the boys' phones, it's peace of mind.' She paused. 'So he's still lashing out at you then?' Gemma asked, pursing her lips together.

'He's lashing out at all of us; he's horrible to Jack. He won't go to the counsellor. I just don't know what to do with him.'

'Just be patient, it's going to hit him the hardest because he understands loss more than the younger two.'

'But I can't let him create a toxic atmosphere, things are hard enough in this house right now. He can't keep using his family as a punchbag.'

'Just give him time,' Gemma encouraged. 'He's at a really difficult age and then when something like this happens – his feelings are bigger than him, it's only natural that he doesn't know how to deal with them.'

They heard footsteps on the stairs and they quickly ended their conversation as Milly and Jack came into the kitchen. Milly was wearing her marshmallow pink ballet tutu with a pair of red sports socks. Rowan had started her in ballet lessons just before the accident and Milly adored the tutu and had even worn it to bed the day it arrived. Her face fell as she looked around the room. 'Where is Lena gone?'

'She had to go home, love,' Aidan said.

'But I want to show her my pwetty costume!'

'Well, your Auntie G would like to see it,' Gemma said. 'Give me a twirl.'

Milly's face lit up once more as she began twirling gracefully around the kitchen. Just below the layers of netting, an angry scar on her thigh was visible; a reminder of all that had happened. As Aidan looked at his daughter spinning around the floorboards in her stockinged feet, his heart surged with pride. Milly was his child, he was certain of it.

23

HELENA

Helena caught James by the elbow, to assist him as he lowered himself stiffly into the passenger seat of the car. She took his crutches and placed them in the boot, then she climbed into the driver's seat.

'Well, that went well,' James said sardonically, pulling his seat belt across his body and slotting it into the buckle.

'What did you think was going to happen? Look, we both knew coming here that it was never going to be easy,' she replied as she started the engine. She indicated and checked her mirrors before pulling out into Ledbury Road.

'Well, I didn't think it would go that badly,' James retorted, looking out the window where luscious autumn leaves had rained down from the trees and carpeted the footpaths in colours of saffron and rust.

'Put yourself in his shoes,' Helena said. 'Imagine what a shock it would have been for him to hear those words. Telling him that he might not be Milly's dad will have completely shattered his world. After everything he has been through in the last few weeks, who can blame him for reacting like that?'

'I know it's difficult for Aidan – he's been through so much – I feel awful for him, I really do, but I've been deceived too. I can't just stand by and do nothing and lose out on being a part of my daughter's life!'

Helena felt a pang of sorrow at his use of the word 'daughter'. She still felt despair balled up inside her, sitting in her stomach like curdled milk whenever she thought about the baby she would never carry. 'Well, he isn't going to just roll over and let you into her life.'

'So what can we do then?'

There it was again. He was using 'we' instead of

'I'. She knew she had started them on this journey, but she felt as though she was being pulled along a road she didn't want to go down. While she was just beginning to get her head around it all, James was ten steps ahead of where she was. He was racing along and she felt she was running after him, trying to keep up.

'I'm not sure, to be honest,' she sighed as they stopped at a red light. They had told Aidan that they wanted him to know the truth – 'no more lies', James had said to him – but was there not a part of her that yearned for a connection – no matter how tenuous – with Milly? Seeing that child again, it felt like she was under her spell. The pudgy softness of her small hand as it had slipped inside her own, Milly's sweet excitement rushing up the stairs to put on her ballet costume to show Helena; she was so innocent. To think that beautiful little girl shared the same genes as her husband... She couldn't help but wonder what would it be like to have her in their lives? She could imagine snuggling up with her on the sofa, watching Disney movies and sipping hot chocolates together. She would play princesses with her, they could dress up. When she was older, she would take her shopping and they would get mini-manicures together. It was like a fantasy that seemed so close, yet so far out of reach. The more she got carried away by the idea, the more the tapestry of the dream was sewn in her head, but Helena knew she had to stop it, she couldn't risk getting swept along by the current of James's actions, it was too dangerous.

'But he doesn't even believe us, he thinks we're making it all up,' he continued, pulling her out of her thoughts.

'Today was a shock for him, James, maybe when he calms down, he might be more willing to listen to what you have to say.'

'Aidan isn't the only one suffering here, I'm losing out too,' he said as the lights turned green and they set off again.

'It isn't that straightforward,' Helena reasoned. 'Aidan has raised her as his own all her life – I'm assuming Rowan put his name on her birth certificate. He loves that child just like he loves Callum and Jack, no matter what the paternity results say. He's not going to let us waltz in and take her off him.'

'She's the image of me – it was like looking in a mirror,' he said wistfully. 'I know you saw it too, Helena. I don't know how I didn't recognise it straight away when I sat in Rowan's car that morning.'

He was right. The resemblance was uncanny. James had a cow's lick to the right of his forehead and when they had been standing in the kitchen, she had noticed that Milly's hairline followed the same pattern. As well as sharing his blue eyes and dark features, they had similar mannerisms too. Milly blinked rapidly when she got animated about something and James did the exact same thing whenever he was excited.

'Now that I've seen it, it's all I can see. My child has been right there all this time and I didn't even know... Just think, Helena, what would it be like to have her in our lives? Imagine it – imagine being able to tuck her up in bed at night and read her a story or watch her opening her presents on Christmas morning – having all the excitement of Santa Claus.'

Helena had thought about nothing else; that was the problem. She had imagined the scenarios and images that James was planting in her head a million times already. Yes, the lure of having Milly in their life was a seductive notion, but she was terrified to open herself up to the possibility because her heart wouldn't survive another crush.

'We could have all of that,' James continued. 'It's like we're getting another chance at being parents – another way of doing it. It's not the way either of us imagined it and I know it won't be easy, but I think, with time, we could make it work.'

There it was again. She felt as though she was a passenger in a car that was travelling too fast. James was spinning a fantasy and had cast her along in its threads. He was talking about the three of them as a unit, but at the end of the day, Milly was James's child – not hers. And her heart was already so sore as it came to terms with the dreams of motherhood that would never happen for her. Did she really want to be a part of this? Yes, she had started this whole thing, she was the one who had lifted the lid on Pandora's box, but she hadn't been prepared for the strength of James's feelings. His desire to have a child at all costs.

'She's a living, breathing child,' Helena said cautiously. 'We have to think of her too, we need to be careful – Aidan is the only father she has ever known. And what about Callum and Jack? This would devastate them too. She's their little sister, for God's sake.'

'I get that – I would never try to take her off Aidan, that would be cruel, but I think we could work something out.'

'Like what?' Helena exhaled heavily.

'I don't know... some kind of arrangement... maybe she could stay with us every second weekend or something...'

'Can you imagine how traumatic that would be for poor Milly? At the moment, she associates you with the car crash that killed her mother! She's too young to understand. We would be ripping her away from her family!'

'It wouldn't be like that, Helena, we'd do it slowly.'

'But how? Aidan won't even talk to us!'

'Well, actually... I think we should get legal advice.'

Helena felt a tightness in her chest. 'Oh, James, do you really think that is a good idea? I think you need to bide your time and maybe then we could come to some kind of arrangement with Aidan. When all the drama and anger has died down and he has had time to process it, he might be willing to allow us access to Milly without bringing lawyers and solicitors into it.' The last thing any of them needed right now was a court battle, Aidan had been through enough.

'But I've already lost enough time with her, I don't want to lose any more!' James snapped. 'If Aidan's not going to listen to what we're saying, then what choice do I have? I have to fight for her – she's my daughter, Helena!'

'This could all get really messy,' she pleaded. 'We have to be fair to Aidan.'

'I can't let him rob me of what might be my only chance to be a dad!' James blasted.

Helena felt the old wound of her infertility struggle begin to sting once more. Previously they had shared that pain together, but since James had learnt he had a child of his own, the cut was deeper. It was painful to realise that their inability to conceive a child was solely her fault. He had another shot at this, but she would never get the chance to carry her own child. Helena had never felt more alone.

'I think we should give him a few days to process it and then we can see if he'd be willing to talk to us again – maybe when he calms down, we'll be able to have a rational conversation.'

'No way, Helena. The softly-softly approach won't work here. He's going to try to protect what is left of his family at all costs. I know it's awful and I hate that we're doing this to him after everything that has happened, but we don't have any other option, we have to go legal, it's the only way—'

'Just think about it, James,' Helena tried. She felt so torn; Aidan was a good man and he didn't deserve this, but she also knew that if someone told her that she had a secret child somewhere after everything they had been through she would stop at nothing to fight for her own child, so it was only natural that James was feeling this way. 'This could all blow up – once you go legal, there's no turning back, who knows what will happen...'

'I've missed out on enough time, Hel, I'm going to contact my solicitor.'

Her heart started to hammer. She felt as though

the car had picked up speed and now it was out of the control. He was like a man possessed, ploughing ahead, not caring about the shrapnel flying in his wake. But she only had herself to blame. She had done this to everyone – it was because of her that this was happening. All actions have consequences and now she was reaping what she sowed.

24

AIDAN

After Gemma had gone home, Aidan moved around the kitchen clearing off the dirty plates. He put them in a pile on top of the dishwasher, then began unloading the clean dishes. He was still trying to get his head around everything that had happened that morning. Every time he thought about it, he felt the anger rise within him again. The audacity of that pair coming into his house! He never would have thought them capable of doing something like that. How could they live with themselves? Even though deep down he knew what James was saying wasn't true, it had put doubts in his head and he felt completely rattled. Milly had just turned three, so it was nearly four years since she was conceived, and when he thought back to that time in their lives, when James claimed to have slept with his wife, all he could remember was a hazy blur of busy family life. He had been commuting to and from Seattle at the time and they had had the two boys; they were leading busy lives, but he couldn't pinpoint anything wrong or something that in hindsight might have been a sign. There had been nothing to suggest that Rowan was feeling vulnerable and lonely, like James had suggested, and Aidan certainly had no idea that she had sought solace in the arms of her old friend. How had he missed the signs, or maybe he didn't know his wife at all.

'I thought we were going on a cycle?' Jack said, coming into the kitchen and disrupting his thoughts.

'Sorry, it's been a weird day,' Aidan said. 'Weird' didn't even begin to describe it.

Aidan had just finished unloading the clean dishes and was ready to load up the dirty ones when the doorbell went again.

'It's like Grand Central Station here today,' Aidan muttered. 'Can you get it, Jack?'

Jack did as he was told and went down the hallway.

'Dad,' Jack called to him a few moments later. 'You need to come here.'

Who the hell is it now? Aidan thought as he made his way down the hallway. If it was some door-to-door salesman trying to sell him cheaper electricity, he wouldn't be held accountable for his actions... As he neared the door, he was shocked to see two uniformed Gardaí standing on his front step and in between both of them, suddenly looking so small, was his son.

'Callum?' Aidan said, searching the boy's face, hoping there was a perfectly reasonable explanation as to why his son was in the company of An Garda Síochána.

Milly appeared beside them, her face agog at the uniformed Gardaí.

'Dad, what's going on?' Jack asked, his face full of concern.

'Jack, can you and Milly go into the kitchen please.'

'But I want to know what's going on?' he protested.

'Just go back inside,' Aidan said more sharply than he had intended.

'I'm Garda Frank Maguire from Donnybrook Garda station and this is Garda Flood the Juvenile Liaison Officer.' The male Garda gestured at his female colleague. 'Are you Aidan Whelan, father of Callum Whelan?'

Aidan nodded. 'What's going on?'

'Can we come inside?' Garda Flood asked.

'Sure,' Aidan said, standing to the side to let them into the house. He led them into the living room, that was originally a drawing room in times gone by. They put their Christmas tree here every year, but other than that they never used the room because it was so cold and dark. He had arrived home from work a few months ago to find Rowan had taken a figary and painted it kingfisher blue, but it just served to add to the gloomy feel of the room.

'Mr Whelan, we received a call from BetterValu supermarket earlier – your son was caught shoplifting in their store. He had a can of Coca-Cola and a packet of crisps concealed in his jacket.'

Aidan turned to Callum in disbelief. 'Is this true,

Callum?' Aidan searched his son's face, hoping it wasn't true, but one look confirmed it all.

'I didn't do it,' Callum protested, his face creased with anger, but they all knew it was a lie.

'We have CCTV footage,' Garda Maguire continued.

'Why did you do it, Callum? I put money on your Revolut card at the weekend! If you needed more, you just had to ask.'

Callum remained stubbornly silent.

'Perhaps Callum you could leave us to talk to your dad alone for a few minutes,' Garda Flood suggested.

'Go upstairs to your room,' Aidan ordered. 'I'll deal with you later.'

Callum trudged out of the room.

'Mr Whelan,' she continued once Callum had left, 'we often find that when children of this age shoplift it can be for one of two reasons: sometimes it's simply boredom, it's something to do for a bit of a thrill with their friends, or other times there can be an underlying reason – a cry for help so to speak. In this case, Callum acted alone, which makes me think that it might be the latter. Has anything happened to Callum lately?'

Aidan took a deep breath. Where would he even begin? 'His mother passed away recently – you might have heard about it – the car crash on the Coast Road?' He still hadn't got used to saying these words out loud – he still couldn't believe it had happened.

Garda Maguire nodded his head. 'I remember it; some of our colleagues in the station attended the scene, you have my condolences, Mr Whelan. It sounds like young Callum has been through a lot in recent weeks.' His tone softened. 'Look, I'm pretty sure that because we have recovered the stolen items and as it is his first offence, if you could get Callum to apologise to the store owner, he might be willing not to press charges,' he suggested.

Aidan nodded. 'Of course. I'll make sure he does that.'

'Today is an informal caution, but I have to warn you that if something like this happens in the future, it will be treated very seriously,' Garda Flood spoke. 'Shoplifting is a crime – it's a scourge for small businesses and that's why we treat it seriously. We need to give Callum a strong message here today that this behaviour will not be tolerated. Hopefully this will be enough of a deterrent and we won't need to get involved again.'

'I'll talk to him,' Aidan said gratefully. 'And thank you.'

They stood up and Aidan led them out to the hallway.

'We wish you all the best and we're sorry again for the loss of your wife,' Garda Flood said as they went back through the front door.

'Thanks,' Aidan mumbled after them. He closed the door behind them and drew his hands down his face, wondering when this day was going to end. He almost wished he had never woken up that morning. It had gone from bad to worse. First there had been James and Helena's outrageous claim and now it felt as though he was losing his son too. He climbed the stairs, feeling as though he was being assailed from every angle. He walked down the landing and knocked on Callum's door. There was no answer, so he pushed the handle.

'Get out,' Callum shouted at him before he had even stepped inside.

'I need to talk to you,' Aidan said, entering the room.

'I don't want to talk to you.'

Aidan ignored him and sat down on the side of his bed. 'Look, Callum, what happened today? Why did you do it?' he tried.

Callum remained infuriatingly silent. This wasn't Callum – this wasn't the boy he knew. He seemed so far out of reach and Aidan didn't know how to get through to him. Aidan would never have believed a child of his would be capable of doing something like this. He and Rowan had always instilled healthy values in their children – once when Callum was two, he had taken a packet of sweets from the supermarket, but Rowan had brought him straight back as soon as she realised and made him hand them over.

'I'm worried about you, I know you miss your mam, I miss her too.' Aidan placed a hand on his shoulder, but Callum shrugged it off. There was a time when Callum had idolised him, he would follow him around with his toy lawnmower when he was cutting the grass, or the two of them would watch the rugby together, shouting at the TV as Rowan rolled her eyes. Those days seemed so far away now. When had they lost that connection? Had it been the crash or had it happened before then and Aidan had just never noticed?

'Shut up, Dad,' he roared with angry tears brimming in his eyes. 'Stop talking about her!'

Aidan had never felt more useless in his life. He couldn't think of anything else to say or do to fix this, so he decided to give Callum what he wanted and left him alone in his room. He returned downstairs, where Jack was spreading a thick layer of Nutella onto two slices of toast.

'We were hungry,' he said by way of explanation.

Aidan realised with a pang of guilt that he had forgotten to give them lunch. They hadn't eaten anything since their pancakes at breakfast time and it was now late afternoon.

'Dad?' Jack asked nervously, handing a slice of toast to Milly. 'Why were the Guards here?'

'They just wanted to talk to me about something.'

'But why was Callum with them?' he went on. His forehead was furrowed anxiously and Aidan knew that he was scared.

'Because he just happened to come home at the same time, you don't need to worry, Jack, everything is okay.' Aidan forced a smile on his face and he saw his son's face begin to relax too.

Jack and Milly sat down on the sofa with their toast and watched some YouTuber on the TV, their plans for a cycle forgotten about.

Aidan surveyed the messy kitchen, which he still hadn't got around to cleaning. He was exhausted and couldn't face doing it now. He just wanted this day to be over and the next one and the one after that too. Everyone said that time helped, but even if he could skip forward into the future, he wasn't sure if things would ever be okay again.

* * *

Aidan was exhausted by the time he was going to bed that night. His head was tormented, and a pounding headache rattled his brain.

He entered Milly's room to check on her as he did every night. She had the blankets kicked off as usual, so he pulled them up around her and tucked her up. He looked down at his daughter who was sleeping peacefully, clutching Mousey in the crook of her arm. Her mouth was open slightly and her hair falling down over her face. She looked angelic, illuminated by the fairy lights that Rowan had strewn all along her toddler bed.

He stared at her for a moment as he tried to look at her objectively. Was there any resemblance to him at all? Anything? She looked so like Rowan, whereas the boys were like him, with paler skin, fair hair and blue eyes, but when you put Milly and the boys side by side, you would know that they were brother and sister – they shared many common features. There was definitely a resemblance there. He was sure of it.

25

HELENA

The rest of the weekend seemed to drag. James moved around the house full of nervous excitement that his plan was moving forward. Even though it was a Saturday afternoon, he had called his solicitor as soon as they had come home from Aidan's house. He wasn't going to waste time waiting until the working world reopened after the weekend. He had managed to set up a meeting for first thing on Monday morning and Helena was dreading it. It seemed she was being dragged along on his crusade, whether she liked it or not. She was already so entrenched, in far deeper than she had ever wanted to be, but she had no one to blame but herself.

Why on earth had she done that test? Why couldn't she just have left everything as it was and she wouldn't be facing this nightmare she now found herself in. She was due back in to the surgery soon, but she had called Ken and told him she would need more time and he had readily agreed. She knew she was in no fit state to return to work. She wasn't sleeping at night, she was barely eating. She felt guilt gnawing away at her constantly. She really hadn't thought the consequences through properly; she had been so sure that the test would tell her that James wasn't Milly's father and then, when the truth had been revealed, she had assumed that James would be more reticent, like her, wrestling and wrangling with his conscience about what the right thing to do was, but he showed no apprehension and actually seemed certain that it was his duty to fulfil his claim on Milly. He would pause and lean onto his crutches, saying things like, 'Imagine Christmas, Hel, we might have her in our lives by then – just picture it, baking cookies for Santa and then helping her to open her presents,' or other times he talked about the legal side of things, 'We've a really strong case,' he would argue.

'No judge could possibly refuse to let us be in her life.'

Helena wanted to cover her ears with her hands and block out his words and stop all of this madness. Had he forgotten that their marriage was still as delicate as old china? He seemed to think that because there was a chance to have a child in their lives, all their problems had been solved, but the truth was, Helena had never felt more distant from her husband or unsure what the future held for them.

* * *

On Monday morning, Helena woke feeling as though there was a weight sitting on her chest, pushing her down on the bed. She had slept fitfully that night, flitting in and out of sleep, slipping in between dreams and nightmares. She had woken in a sweat after one particularly awful one where James was literally pulling Milly out of Aidan's arms and Milly was screaming at her, 'Help me, Lena.' She hoped that maybe the solicitor would talk some sense into James, advise him that it was better to tread carefully and take a considered approach instead of attacking Aidan with all guns blazing. Although she knew that by having proof that he was Milly's biological father, James had already overcome the biggest hurdle and stood a really good chance of gaining access.

She could already hear James moving around down below, getting ready for the meeting. She pulled back the duvet and trudged into the en suite. She showered and dressed, choosing a silk shirt and slim-fitting three-quarter-length trousers from her walk-in wardrobe. Putting on a blazer, she squared her shoulders. As she looked at her reflection in the mirror, the confident woman staring back at her belied the mess that she was inside.

'Good morning,' James said brightly as she came into the kitchen a while later. 'How did you sleep?' He was sitting at the table eating a bowl of granola. His mobility was coming on well; he had had several physiotherapy sessions and was making new gains every day. Although he was still sleeping in the living room, Helena reckoned it wouldn't be long until he was back using the stairs again. She had helped him to set up a workstation in there too and she would see him clacking away on his laptop and taking calls from Colm, but she knew he was itching to get back into the office again.

'Not great,' Helena admitted, hearing the wobble in her voice.

'Are you okay?' he asked.

She sighed. 'Are you sure we're doing the right thing, James?' She had been asking herself this question all night long.

'I don't understand – I've watched you be completely broken over the last few years trying to have a child and now we have a chance to have one – don't you want Milly in our lives?'

'Of course I want to have a child, James!' she replied with emotion threading her words. 'But not like this. What about Milly – is it right to do this to her and the boys too… It's too high a price to pay! I keep thinking of Aidan and all that he will be losing – it's cruel.'

'We're not trying to take Milly off him, Helena, I just want to have her in my life. Put yourself in my shoes, if you suddenly discovered you had a child out there wouldn't you do all that you could to be a part of their life?'

He had been saying a version of these words ever

since he had learned about the paternity test result and she had no answer for him because deep down she knew she would do the same. She would do whatever it took – she would travel to the ends of the Earth – if there was a chance to carry a child of her own. It could never happen for her, but James had got a chance and she couldn't blame him for wanting to grab it with both hands.

Helena knew she had a choice to make: she could either walk away from all this drama or stay with James in the hope that he was granted some sort of shared custody of Milly and have an opportunity to be involved in a child's life. Wasn't having a child all she really wanted? A part of her asked if it really matter how it happened? She knew from the families that came into her surgery that the days of the traditional family were long gone.

When she was growing up in Ballycladdagh, the tiny coastal village of her birth, everyone at her school was from a wholesome two-parent family: mother, father and children. People didn't separate and there were no single parents, unless they had been widowed, but times had changed for the better and nowadays there were lots of blends in between.

There were step-parents and stepchildren, half-siblings, children who spent one weekend with one parent and the next weekend with the other, children raised by grandparents, children born to same-sex couples, children that had been born by surrogate – she had seen it all. Would their situation really be so different? So what if they wouldn't be the conventional family that she had always pictured in her head, maybe she needed to get past those ideas. But no matter how she tried to convince herself that if she wanted a chance to be a mother, then this was her only shot, it still wouldn't sit right with her.

* * *

Later that morning as Helena turned her Volvo jeep onto Fitzwilliam Square, where the offices of Ward & Jones solicitors were located, her heart rate started to ratchet. They had only ever used Laurence Jones for the conveyancing on their house, Helena wasn't even sure if he would have the necessary expertise to help them, but James had been confident that it was the best place to start. She pulled up outside the Georgian terrace and fed the parking meter with coins.

She displayed the ticket on her windscreen, then helped James out of the car and onto his crutches. She linked his arm as he made his way up the granite steps, then he pressed the bell. As they waited to be let in, Helena felt as though there was a rock sitting in the pit of her stomach.

'Good morning,' the receptionist greeted after a few moments after she had opened the door to them.

'We're here to see Laurence Jones,' James began.

'Take a seat in our reception and I'll let him know you're here.' She smiled kindly at them.

They sat down in the reception area, where they were immediately overpowered by the fragrance emanating from a large bouquet of lilies that sat atop the fireplace. The smell made Helena feel nauseous.

'James, Helena,' Laurence Jones said appearing in the reception area a few minutes later. They shook hands. 'If you'd like to come with me.'

They followed him over the plush carpet down to his office. They went inside and Helena looked around at the dark mahogany bookshelves that were stacked with heavy leatherbound legal tomes. Although it was a generously proportioned room, it felt small, almost claustrophobic.

'I must say I was intrigued when you called me on Saturday, James,' Laurence began. 'Do you want to fill me in on the background first?'

Helena knew that James hadn't given him the full details yet and she cringed as he took a deep breath and began telling him the sequence of events that had led them here. He looked sheepish as he told Laurence about the one-night stand and everything that had happened since. As Helena listened, it sounded like something out of a soap opera, it was all so far-fetched and unbelievable. She saw Laurence Jones was doing his best to keep his expression neutral, but he couldn't mask the shock in his eyes. She couldn't believe how much the landscape of her life had altered in such a short period of time.

'I don't normally specialise in family law, but there are a few things which immediately jump out at me. Firstly, under Irish Law, when a married couple have a baby, the woman's husband is assumed to be the child's father and has automatic guardianship rights even if he may not be the biological father. I need to ask how did you procure the DNA sample from the child? I presume you had the necessary consent paperwork in place from the child's legal guardian?'

Helena felt heat creeping up along her face.

James turned to her, wondering how best to answer the question. She looked down at the floor. James turned back to Laurence. 'Helena took the sample,' he admitted after a moment. 'Aidan had asked her to sit with Milly while he was at the funeral and she did it then.'

'And you had consent from the child's father?' Laurence repeated.

Helena thought she was going to get sick. 'Well, that's the thing...' she began. 'I just took her toothbrush—'

'Without consent?' Laurence reiterated.

Her palms grew clammy as she thought about the false patient identities that she had forged on the consent forms. If anyone ever found out about them, she would be in a world of trouble.

'Okay, I know she didn't follow strict legal protocol,' James interrupted, 'but if Helena hadn't done the test, then I would never have known the truth.'

'I really didn't think it would come back with the result that James was her father and I thought I could forget all about it,' Helena explained. But she realised how pathetic it sounded in the cold light of day.

'But that's not what happened, is it. Instead you have discovered that James is in fact the child's biological father.'

Helena nodded. She wanted the ground to swallow her up. It felt as though the room was spinning around her.

'Look, can you help us or not?' James asked, jumping to her defence with impatience.

'You need to be aware that Helena could be struck off by the medical council for engaging in this type of behaviour.'

'But she wasn't working there!' James protested. 'This has nothing to do with her job as a GP.'

'The man left Helena in the care of his daughter, while he attended his late wife's funeral,' Laurence explained.

'As a friend – not in a medical capacity – Milly had her own medical team at the hospital,' James interrupted. 'Helena was not involved in her care at any point.'

'Nonetheless, some would argue that Helena

abused her position as a medical professional. There are also patient confidentiality violations.'

'Wh-what do you mean?' Helena said slowly. She hadn't even considered this.

'You overhead a medical conversation taking place between the child's doctor and father and then you used that confidential information for your own needs.'

'But her father asked me to be there – I wasn't doing anything underhand by being present,' Helena interjected.

'As a doctor, it could be construed that you had a greater understanding of blood types and their genetic profiles than most laypeople would have. It could definitely be argued that you used your own medical knowledge to take advantage of this man.'

'So what you're saying is that I could lose my job over this?' Helena asked in shock.

Laurence Jones nodded. 'There is a risk. I have to make you aware of every possibility or I wouldn't be advising you properly. You need to be fully prepared for all events if you do decide to proceed with this case. Mr Whelan's team could throw the rulebook at you and they'd have a very good case. It could get nasty. Think carefully,' he warned.

'When you say it like that, you make it sound like we're the ones who are wrong here, but we were lied to,' James protested angrily. 'I've been denied a chance to be present in my daughter's life for the last three years. We're victims here too, y'know!'

Here it was again, Helena thought, James using 'we' and 'our' except it wasn't 'we' and 'our' – she was acutely aware that Milly was James's child, not hers – no matter how much she had imagined it differently in her head.

26

AIDAN

Rowan was in the kitchen. She was standing there in her white towelling robe, making waffles. She had a tea towel slung over her shoulder and the spatula in her hand. She turned around and smiled at them all. 'Surprise, I'm back again!' she said. Aidan felt a huge wave of relief rush through him, as the kids ran over and threw their arms around her. Even Callum had a huge grin on his face. They were all laughing and hugging her tightly and Aidan felt his heart soar. The people he loved most in the world were overjoyed and happy again, the way it should be. 'Come on, Aidan,' Rowan beckoned to him to join them.

He ran over towards them, but suddenly the doorbell rang.

'I'd better get that,' he said, turning in his tracks and heading down the hallway.

Suddenly her face fell. 'Why do you put everything before me, Aidan?' she asked sadly.

The doorbell went again and Aidan woke with a start. He looked around him feeling panicked and realised he had been dreaming. Milly was asleep in the bed beside him, he vaguely remembered her climbing in during the night. He checked the clock on his bedside table and saw that it was nearly eleven a.m. How had he slept in so late?

The doorbell went again and it dawned on him that it would be Rowan's parents. *Shit*, he thought. He had completely forgotten that they had said they would call over to see the children on Monday. He jumped up and pulled on the same pair of joggers that he had been wearing the day before that he had tossed onto the floor going to bed. He pulled a sweatshirt over his head. He glanced quickly in the mirror, trying to tame his hair and make himself look like he hadn't just been asleep. Then he hurried down the stairs, taking the steps two at a time, to open the door to Sheila and Philip, who didn't look impressed to have been kept waiting.

'Did we wake you?' Philip asked straight away. No 'good morning' or 'how are you?'

'No,' Aidan lied. 'I was out the back, I didn't hear the bell.'

'We thought you might have gone out,' Sheila said, 'but your car was in the driveway. Where are the children?'

'They're still asleep.'

'At eleven o'clock? They must have had a late night.'

They could never resist getting a dig in. Their latest issue was that Aidan still hadn't taken the children to the graveyard to visit Rowan's grave. The truth was that Aidan couldn't face taking them to look at their mother buried under the cold, sticky earth, he didn't feel able for it.

He led them to the kitchen and Aidan watched as Sheila surveyed the mess. He wasn't sure if it was his imagination, but he thought he saw her raising her eyebrows in Philip's direction. The last time they had called, she had not-so-subtly suggested that he hire a cleaner, but cleaning was the last thing on his mind; these days he was just trying to survive.

'Can I get you a tea or coffee?' Aidan asked.

'I'll have a coffee,' Philip replied, sitting down at the island. He noticed Philip eyeing the blank space on the wall where he had taken down their wedding photograph.

'Nothing for me thank you,' Sheila said, pulling out a stool and joining him.

Aidan set to making a coffee for Philip and himself. He needed it. The headache that had pounded his head all weekend still lingered and his head was fuzzy from the dream and being woken so abruptly.

He made polite conversation and was relieved when Milly appeared a few minutes later. She would help distract Rowan's parents.

'Ganny and Gandad!' she cried, running into the kitchen.

'Hello, darling girl, how are you?' Philip said, getting up from the stool. He lifted her up and swung her around.

'She's the image of her mother at that age, isn't she, Philip?' Sheila said sadly. 'It's like stepping back in time.'

'She is, my love,' Philip replied. 'So have you any news for your old, Grandad?' Philip asked as he sat back onto the stool with Milly on his knee.

'The police came to our house – there was a girl one and a boy one.'

Aidan cringed. He had hoped he could avoid Sheila and Philip finding out about it.

'The police,' Sheila gave a nervous laugh. 'Are you sure, Milly?'

Milly nodded her head definitively.

Philip turned to Aidan. 'Was it something to do with the accident?'

Aidan shook his head. 'I had a bit of bother with Callum on Saturday,' he admitted.

Sheila's face fell. 'What do you mean?' she asked.

'He was caught shoplifting.'

'Callum wouldn't do that!' she replied with confidence.

'Unfortunately he was caught with crisps and a can of Coke concealed inside his hoodie.'

'Oh for God's sake,' Philip spluttered. 'That's ridiculous, he was probably just carrying them in his pocket – you know what teenagers are like.'

'The Gardaí said he walked out of the shop without paying.'

'He probably just forgot to pay. The boy made an honest mistake. What were their names - those two Gardaí? I have a friend in the golf club who is a superintendent. I won't have my grandson branded like some sort of... some type of... of... criminal – it's ridiculous.'

'They have it on CCTV, they seem pretty certain,' Aidan continued. Although he himself hadn't wanted to believe it was true, he had had to accept what the guards had told him.

'Well, even if it's true, why cause all that drama for the sake of a couple of euro? Could you not just have given the shop owner the money owed, maybe a little extra for the hassle, and we could forget all about it?' Philip continued, turning the blame onto Aidan.

'It's not that simple,' Aidan explained. 'It doesn't matter if he stole two euros' worth of stuff or two hundred euros, they told me they have to be seen to come down hard on shoplifting.'

'Why would he do it?' Sheila asked, clearly bewildered. 'He gets pocket money, doesn't he?'

Aidan nodded. 'That's the thing...' he paused, 'they think it was a cry for help—'

Sheila's jewelled hand fluttered to her necklace and she began sliding its diamond pendant back and forth across the chain. 'Oh the poor boy, he's really suffering. He was very close to his mother.'

'Well, did you talk to him?' Philip demanded. 'Find out what is going on with him?'

'I tried, but he keeps shutting me down. He won't open up to me.'

Philip shook his head in exasperation.

'Maybe he should come to stay with us for a while?' Sheila suggested. 'He might just need a little time and space away.'

'He's not going anywhere,' Aidan said quickly. He knew what Sheila and Philip were like, they had this way of suggesting they were helping you when really it was them trying to be in control. When he and Rowan had been getting married, Philip had offered to pay for the wedding and then had invited half of his golf club. Aidan hadn't recognised most of the guests at their reception. When they had been buying the house and Aidan was arguing that they couldn't afford to live on Ledbury Road, Sheila and

Philip had fronted the money, just so Rowan could have her own way. There was always a catch with their generosity. It had been the same way his entire marriage.

'You don't need to be so defensive. I'm only trying to help you, Aidan. You're so busy with the younger two, maybe a little one-on-one attention is what Callum needs right now.'

'This is his home,' Aidan said with a steely resolve, just so there was no doubt in their minds.

'But if you're not able to cope…' Sheila continued, throwing the accusation out there, leaving it dangling in the air, turning it sour.

'Of course I'm able to cope,' Aidan retorted bitterly. 'Callum has lost his mother and he's a teenager – it's bound to be tricky. It's going to take a while for him to process it,' he said, repeating the advice that Gemma had given to him.

'Well I won't stand by and watch my grandson turn into a delinquent because you weren't able to keep him in line!' Philip blasted.

'It was one incident, let's not get carried away,' Aidan said with more assurance than he felt. 'I'll try to talk to him again.'

'Well, you better regain control over his behaviour before this gets any worse,' Philip warned.

'Just think about it, Aidan,' Sheila tried to persuade him once more. 'It would only be for a few days… you wouldn't even notice he was gone.'

'Callum is going nowhere!' Aidan said resolutely. As much as Callum was hard work at the moment, something told him that his son needed him now more than ever. 'This is his where he belongs – with me, Jack and Milly.'

27

HELENA

They had driven home from Fitzwilliam Square in silence, each of them processing their thoughts after the meeting with Laurence Jones. Helena had let them into the house and wordlessly they had both sat down at the kitchen table.

Wedges of white autumn sunlight spread out across the kitchen tiles. The tension was sitting thickly in the air, so thick that Helena was sure if you took a pair of scissors, you would be able to cut right through it. The meeting had been an eye-opener for her. Up until then she had thought that destroying Aidan was their biggest worry, now she realised there was so much more at stake here. She had thought they would be able to keep the matter between their respective solicitors, but Laurence Jones had informed them that if they did decide to proceed, then their next step would be to make an application to the District Court. The thought of their deepest darkest secrets being aired in the midst of a court battle was awful. She was also worried about her professionalism being called into question. The thought of her family and colleagues learning what she had done filled her with shame.

'So what do you reckon? It sounds like we've got a good case, doesn't it?' James began.

Helena felt as though they had been at two different meetings. She had been thinking over everything that Laurence Jones had told them, with something close to despair.

'What's wrong?' he asked, picking up on her muted reaction. 'You're not happy?'

'I don't think I can do it,' she said.

'Of course you can, I know it seems daunting right now, but it will all be worth it when we have little Milly in our lives, I promise you,' he coaxed. He reached across the table and gave her hand a squeeze, but she quickly pulled it away from him.

'You're the only person who wins in this, James – Aidan loses out, Milly too, even I will lose out.'

'Why would you say that?' he asked, sounding wounded.

'You heard what Laurence said: there's a risk I could be struck off! I can't take that chance. I spent so many years studying, working crazy hours as a junior doctor, then doing my GP training. But it's more than that – I love my job, I love helping my patients. I've been out of work for three weeks and I can't wait to be back. I'm sorry but I can't put all of that in jeopardy. I've so much more to lose than you.'

'Laurence was just pointing out the worst-case scenario – that's his job, it doesn't mean it is actually going to happen.'

'But it could. And even if I didn't get struck off, something like this would ruin my career if people found out. It would be all over the press. Imagine what my colleagues would say? Or my parents? They'd be horrified. And by the way, even if we decided to go ahead with the court application and were successful, have you even considered what we would tell our families? How would you begin to explain Milly's sudden presence in our lives to them?

You'd have to go right back to the start and tell them about the one-night stand – they think that Rowan was just giving you a lift on the day of the crash. Imagine what they would say if they knew all of this?' Helena's elderly parents were extremely religious and she knew this wouldn't sit well with their traditional values at all. 'It would kill Mam and Dad and I don't think your parents would fare much better.'

'If we want to be happy then we can't live our lives worried about what other people will think. Come on, Hel,' he coaxed, 'I know it will come as a shock to a lot of people – hell, it's even come as a shock to me – and maybe some people won't be supportive of us, but this is our one and only chance to be parents and if people aren't happy for us, then they're not worth having in our lives,' James went on. 'Who cares what people think! They don't know the full story. They don't know us, they don't know what we've been through or how much we want a child. We're doing the right thing. I know this is horrible and a stressful situation, but the end result will justify the means.'

'It's different for you, James. You might be her father, but even if you're successful, it doesn't change the fact that I'll never be her mother – she's *your* daughter, not mine.' She'd finally said the words that she had been skirting around but she needed to make James see it. No matter what way he tried to dress it up, Milly would never be her daughter.

'But you're my wife – we're in this together. We'll be a family together When I woke up in hospital after the crash, I knew I had got a second chance. When something like that happens to you – when you look death in the eye like I did – you know you will never take another day for granted again. We get one life and I want to live mine with no regrets and I swore I was going to do everything I possibly could to live my life properly.'

'Just listen to yourself, James, you are consumed by this! Too many people will get hurt; there's Aidan, Callum and Jack, there's me and the risk to my job, and of course the child caught in the middle of it all, Milly. She's too young to understand, she's been through enough. If you really cared about Milly, you would put her first and do what's right for her instead of yourself.'

'We would do it slowly, just an hour here and

there initially and then build it up. She wouldn't even realise what was happening.'

'And would you get her to call you Dad as well?' Helena pushed.

'I never even thought about that... but let's not get hung up on the technicalities. I don't care what she calls me, I just want her in my life.'

She shook her head. 'I don't think I can be a part of it.' How she wished she could just climb on board James's train and fight for this chance to be parents. She wanted everything that he wanted; she wanted a child for them too, but this wasn't the way it was supposed to be. She didn't want their chance at parenthood to come about at the expense of somebody else. How would they begin to live with themselves? Helena knew she could never be happy knowing they had done that to Aidan.

'Why the hell did you start all of this if you weren't prepared to stay the course?' he blazed. 'You're in this too whether you like it or not. You're the one who told me about the paternity test. You started all of this!'

'I know and I'm sorry, I wish that I'd never done that damned test.'

'How can you say that? She was my child all along and I never even knew it, you'd rather I had been kept in the dark?' he asked in disbelief. 'You can't just bow out now when the going gets tough –.'

'I know it's all my fault, but it's not too late, we can stop this from going any further before we ruin any more lives. It isn't about us, it should be about Milly and what she wants. She's grieving for her mother, you can't force the issue now. We've told Aidan the truth, so it's up to him what he wants to do with this information.'

'I can't believe I'm hearing this!' James shook his head, with fury lighting his eyes. 'What did you expect me to do with the knowledge that I had a child?' he shouted. 'Did you think I'd just continue on and forget all about it? I don't get you, Helena. You can't just give me a chance of making my dreams come true and then snatch it away from me again!' he blasted.

'I just never imagined it would go this far.' She couldn't hold it together any more as her voice dissolved into tears. She wanted all this madness to stop. She wanted her old life back. Even in her darkest hours of infertility struggles, she had never felt as low as this. 'I just hoped we would have been able to deal with Aidan on our own without bringing solicitors and court hearings into it.'

'Well then you're very naïve. Did you think Aidan was just going to roll over and hand her over to us? Come on, Helena, get real! We have to fight for her!'

'I don't think I can,' she whispered.

'Well I'm not going to give up on her, I'm not going to be made a mug of any more. With or without you, I'm going ahead with the application.'

28

AIDAN

Aidan was standing in the kitchen trying to brush Milly's hair. He pulled the hairbrush down through the dark strands where it snagged on a knot and she let out a yelp, 'Owwweee, Daddy, op! Op!'

'Sorry, love, I'm trying not to hurt you. I promise I'll try to be a bit gentler.'

Brushing Milly's hair was the one thing Aidan dreaded. Over the last few weeks, he had got to grips with making dinners, vacuuming and putting on the washing machine, but doing Milly's hair was something he seemed to fail abysmally at. Women had a lifetime of practice before they had to start doing their daughters' hair, but for a man it was a whole new experience, he thought grimly. He made hapless attempts every morning at ponytails or sticking hair-clips in to tidy it up a little, but she still never looked neat, like the other girls they would see.

It was over a month since the crash and it was the day that the children were due to return to school. It was also to be Aidan's first morning back in work. He felt his stomach lurch whenever he thought about it. It was Gemma who had suggested that maybe it was time. 'It'll be a good distraction,' she had said. Aidan had been waiting for the right time, but he now realised that was never going to happen. There was never going to be a right time.

The kids had missed so much school already and he didn't want them to fall behind and have to contend with that as well as everything else that had happened to them. He also knew it was probably time to return to work; there was only so much bereavement leave his company would give him. Hadn't he once been that same boss that had said to members of his team to 'take as much time off as you need' when they were going through something but really, he expected them back in the job in a few weeks? Any longer and he thought they were taking the piss.

Aidan now understood that there was no time limit on grief. People said that time healed, but he could imagine himself a year down the road – even ten years down the road – still feeling the same way, completely floored and shocked by what had happened to them. It felt wrong to move on again, how could they do that? Returning to normal life seemed like admitting acceptance – like he was giving the world permission to continue on when his life had come to a standstill. People would think that by getting on with their lives they were okay; that they were picking up the pieces and getting through it, but Aidan didn't think they would ever be okay again. He still felt angry and cheated that this had happened to his family, he wanted people to know that it wasn't all right – he wanted them to understand just how awful the last few weeks had been.

He was also scared to send the children back to their ordinary lives when everything had changed so much. It was like part of their shell had been removed and they were a little bit more vulnerable, a little more exposed to the frailties of life. They now knew that bad things could happen and when they did, he wouldn't always be able to fix it or be by their side them to protect them.

He twisted the elastic around Milly's hair, wincing as it snagged on a strand. Then he turned her around to face him. He looked at her lopsided pigtails and sighed. Poor Milly, she would have to endure a lifetime of bad hairstyles at his hands.

'You look beautiful,' he said. 'Go grab your lunch bag.' He watched his daughter run off towards the cloakroom. She still had her cast on, but it hadn't slowed her down.

He hadn't heard anything further from James and Helena. As the days had gone past and he had time to process everything, he was feeling more and more outraged by their visit. At first their audacity had landed like a sucker punch that he hadn't had time to prepare for, but as he had begun to digest it, he was disgusted at how pathetic they were. They were so hellbent on having a child that they didn't care whose lives they trampled on. James had destroyed enough of his life, and he certainly wasn't going to allow him to do any more damage.

He looked over at Jack who was munching his way through a bowl of Cheerios at the table, but his spoon seemed to be permanently dangling in mid-air. It was as though the distance between the bowl and his mouth was an eternity.

'Jack, hurry up and finish your breakfast, we need to leave in five minutes!' Aidan warned. 'Callum?' he called upstairs. He had woken Callum an hour ago, but he had yet to make an appearance in the kitchen. 'We're leaving in five minutes.'

Callum's behaviour was still proving difficult. He had accompanied his son to the BetterValu supermarket to apologise to the store owner, but he had refused to set foot in the place.

'Why the hell did you come here if you're not even going to bother getting out of the car?' Aidan had asked as they sat in the car park, growing angrier with every passing minute.

He'd shrugged. 'I didn't want to come, you made me.'

'Are you going to go in?' Aidan had tried again, but Callum had remained stubbornly silent, so

Aidan had stormed out of the car, slammed the door behind him and marched into the supermarket.

Why couldn't Callum see the bigger picture here? he'd wondered, feeling anger blistering through him. The Gardaí had told them that a simple apology could prevent this from escalating further. Callum didn't realise how much was at stake.

A lady on the checkout had told him that the store owner was in the frozen food aisle. He'd found him, a small man in his mid-sixties, piling bags of frozen peas into a freezer. Aidan had apologised on Callum's behalf, explaining the situation about Rowan's death and promising that it would never happen again. The store owner had been very gracious about it, all things considered.

'If you so much as set foot in that shop again, you'll never leave the house,' Aidan had warned as he returned to Callum in the car.

'Whatever,' Callum had retorted, as he'd looked out the window.

Aidan had gripped the steering wheel tighter. They drove home silently together and when they reached the house, the tension had wound itself so tightly around Aidan, that he felt like punching something. He knew his angry reaction was inflaming the situation; Rowan would have told him to calm down and deal with it rationally, but he couldn't help it. How dare Callum think this was okay. Once they'd got in the house Callum had stormed upstairs, while he had gone in to Gemma, who had been minding the younger two.

'I just can't get through to him,' Aidan had said, coming into the kitchen, tossing his keys down on the island. 'We're trying to help him here, but how can we do that when he won't even help himself?'

'I know it might not feel like it, but you're doing a good job, Aidan,' she had said. 'Don't beat yourself up. Give him time.'

'Daddy, can you help me?' Milly asked, pulling him out of his head.

'Sure, sweetheart.'

He helped her to slide her arms into the sleeves of her coat.

'Hurry up, boys,' he called upstairs to where Jack had gone to brush his teeth and he was still waiting on Callum to appear. 'We're leaving now.'

He held Milly's hand and led her out of the house. As they descended the front steps, he saw their postman coming up the driveway towards him.

He handed Aidan a letter. 'I need you to sign for this,' he said.

'Sure,' Aidan said, signing the handheld device where indicated, wondering what was so important that he had to sign for it. He realised with a sinking feeling that it was probably some official paperwork to do with Rowan's death. Over the last few days, there had been so many letters arriving from insurance companies and other financial institutions regarding policies they had had in place in the unlikely event of one of them dying young. The types of things you set up to be sensible, but you never expect to use.

He took the envelope and held it between his teeth as he opened the car and strapped Milly into her seat. Then he sat in the driver's seat and ran his finger beneath the gummed seal, while he waited for the boys to come out of the house. He took out the letter that was inside and unfolded it. He quickly scanned through it and felt his heart stop with every word he read. Surely it was wrong. He tried reading it again, but the words seemed to be swimming on the page before him. The car doors opened, and Jack climbed in beside Milly and Callum sat into the passenger seat. Aidan quickly folded the letter and slipped it back inside the envelope. His fingers were trembling as he turned the key in the ignition.

29

HELENA

Helena pounded the pavement, her feet synched to her breathing as she ran. They were experiencing something of an Indian summer, and the streets were busy with people enjoying a last blast of heat before the winter chill won out. Office workers spilled out of cafés on their lunchbreak. She weaved her way through people on the pavement. It was a long time since she had run, and her fitness wasn't what it used to be. She had stopped running for a while; after hearing somewhere that it wasn't good for women trying to conceive, she had abandoned it a few months back. She had read so many theories and tried so many alternative therapies along her infertility journey, desperately going along with them, hoping that that one change would be the thing that made the difference, but it never had. She felt her lungs burn as she breathed in, but she enjoyed the release it gave her body, the headspace it gave her mind to process everything. Not to mention an hour out of the house, where James was still laid up.

Things were still tense between them since he had told her about his plans to use the court system to get access to Milly. He wanted a shared-access arrangement; he said the details would need to be ironed out between both parties, but he was hoping to have Milly feature permanently in their lives. He was angry that Helena wasn't on board with his plans, and she couldn't blame him. It was her fault that they were on this road – she had pulled back a curtain and given him a glimpse of a life he could have, and now she wanted to close it again and forget all about it. How could she expect him to do that?

But no matter how much he argued with her or to tried to convince her that it was too late to back out now, that it was she who had opened this can of worms, Helena still couldn't support it. Sometimes in life the fairest thing wasn't always the right thing.

How could they uproot Milly from the only father she had ever known, especially so soon after the loss of her mother? And what about Callum and Jack too and their wider family, how would Aidan explain to them why James was laying claim to Milly? He would have to taint the good memories that they had left of their mother with the less savoury news that she had been unfaithful. Then there was the risk of being struck off the medical register and the shame Helena would feel when her colleagues found out about it all. She just wanted things to go back to the way they were before, but James was obsessed with the idea of having Milly in their lives.

She stopped to let a beeping bin lorry reverse into a side street, taking a moment to catch her breath. Then she continued on, passing a woman coming against her on the footpath.

'Dr O'Herlihy?' the woman called after her.

Helena stopped and turned around; it took her a second, but then she recognised who it was. 'Julie?' she said. She immediately cringed, thinking back to that day in the surgery when this woman had cried in front of her, and Helena had fallen apart alongside her. Helena hadn't realised it at the time, but that had been the start of it all – the beginning of the end. It felt like a lifetime ago now, her world had changed beyond recognition since then. 'How are you?' She breathed deeply, trying to catch her breath.

'I'm good,' Julie grinned. 'I was in the surgery last week actually.'

'Oh yeah?' she panted.

'I asked to see you, but they said you were off, so I saw the locum instead.' The woman was grinning manically at her and Helena knew there was more she wanted to say. 'I know I shouldn't be telling people yet, but seeing as though it's you...' She leaned in conspiratorially. 'I'm pregnant again,' she announced, her whole face beaming with pride. 'I was in having it confirmed.'

The traffic seemed to get louder and the white sunlight blinded Helena's eyes. She suddenly felt very hot – the combination of the heat from the run and the searing sun made her feel as though she might pass out. She couldn't catch her breath; her lungs had seized.

'Are you okay?' Julie asked, her face full of concern.

'Sorry, I pushed a bit hard.' Helena reached out

and gripped onto a nearby lamp post to steady herself and fanned herself with her hands. 'Congratulations.' She tried to smile. She meant it, oh she really did, she was so happy for this woman who had experienced her fair share of pain too, but her heart also felt like someone was holding it at either side and twisting until it was completely wrung out.

'I know it's early days,' Julie continued excitedly. 'I'm only six weeks, so I've a long road ahead of me... After the miscarriage I didn't think it would happen so soon. We're both over the moon,' she gushed. She put her hand on her tummy, where inside her miracle was growing – her chance of happiness was unfurling like the tiny buds in the spring.

Helena nodded. 'That's wonderful news, I hope it will all go really well for you.'

'Me too,' Julie sighed. 'I'm a nervous wreck, every twinge has me running to the bathroom. I don't think I'll relax until I'm holding my baby in my arms.'

'That's understandable... Look... I'd better go,' Helena said, still trying to catch a breath.

'Oh sorry, I know what you runners are like

about your times, so I'll let you get back to it,' Julie laughed.

Helena wished her well and tried to continue on, but her rhythm was all wrong. She couldn't get her legs to work properly; they felt leaden. Her head was in a spin. She didn't want to be that bitter person that was jealous of other people's happiness, but it seemed that everyone else got their happy ever after except her. She had spent so long wondering when it would be their turn. Helena had always believed that if you wanted something badly enough and worked hard to achieve it, it would pay off. Sometimes it might take a while, but you would see the results eventually. It was a mentality that had served her well throughout her life – it had got her through medical school, running a marathon – everything. And she had been sure that because their journey to have a baby had been so arduous it would all come right in the end – they *deserved* it, but then it still hadn't happened, and it would never happen now. Her friends had rallied around saying things like 'keep your chin up' and telling her to stay positive. 'It *will* happen,' they had promised as if they had a crystal ball, and she had stupidly believed them.

They filled her head with stories of friends and relatives who had all but given up hope of conceiving a baby when suddenly they had fallen pregnant. Miracles happened every day when you least expected them, you just had to be open to them, they said. And she had tried, she had tried so bloody hard, but she now knew that people lied, they fed you stories full of hope because they didn't know what else to say.

Carrying a baby was the most fundamental part of being a woman; it was the reason women were on this earth, to keep the human race populated. So why wasn't her body capable of doing its job? Why couldn't she do what millions of women did every day and had done for thousands of years? Why could women who took heroin, who drank bottles of vodka daily, women in desperate abusive situations, or living in countries ravaged by famine or war, conceive and carry a healthy baby while, despite giving her body every opportunity and having a pretty good lifestyle by most people's standards, Helena still couldn't?

It had happened once, her miracle. After several early miscarriages, she had got to the magical twelve-week mark, where the chances of miscarriage are drastically reduced, and she had been so sure that it was meant to be that time. Finally, *finally*, it was their turn. At last. She had waved to the blurry shape of her baby on the monitor during her scan, feeling her heart swell with love for her much-longed-for baby, with tears of gratitude pooling at the corners of her eyes. Until the cramps had arrived and then the bleeding had followed, and she knew her dream was being snatched away from her once again. She had found out in the blood tests they had carried out afterwards that he was a little boy. She had called him George. She had never told anyone that; not even James knew that she had named him.

The pain lanced through her as it always did whenever she remembered him. She knew James thought he could fix the hole in her heart with Milly, but it wasn't a case of simply replacing one child with another. No matter how much she yearned for a baby, she knew the pain of losing a child, how could she inflict that on another person? She couldn't do that to Aidan.

Somehow Helena managed to make her way home, she didn't remember getting there – her head was too full. She let herself into the house and heard sounds of the TV coming from the living room.

'Helena?' he called out to her.

She couldn't bear to see him, so instead she continued through the house and out into the garden. She sat down in the chair under the branches of the oak tree as they swayed gently in the breeze and closed her eyes. George would be a boisterous toddler now, taking wobbly first steps, trying to lift pudgy legs to climb steps. Eating everything he could find, soil and stones, exploring the world with his mouth. She could imagine leading him through the garden, lifting a rock to show him the creepy-crawlies beneath or watching an earthworm shrink away from them. He would trip going up the garden steps and she would pick him up, sit him onto her hip and soothe him. She would carry him inside and kiss away his tears and put a plaster on his grazed knee. She would sing to him until he stopped crying and tell him he was the bravest boy and that she loved him so, so much.

30

AIDAN

Aidan walked across the open-plan office in a daze. His colleagues rushed over to greet him as soon as they saw him. He vaguely remembered seeing some of them at the funeral through his haze of grief. He stood there going through the motions, listening to their platitudes and their awkward attempts at making conversation until eventually they all left him to get on with things and he went into his office and shut the door behind him.

He waited as his laptop powered up and exhaled loudly as he watched hundreds of emails begin to download. He looked around the office with its views across the IFSC and the wide mouth of the Liffey snaking through the city. Everything had changed and yet nothing had. His team had kept the show on the road in his absence, the job hadn't come to a standstill, and he realised that they could survive without him. That thought would have bruised his ego just a few months back, but now he really didn't care.

The things that had once seemed important, now seemed so trivial. All those urgent deadlines, always hungry to win the next client and then the one after that, the approval from Richard and the rest of the board – it had been like a drug. He was always too busy. Too important. Life had been turned on its head and he now realised none of it mattered – not the accolades or the approval. Why had he spent so many hours toiling away at this desk when he had a lovely family at home waiting for him? Why had he been so concerned with his appearance here instead of to the people who mattered to him? He should have been home earlier in the evenings, been there at dinner time or to help Rowan with bath-time when the children were smaller. And would it really have killed him to take a half-day here and there to surprise the boys by collecting them from school or to see their school concerts? Would Rowan still have slept with James if he had been more present in their marriage? That was the question that would torment him forever more. It was hard to accept that maybe if he had had more balance in his life, then things might have been different. Yes, he needed to earn a living, with three children to feed and clothe, but he didn't have to work at the intensity that he had been working at before the crash. His head was full of 'what ifs'.

And now this letter had arrived and knocked him completely off balance. It was sitting in the pocket behind the lapel of his suit jacket like a grenade. He was about to reach inside to take it out and read it again when suddenly there was a knock on the door.

'Aidan, how are you doing?' Richard asked, sticking his head around the frame. 'It's good to have you back.'

'I'm doing okay, thanks.'

'How are the children?'

Aidan thought about Milly's wobbling lip as she had clung to his hand that morning as he led her into the crèche. She would now be attending it full-time while he was at work. She hadn't wanted to leave him, and he hadn't wanted to leave her either. The minders had had to peel her off him and he had had to leave her there, screaming after him. At the school, Jack had looked so downtrodden, and Callum had wordlessly slammed the car door as he had dropped them off at the gate. Gemma was going to pick them up for him today and his mother had said she would step in too but he hated the fact that he couldn't be there for them.

'They're doing all right; it's a big adjustment for them.'

'I can imagine,' Richard said, shaking his head sympathetically. 'I know it'll be tough trying to juggle it all with the children and everything, so feel free to take your laptop home if you need to leave early or whatever.'

'Thanks, I appreciate that.'

'Well, I'll let you get stuck in.' Richard closed the door and left Aidan alone once more.

When Richard was gone Aidan took the letter from his pocket and reread it again, still feeling that same disbelief as he had when he had first read it that morning:

IN THE MATTER OF PART VII OF THE STATUS OF CHILDREN ACT 1987

NOTICE OF MOTION FOR THE TAKING OF BODILY SAMPLE

BETWEEN

James O'Herlihy Applicant

AND

Aidan Whelan Respondent

TAKE NOTICE that an application will be made to the Court on 6th November 2021 on behalf of the above named James O'Herlihy for an Order directing that DNA tests be carried out in respect of the persons whose names are set out below for the purpose of ascertaining the parentage of Milly Whelan of 14 Ledbury Road, age 3.

1. Aidan Whelan, 14 Ledbury Road, Ballsbridge, Dublin 4.

2. James O'Herlihy, 39 Abbeville Road, Ranelagh, Dublin 6.

Dated this 24th day of October 2021

How was this happening? How could James and

Helena do this to his family? Why were they putting them through this on top of everything else that had happened? It was now dawning on Aidan with searing clarity that they must be feeling pretty confident in their claims if they were willing to go down the legal route. Their far-fetched story when they had turned up at the house that day had seemed ludicrous to his ears, but maybe they had been telling the truth? But no, Milly was *his* daughter – he knew she was – he was named on her birth certificate. He felt as though the walls of his life had crumbled with Rowan's death and subsequent knowledge of her liaison with James, but now the foundations were crumbling too, and he was sinking beneath it all.

Even though he didn't want to get further embroiled with James and Helena, legally he knew he had a duty to respond. He couldn't just ignore this letter, hoping the situation would go away, no matter how much he wished he could. He had to protect his family at all costs, so he picked up the phone and dialled the number of his solicitor, Brendan Waters. He had been in touch with Brendan several times recently in terms of the legal aftermath of Rowan's death as he guided him through her will and other policies that they had had in place, but he felt mortified as he explained about Rowan's one-night stand and James's claim that he was Milly's biological father. It was humiliating admitting that his wife had turned to another man. Finally, he told Brendan about the application James had made to the court to have a paternity test carried out by both parties.

'We can ask to have it struck out on grounds that it's vexatious, but I must say it is very unlikely the judge will agree to that. The UN Convention on the Rights of the Child recognises a child's right to know their parents – children have a right to accurate information. The judge will want to be seen to be fair to both sides and a DNA test is relatively easy and is the most straightforward way in matters like these. Mr Whelan is either lying or he's not,' he added simply.

'But what if I refuse to do the test, they can't pin me down and take a sample – aren't there rights about things like this?'

'That is true, but you must be aware that if you refuse to do a test, the court can draw whatever conclusions it sees proper in the circumstances of the particular case. The judge will ask themselves why you are refusing, could it be that you are afraid of what the results might show? It's a gamble and I wouldn't advise it.'

'They did a test on my daughter without my consent, surely that's illegal? I trusted Helena and she took a conversation that I had with one of Milly's doctors and used it against me. They have broken so many laws here that I don't know how we're not the ones taking them to court!'

'We can certainly lodge a counter-claim, but it won't change the outcome if it is proven that Mr O'Herlihy is Milly's father then—'

'He's not,' Aidan interrupted.

'Very well then, you've nothing to worry about,' Brendan stated.

Aidan ran his hands down along his face after he had hung up. It felt as though his whole world had been shifted. It was eating him up inside. He was now doubting one of the most fundamental things in his life – he was doubting whether Milly really was his daughter, and it was terrifying.

31

HELENA

Helena took a deep breath as she climbed the steps leading to 14 Ledbury Road. She stood with her hand on the brass knocker, contemplating what she was about to do. She didn't know why she was there or even what she was going to say. She had been out for a run and she had found herself being pulled towards Aidan's house, as if a magnetic force was calling her. She hadn't told James she was going there – she didn't even realise that she was coming here until she found herself standing on the steps. Something inside had told her that she should do it and before she could talk herself out of it, she rapped the knocker hard. She could hear vague sounds of life coming from inside the bowels of the house as she waited.

What are you doing, Helena? she asked herself. This was wrong, especially now that James had an initiated a legal case. Laurence Jones would be horrified. She could potentially be jeopardising everything, but she needed to see Aidan. She had no idea what she was going to say when she saw him but she had to say something. They had become close in the time they had spent together in the hospital and the guilt over her role in Milly's paternity test was tearing her apart. She owed him an explanation.

The door was pulled back and Jack was standing there. Shoes lay kicked off just inside the door. She saw Milly's pink scooter, with purple tassels hanging from the handlebars.

'Hi, Jack,' she began, her voice dancing with nerves. 'Is your dad home?' He looked so like Aidan with his sandy-coloured hair and the sprinkling of freckles across his cheeks from the summer.

'He's in the kitchen,' he said, stepping to the side to let her into the house.

She paused momentarily wondering if she should be doing this. It wasn't fair to ambush Aidan like this, but she just wanted to explain – she needed him to know that although she had played a part in this, it didn't sit easily with her.

She stepped over the shoes and made her way down the hallway with Jack following after her. She could hear the sound of the TV playing some kids' show with a squeaky-voiced character. She entered the kitchen, where Aidan was standing with his back to her at the cooker. He hadn't heard her come in over the noise of the TV. The island was cluttered with plates and bowls, cereal boxes and cartons of milk and juice. There were piles of laundry sitting in baskets on the table. Toys were thrown around the place. A plastic skeleton sat on one of the stools and a half-carved pumpkin stood beside the sink. Helena guessed the kids had been getting ready for Halloween.

'Dad,' Jack called to his father. 'There's someone here for you.' Then he flopped back down on to the sofa in front of the TV. An older boy was sitting beside him typing on his phone, she guessed this was Callum. He was the image of his mother.

Aidan turned around from the cooker, but before she could meet his eyes, she felt something hard collide with her legs. She looked down and saw Milly had entered the kitchen and had wrapped both her arms around Helena's thighs. She was wearing a calamine pink tutu and she looked as sweet as spun sugar. Helena noticed her cast had been removed. She was grinning with those perfect baby teeth of hers and her eyes peeped out from beneath a fan of dark lashes. Helena felt her heart stumble once more.

She looked up in time to see Aidan's face fall as he saw her standing there. 'What the hell are you doing here?' he began. 'You've some nerve—'

'I want to explain,' she said quickly, heart in mouth.

She noticed Jack and Callum watching them warily from the sofa, wondering what was going on. Sensing the tension, Callum got up and wordlessly went upstairs.

'Lena,' Milly said, 'will you do my hair? Me going to ballet today. Daddy does my hair, but he's not good. Only girls can do hair good.'

'Sure,' Helena replied because everyone was staring at her and now she realised what a bad idea this was. What had she been thinking coming here, barging into their weekend? This was crazy. Aidan wouldn't want to hear what she said. Deep down, she knew there was nothing she could offer or say to explain what they were doing to him. Why would he care if she was beating herself up about her role in all of this or that she was so wracked with guilt that she couldn't sleep at night?

'I get the brush and my Elsa clips,' Milly said, dashing out of the room.

'I'm going outside to play football,' Jack said, excusing himself.

'What do you want?' Aidan began once they were alone. He lifted the remote and silenced the TV.

'I just wanted to explain,' Helena began. 'What we said that day... Aidan, I know it was a shock, but it's the truth. I just thought that it might help to be able to see where we're coming from.' She took a deep breath wondering if she was doing the right thing. 'As you know James and I have been trying to have a child for a long time now. We've been through so many rounds of IVF, we've miscarried babies and recently our fertility clinic told us that the only way we can have a child is to use a surrogate. My body can't seem to hold onto babies,' she added bitterly.

Aidan narrowed his eyes. 'Am I supposed to feel sorry for you?' he asked.

'That day in the hospital when you said about the blood types,' Helena continued, 'I don't know what came over me, I couldn't help it – it was like it was a sign or something... and I'm sorry – I had to keep digging, it was like I became obsessed with finding out the truth.'

'I thought you were my friend, I trusted you. I thought you were on my side. In the hospital, you were so supportive – I was so grateful for you, but then you do this...' He shook his head. 'It was bad enough finding out that James slept with my wife, but this is so much worse, Helena, you're trying to take away my daughter too,' Aidan said unable to disguise the emotion in his voice.

Guilt curdled up inside her. She hated herself for what she had done to him. She could see he was close to breaking point. 'I didn't think it would show that James was the father, I swear to you, Aidan,' she pleaded. 'I really thought you had made a mistake with your blood group or something. I was just as shocked as anyone when the results came back.'

'So just because you can't have a child of your

own, you think you can take mine?' he spat. 'That's not how it works, Helena. Milly is mine no matter what you think your DNA test says – she's still my daughter.'

'I'm so sorry,' she whispered.

'It's too late for that now. You can't just apologise your way out of this mess, this is all your fault. I trusted you – when I was at my lowest point in the hospital, I thought you were a friend. Have you any idea what I'm going through here?'

'I never thought it would go this far.' Her voice choked. 'I guess James sees this as his only chance at fatherhood and he's like a man possessed. I honestly never thought he would bring solicitors into it.'

Aidan was incredulous. 'What did you think was going to happen? Why the hell did you do it? Surely you must have thought about it from both sides,' he blasted. 'What do you want, Helena? Why did you come here today?'

Helena had no answer, she didn't know why she had come here. Had she needed to see that he was okay or maybe some selfish part of her was hoping that Aidan might absolve her? 'It was never my intention to hurt you, I'm so sorry. You have to believe me, I wish I had never done that stupid test. If I could turn back the clock, I would.'

'I don't get you, Helena. You started all of this and now you're telling me you regret it? Are you trying to make everything worse? My life was ruined on the day of the crash. My wife is dead and my children have lost their mother. Do you have any idea what it is like to hear your kids crying themselves to sleep at night and not be able to fix their pain? Do you know how awful it feels knowing that your children have to bear that trauma for the rest of their lives? I lost all the good memories we had together because everything has been tainted. You've taken all of that away from me. I don't get a second chance with Rowan, or an opportunity to hear her side of the story. I'll never be able to think of all the good things about my marriage ever again, without remembering all the hurt and the lies. Haven't you caused enough trouble? How can you live with yourself? You're like scavengers, picking apart what's left of my family. What more do you want from me?'

'I guess I was hoping that maybe we could all sit down and talk with one another. I don't know... maybe we could come to some sort of... arrangement... without bringing courts and stuff into it...' It was only upon saying it out loud that she realised how pathetic is sounded.

Aidan sneered. 'Even if the test does come back and show I'm not her dad, do you honestly think I'll just hand her over? No way, I will fight you every step of the way on this. Tooth and nail. I'm her father no matter what happens. I lost my wife, I won't let you take my daughter too.'

32

AIDAN

It was Jack's eleventh birthday and Aidan had just seen off the last of the guests. He knew today was going to be tough for Jack, facing his first birthday without his mother, and he'd wanted to try and make it as special as he could for him. His own parents and Gemma, as well as Sheila and Philip, had all come over to wish Jack a happy birthday and he had invited some of the boys from his class for a small party. They had all been charging around the house upstairs, with Milly running after them. Callum had been holed up in his room as usual.

Rowan had always made a big deal of birthdays. She baked their birthday cakes herself and would have had the kitchen decorated with bunting and balloons. As it was a Wednesday, Aidan had taken a half-day from work to get organised and in his rush out of the office on time, he hadn't managed to get any decorations. He had quickly stuck up a couple of balloons he had found in the drawer when he got home. Gemma had offered to bake the cake, so at least that was one less thing to worry about.

'This looks great, Aidan,' his mother had enthused, looking at the platter of party food he had spread out on the centre of the island for people to help themselves to. She'd picked up a cocktail stick and used it to spear some sausages onto a plate for herself. 'Will you have some, Philip?' she had said, gesturing towards the food.

Philip had eyed the food as though it was contaminated. His face was scrunched up angrily and Aidan had a feeling that one of the outbursts that he reserved especially for him was coming on.

'Sheila?' Agnes had tried then, when it was clear that Philip was boycotting the food.

'Thanks, Agnes,' Sheila had mumbled as she used a cocktail stick to pick up a spring roll.

They'd all fallen into awkward silence, nibbling away at their food.

'I see you've been making some changes,' Philip had said finally.

'Huh?' Aidan had asked, trying to swallow the sausage that he had just bitten into.

'I noticed it the last time I was here but couldn't work out what was missing...' He was eyeing up the space on the wall where their wedding photo used to hang, and Aidan had suddenly realised what he was angry about. 'She's not even cold in the ground and you've stripped all memories of her from her own home.'

'Now hang on a minute, Philip, I still have the photo, it's just painful, you know... every time I look at it... well, it hits me all over again...' Aidan had tried to explain.

Agnes had nodded sympathetically.

'You can't just forget about her,' Philip had continued. 'It's important that the kids still see photos of their mother.'

'Nobody is going to forget her,' Aidan had said, defending himself. 'I just need a little time. It's still so raw.'

'Everyone grieves differently, Philip, I don't think Aidan meant any harm,' Bill had interjected. 'We're all missing Rowan.'

'I think at this stage of his life, your little boy is big enough to stand up for himself, don't you, Bill?' Philip had barked back at him.

His clearly chastised father had looked back down at the plate that was balanced on his palm as silence fell on the room once more. Just then, they had been interrupted by the doorbell and Aidan was glad of the excuse to escape the atmosphere in the kitchen.

Bloody Philip, he'd thought angrily as he'd walked down the hall, could he not keep a lid on it for one day?

Aidan had opened the front door to see the postman standing there. He'd handed him a registered letter and Aidan's heart had sank as he'd signed for it before taking it from him. He knew what it contained. All parties had been told to expect the results this week.

'Should we do the cake?' Gemma had suggested as he'd returned to the kitchen.

'Good idea,' Agnes had agreed readily. 'I'll go hunt down the kids.'

Aidan had slipped the letter inside a drawer and tried to push it from his mind. Today was all about Jack.

Soon the children had all rushed into the kitchen, shepherded by Agnes, and the adults had plastered smiles on their faces and gathered around to sing Jack a happy birthday.

By the time Aidan had finished cleaning up, his head was thumping with a headache. He saw Milly had started to nod off on the sofa, exhausted from the all the fun, so he carried her up the stairs and placed her down on her bed. He left her in the leggings and T-shirt that she had been wearing that day and just removed her shoes. He placed Mousey in beside her and tucked the duvet right up underneath her chin, before kissing her smooth forehead. He brushed back her hair with his fingertips, caressing her skin that was so soft, like only a child's could be. She looked just like her mother, but a chubby-cheeked version.

He thought about the letter that was waiting downstairs for him. He hadn't opened it yet; he wanted to wait until the kids were in bed so that he would have the space if necessary to deal with whatever it contained. He was swinging wildly between absolute certainty that Milly was his child, to the terror of *what if...*? As the days of horrible waiting had passed, Aidan felt his assurance that he was her father start to falter. Horrible thoughts and doubts were worming through his brain, keeping him awake in the dead of night.

It was now late November, and it was almost three weeks since the court hearing. It had gone as Brendan Waters had predicted it would; even though his solicitor had done his best and argued that James was being vexatious, the judge had sat up and listened carefully to the circumstances of James's claims and had even raised his brows when he heard James and Rowan had been travelling in the car together at the time of the crash. It wasn't a surprise to anyone when he upheld the motion and ordered both men to do a paternity test. So, two weeks ago, Aidan had brought Milly to the clinic designated for the sampling appointment to have the test done and witnessed. He couldn't believe how straightforward the whole thing was; he had had visions of hauling her into a lab somewhere and holding her down while she was prodded with a needle, but it only took a simple cheek swab. Milly had squirmed for a moment as the doctor had run the swab inside her cheek, but it was painless. Aidan had done the same himself and then, while Milly played with Lego in the corner, the doctor had explained carefully that fifty per cent of the genetic markers of a child come from each parent, so if half of his markers didn't match Milly's, then they could exclude him from being her father.

'I wuv you, Daddy,' Milly said with a breathy sigh as she sank down on the pillow.

'I love you too, darling girl,' he whispered, watching her eyelids grow heavy. 'Sweet dreams.'

He stayed sitting on the edge of her bed for a few minutes, tracing his finger along her cheekbone until her eyelids grew heavy as she fell into a deep sleep. He observed her for a moment to see if he could see any part of himself in her. Something that would give him hope. Milly's nose had the same upturned slope at the end, just like his and they both had blue eyes; although she was more like Rowan, she definitely had some of his features too.

Aidan went into Jack's room next. He was lying on the bed reading a David Walliams book.

'Hey, birthday boy, it's time to get some sleep,' Aidan said, coming over and sitting down on the edge of his single bed. Jack slotted his bookmark in between the pages and closed the book. Aidan noticed a crumpled-up T-shirt stuffed beneath his pillow. 'Hey what's that?' he asked, pulling out the sage green, cotton T-shirt that had a picture of a roaring lion emblazoned across the front. It had belonged to Rowan. He could still see her wearing it with her jeans, her hair piled up messily on top of her head.

'It still smells like her,' Jack admitted, with tears filling his eyes.

'Oh come here,' Aidan pulled him into a hug.

Jack resisted at first, but after a moment Aidan felt his small body soften as he gave up the fight. 'It's not the same any more,' he sobbed. 'Mam always put balloons up around our beds for our birthdays and Auntie G made me a chocolate cake and I hate chocolate cake.'

Aidan exhaled heavily. 'We're all trying our best, Jack. It's hard for me to remember everything, your mam was much better at those things.'

'She knew the way I liked things. You keep giving me ham sandwiches for my lunch and I keep telling you that I don't like ham and sometimes she put little notes in my lunch box too.'

'What did they say?' Aidan asked, feeling crestfallen. He had wanted today to be special for Jack but it felt as though he was falling at every hurdle.

'Just things like, "I love you" or "Have a nice day" or "I'll have your favourite muffins for you after school".'

He never knew that she had done that, all these little things that helped to make their childhood special. She had been a great mother. It was just the wife bit she had struggled with, he thought grimly.

'When will I stop feeling sad?' Jack went on.

The question blindsided Aidan.

'I really miss her,' Jack said tearfully.

'I know,' Aidan agreed. 'I miss her too.' It was the truth. Despite everything that had happened, he knew he would forgive her everything if he could get another chance to have their family back together, the way it used to be again. 'I wish I could tell you that you will feel better next week or next month, but the truth is you'll probably always be sad when you think about your mum.'

'But it's not fair,' Jack said angrily as fat tears began to course down his small face. 'Why is it my mam and not someone else's?'

'I've no answer to that,' Aidan said truthfully. 'Sometimes life is really unfair.' He felt dampness against his cheek and he realised that tears were spilling down his own face and landing in Jack's hair. He stroked his son's sun-kissed face. His freckly skin wasn't like Milly's, which turned a golden olive shade with the merest hint of sun.

When Jack had finally exhausted himself from crying and had fallen asleep, Aidan tucked him underneath the blankets and crept out to the landing, pulling the door behind him so just a chink of light from the hallway would shine through. He made his way down the landing and paused outside Callum's door. Callum closeted himself up here night after night and never joined the family any more. Aidan placed his hand on the handle, wondering if he should go in to say goodnight but then decided against it. He was exhausted and it would only end in a row, like it always did.

He descended the stairs and entered the kitchen. The early winter evenings were beginning to close in, and darkness had dampened down the daylight several hours ago. Aidan had a list of things he needed to do; life seemed to be a never-ending hamster wheel of work, dinner, school lunches, laundry, so that Aidan fell into bed exhausted every evening, but right now he couldn't face any of it and instead he took the envelope from the drawer and turned it over in his hands. He placed it down on the countertop and walked over to the high cupboard above the fridge where they kept the spirits. He lifted down a bottle of Hennessy and poured himself a generous brandy. It had been a long time since he had had a drink, but he needed something to fortify him. The amber liquid burned its way down his throat as he lifted the envelope once again. He clutched it in his hands, torn between wanting to know what was inside, and not wanting. But the wanting was stronger.

He took a deep breath and slid his finger along the underside of the gummed seal of the envelope. He hesitated on the last part; whatever was inside this envelope could potentially change everything. Now that the time had come to open it and he was a step closer to resolving this whole nightmare, he wasn't sure that he wanted to do it. What if the results weren't what he wanted them to be? But something deep within told him that everything would be fine – there was definitely a resemblance between him and Milly, but it was more than that – she *felt* like his – it didn't get any more certain than that. His gut – a connection pulling inside him – told him that she was *his* child.

He took another sip, feeling the alcohol warm his insides, until the curiosity finally got the better of him and he inserted his finger underneath the final part of the flap and ripped the seal apart. He automatically found himself making the sign of the cross before gently pulling out the letter that was inside. He took a deep breath and then unfolded the sheet of paper. His eyes immediately went to the end of the letter where the result would be. The words jumped around the page.

He shook his head and read it again, but the letters stayed the same. His eyes fixed on the words:

The alleged father is excluded from being the biological father to the child. This exclusion is based on the lack of genetic markers that must be contributed to the child by the biological father. The probability of paternity is 0%.

The words burned through him, and he felt a ringing in his ears. This could not be happening. And yet it was. It was printed on the page before him – he was not Milly's biological father. The shock hit him full force in the stomach like a punch. His ears filled with blood, and everything seemed to be miles away. His legs grew weak and he manoeuvred himself backwards until he found himself sitting in a chair.

How could it possibly be right? But that's what it said, there it was written in the cold harsh reality of black ink. As Aidan clutched the paper in his hands, he couldn't help but wonder if Rowan had known the truth all along? How could she do that to him?

He thought of his beautiful daughter who was sleeping soundly upstairs, oblivious to the fact that the very foundations of their world had just been decimated. He thought of her cheeky smile and those beautiful dark eyes, her silky skin and her joyous giggle that filled his heart. He thought about all the things he adored about her and felt panicked. What was going to happen? And how on earth was he supposed to hold onto Milly now that his worst nightmare had materialised? Would she be ripped straight from his arms, from the family that loved her dearly, and sent to live with a stranger? He couldn't allow that to happen, he had to fight to protect his daughter. He would do whatever it took to keep her within the only family she had ever known.

33

HELENA

Although the results didn't come as a surprise to Helena and James, a thick layer of tension had settled on the house like rubble after an earthquake since the arrival of the letter in Abbeville Road.

James was holding the sheet of paper in his hands like it was a trophy.

'There it is now…' he stabbed the paper with his index finger, 'it's there in black and white for the whole world to see. Let's see who Aidan's accusing of causing trouble now!' he said smugly.

'That's not fair, James,' Helena argued. 'Haven't you any compassion for the poor guy? He's raised Milly as his daughter for her whole life – he is her father. This is going to crush him!' She couldn't bear to think of what Aidan must be going through behind the walls in his own home right at the same moment, dealing with the hammer-blow that the results would be for him. She hated herself for her role in all of this.

'But we tried telling him and he wouldn't listen!' James went on unperturbed. 'Does he really think we'd lie about something like this? I'm going to contact Laurence Jones first thing in the morning and get the ball rolling.'

Helena felt her heart stop. 'Oh, James, please don't rush this. Just stop and pause and give everyone time to get their heads around it first,' she begged.

'No way.' He shook his head. 'I won't be robbed of any more time with her, Helena – I'm going for full custody.'

Full custody? What had happened to a shared arrangement? This would finish Aidan off entirely. How could James do that to him? Did she know her husband at all? When had he turned so cruel, so heartless? Helena felt as though she was sinking under oil, she was flailing around beneath it, unable to break through the surface. 'You can't do that!' She was aghast.

'Why not? She's my daughter – we have it officially here.' He lifted the letter and read it once more. 'It says "the probability of paternity is 99.9%", it doesn't get any more certain than that.'

'I know what it says,' Helena shouted angrily at him, 'but you need to be fair, James.'

'Fair to who? Is it fair on me that I've missed out on over three years of my own daughter's life?'

'Fair to all parties. You can't just take her off Aidan. She's lost her mother, he's all she has left. It doesn't matter what the results say, Aidan is the only father that child has ever known. You've got to think about Milly,' she pleaded. James was so black and white – so clinical. He just didn't seem to understand that Milly was a living breathing child with feelings and needs and wants.

'Because she was never allowed to get to know her real father!' he blazed. 'Look, we've been over all of this, we'll do it so gradually that she won't even notice what's happening.'

The whole thing was unbearable. 'I can't destroy

Aidan and Milly's lives any more than they already have been.'

'It's too late for that now, Helena. You can't just wash your hands of it – you started it all. You said having a child was all you ever wanted!'

It was true, everything he was saying was right. She had done this, she had given him a glimpse of the life he could have had if things had been different. She had set him on this path.

'Not like this, I'm sorry, James,' Helena whispered, shaking her head.

'I can't just forget about her.' His tone changed, the anger evaporated. He sank down onto a chair, shaking his head, looking broken. 'You can't expect me to walk away from this now that I know the truth?'

She took a deep breath, preparing herself for what she was about to say, for the vein of sorrow it would open up inside both of them. 'Remember when we lost our baby boy,' she began. She saw the hurt creasing his face as he relived their grief for the baby they had lost at twelve weeks. They had never talked about it. Not once. Neither of them had dared to mention it because they were terrified of the tidal wave of emotion that would be unleashed if they did.

He nodded, unable to form words, his whole face contorted in anguish.

'Remember how broken and awful we felt?' Helena continued. Even though she knew it was agony for both of them, she had to make him see what he was doing. She had to get through to him. 'Remember how our hearts felt physically wrung out from grief? I've never felt so low in my entire life – I wanted to die and never wake up again. Well, that's a tiny insight into what we are putting Aidan through and I don't know about you, but I wouldn't wish that heartache on my worst enemy and certainly not Aidan.'

34

AIDAN

In the office the next day, Aidan tried to concentrate on the spreadsheet before him, but his brain just couldn't focus. He had had to force himself out of bed that morning. He wanted to stay there, hide under the duvet and never get up again, but Milly had climbed on top of him, pulling him up, and as he had looked at her innocent, sweet face, he knew he had no choice but to plant his two feet on the floor and keep the show on the road.

His overriding feeling since reading the letter the evening before was fear. What was going to happen now? Now that all parties knew the truth, where did they go from here? The one thing he did know was that James wouldn't back down; it would only strengthen his desire to have Milly. Aidan wanted to keep everything as normal as possible for the kids for as long as he was able to because he knew there was a day coming when the last remaining fragments of their life, the things they thought were a constant in their world, were going to be ripped apart.

He scrolled down through the figures on the screen in front of him for the hundredth time, but the data blurred before his eyes. To think he had once thought this was the be-all and end-all. How perfect his life had been back then, and he hadn't stopped to appreciate it until it was taken away from him.

His phone rang and he picked it up, not recognising the number.

'Is that Mr Whelan?' a woman asked.

'Uh-huh.'

'This is Theresa Woodward, the principal at St Thomas's. Your son Callum has landed himself in a bit of trouble today.'

Aidan groaned internally. This wasn't going to be good. 'What happened?'

'I'm afraid Callum lost his temper with Mr Leonard, his French teacher, when he asked him to stop banging his ruler against the table in class. Callum was being disruptive, and Mr Leonard requested that he come outside the classroom to have a word with him. Callum stood up and pushed his desk over on his way out. Thankfully, nobody was injured. I know he's been through a really difficult time lately and I understand that he is angry, but we have to set an example to our other students that we can't tolerate any sort of aggressive behaviour towards our teaching staff.'

Aidan was livid. 'I'll be there to pick him up as soon as I can.'

'Well, that's the thing, Mr Whelan...' she paused. 'He just walked out of the school building after the incident.'

'Well, where did he go?'

'We're not quite sure... Mr Leonard tried to follow after him, but Callum refused to come back, and he walked off the school grounds.'

'So, you don't know where he is?' Aidan asked in disbelief.

'I'm sorry, Mr Whelan, once a student leaves the

school premises, they become the responsibility of their parents. Do you want me to call the Gardaí?'

'No,' Aidan said quickly as he thought about the incident in the BetterValu supermarket. Callum's card was already marked with the Gardaí and Aidan didn't want to draw any more attention to his son's behaviour. 'I'm sure he'll turn up. He probably just went home.'

Aidan hung up the phone feeling furious. He had only been in the office for a few hours and now he would have to turn around and go back home again. He lifted his phone and dialled Callum's number, but it went straight to voicemail. He had obviously switched his phone off. Callum was probably sitting up in his room right now watching something on his laptop, completely oblivious to the worry and stress he was causing everyone, Aidan thought angrily. He was digging himself further and further into trouble with his selfish behaviour. They were all grieving – him, Milly and Jack – they were all hurting, but none of them were reacting like Callum, pressing the self-destruct button at every opportunity he got. Aidan couldn't keep excusing his behaviour and picking up the pieces. How was he ever going to get through to him? Aidan began winding up the cord of his laptop charger and put it with his laptop into his briefcase before making his way out of the office.

He sat in the city-centre traffic willing the cars in front of him to inch forward. As the lights changed from red to green and back to red again and he had barely moved, he felt the tension begin to wind its way through his shoulder blades. He tried ringing Callum again, but his phone was still off. What had been going through his mind? Aidan wondered. How could he think it was okay to push over a table and walk out of school? He could get expelled for something like this.

When he got home to Ledbury Road, Aidan let himself inside the house and called out Callum's name, but there was no reply. He made his way to the kitchen and everything was still the same chaos as they had left it as they ran out the door that morning. Dishes and glasses were piled up on top of the dishwasher. Milly's pyjamas lay on the floor.

Aidan went back out to the hall and headed up the stairs, taking the steps two at a time. He entered his son's room. The duvet was thrown back and clothes, shoes, plates and mugs littered the floor, but there was no sign of Callum.

Don't panic, he told himself as he looked at his watch and saw that it was almost an hour and a half since he had received the call from the school.

He took his phone out of his pocket and called his mother. Maybe Callum had turned up at her house. She usually collected boys from school so he might have gone there.

'Mum, it's me—'

'Is everything okay, Aidan?'

'Is Callum with you?'

'No, shouldn't he be at school?'

Aidan sighed. 'He walked out of class earlier and I don't know where he is. I've checked at the house and he's not there.'

'Is there anywhere else that he could be?' Agnes asked, her voice laced with concern.

'I've wracked my brain, but I can't think of anywhere.' It was as if his brain had seized up and wouldn't work properly. Nothing was coming to him. Every time he tried to call Callum, his phone was still off and there was no point ringing his friends because they would all still be in school.

'Do you think we should call the Guards, Aidan? He's fourteen years old, he's too young to be out wandering the streets on his own.' Agnes articulated the same question he was wrestling with himself.

'Let's give him a little longer, I'm sure he'll be back soon.' Aidan knew that once he made that call to report his son missing, things would escalate rapidly, and he wasn't ready for that yet. He prayed Callum would turn up soon and they could avoid dragging the Guards into it.

'But what if something has happened? He could be in trouble, Aidan,' Agnes pressed.

'I'll take a drive around to see if I can find him,' Aidan said to appease her. 'I'm sure he hasn't gone too far.'

'Right, well I'll meet you back at the house, love.' She had her own key so could let herself in. 'I'll call you if he turns up.'

After he hung up, he tried Sheila's phone next to see if Callum had gone there, but she told him he wasn't there either.

'But where would he go?' she demanded.

'I don't know,' he replied, suppressing the urge to remind her that if he knew where Callum had gone, he wouldn't be searching for him now. 'I'd better go in case he tries to ring me,' Aidan said quickly as she began asking more irritating questions which he didn't have the patience for.

He tried calling Callum again but was met with his voicemail once more. He hung up in temper, climbed into his car, and reversed out onto Ledbury Road. He dialled Gemma's number as he drove, just in case he had gone to her house.

'Aidan, how are you doing?' she said when she answered. He had called her the evening before after he had opened the results of the paternity test. She was the only person in his family who knew what was going on and she had been just as stunned by Rowan's duplicity as he was.

He explained then what had happened with Callum.

'I'm sorry, Aidan, he didn't come here. I'll jump in the car and be straight over,' she promised.

He drove up and down street after street, scanning the pavements for a sign of his son. He would spot a teenager and his heart would leap, but then he would get closer and see they were the wrong height, or they were wearing the wrong coat, and disappointment would floor him. After searching for over an hour, dusk was starting to fall. It would soon be time to collect Jack from the after-school club, where he usually waited until Callum's finish time, and then Milly would need to be collected from the crèche. With no sign of Callum, Aidan decided to go back towards home, hoping against hope that his son had shown up by now, even though he knew his mother would have phoned if he had.

He saw Gemma's car in the driveway and as Aidan came through the front door, his mother and sister both shook their heads before he could even open his mouth to ask them if Callum had turned up. His heart sank. Every minute seemed to be lasting an hour.

'I think it's time to call the Gardaí, Aidan,' Agnes said. 'I'm really worried about him. He's been through a lot lately; we don't know what's going on inside his head.'

'Let's just give him a little bit longer and if he still hasn't turned up, I'll call them.' He checked his watch once more and turned to Agnes. 'Look, could you pick up Jack and Milly for me?'

'Of course,' she said. 'Make sure you call me if you find him.'

Aidan and Gemma trudged to the kitchen after their mother had left.

'Did you not get that tracking app I told you about?' she asked him as she filled the kettle with water.

'No, I never got around to it…' he admitted sheepishly. 'His phone is off anyway so it wouldn't work.'

'Oh, Aidan,' she sighed, leaning back against the cupboards and turning around to face him.

Panic was starting to rise within him with every passing minute. Where the hell was Callum? The worries were multiplying inside his head. What if he was in danger somewhere? Or perhaps was afraid to come home because he thought he was going to be in trouble? The thought of his son being out there somewhere, frightened, vulnerable and all alone made him feel sick. He would give him another half an hour and if there was still no sign of him, he would have no choice but to report him missing.

The doorbell went and he and Gemma exchanged a look. *Callum.* Aidan felt his heart rise as he ran down the hall to answer it, but when he pulled it back, he saw that it wasn't Callum. Instead, Sheila and Philip were standing there.

'What the hell is going on, Aidan?' Philip asked, barging straight past him into the house.

'Callum was in trouble in school earlier and he walked out,' Aidan explained once again, even though he had already told Sheila what had happened, 'and now I can't find him.'

'But you told me you were going to get his behaviour under control,' Philip blazed.

'I knew he should have come to stay with us...' Sheila said.

'I know this isn't easy for any of us, but Aidan is trying his best,' Gemma, who had followed Aidan out into the hall, interjected. 'Cut him some slack. He's doing a good job.'

But Philip wasn't listening. 'Callum will end up in a juvenile detention centre if Aidan doesn't get his act together. His mother would be turning in her grave if she could see this!'

Aidan felt the months of anger begin to overspill inside him. He knew he should try to keep a lid on it, but he couldn't help himself. He was like a pot left on the boil that had started to bubble over. 'Rowan wasn't the angel you thought she was, you know!' The words were out before he realised it.

Aidan watched as Sheila and Philip's flabbergasted jaws fell to the floor. Gemma was wide-eyed with shock too.

'What did you say?' Philip said in a voice that was deathly serious. His face had clouded over and he actually looked like he was going to punch Aidan.

'Come into the kitchen, Aidan,' Gemma was saying in a calm voice, but Aidan didn't move. 'Now!' she said more firmly.

Aidan did as he was told as she linked his arm and steered him towards the back of the house. They went inside the kitchen, and she shut the door behind them.

'What was all that about?' she asked horrified. 'You need to calm down, Aidan! They're grieving, their grandson is missing, this is hard on them.'

'Do you think it's easy on me?' Aidan retorted.

'I know they were giving you a hard time, but they don't know anything about that paternity test and it's not going to help matters if you start ranting about their dead daughter. You need to be able to rise above Philip's barbed comments.'

'But you don't understand, he never gives up... and well... I'm tired of it.'

Gemma came closer and placed her arm on his shoulder. 'I get that, Aidan, I do. I know this is so hard on you, especially since nobody except you and I know everything that has gone on over the last few months, but for the sake of the kids at least try to bite your tongue.'

'I'm doing my best, Gemma! God knows it hasn't been easy, so it galls me when Philip is constantly criticising what a bad husband and father I am, when he doesn't have a clue about his daughter's double life!'

'Well, if you feel having her secret out in the open would be for the best, maybe you should tell him?'

Aidan shook his head. 'It wouldn't be right.'

'Well then, you need to accept that, in Philip's eyes, Rowan was a perfect mother and wife, even if you know the truth. Be the bigger person here, Aidan.'

He nodded. 'You're right,' he sighed.

They went back into the hall, where everyone seemed to be staring down at the floor.

'Right, we're going to divide up and search for Callum,' Gemma instructed, taking charge of the situation. 'Sheila and Philip, you go in your car, I'll go in mine and Aidan you wait here.'

35

HELENA

Helena drove down Abbeville Road with its trees now bare as the November chill set in. Drizzle misted the glass and the wipers screeched as they cleared it. Tears clouded her eyes and her stomach felt sick. She couldn't believe that she had done it. It hadn't been planned – she had just walked out of their house.

She had hoped that sleeping on it would help James to see sense, but when she had overheard him on the phone to Laurence Jones discussing their next steps, she knew she couldn't be part of it for a minute longer. Her dad had always said that you had to stay true to your heart in life; if something didn't feel right, then it most probably wasn't and it didn't feel right to Helena to stand by while James destroyed what was left of Aidan's life. 'I can't do it, I'm sorry but what you are doing is wrong...' she had said to him.

'Please don't start that again,' he'd sighed, his tone bordering on exasperation.

'I can't be a part of this any longer...' She shook her head. 'I need time to think...'

'What's that supposed to mean?' he'd retorted.

'I need a break – what happened in work, then the crash, learning about the one-night stand and now this – it's all been too much.' She'd held her head in her hands; saying it out loud felt traumatic. 'I think it would be best for everyone if I go to stay with my parents for a while.' She still hadn't been able to return to work, she was in no fit state with everything that was going on in her life, and now with the arrival of the official court-mandated results, she knew that things would step up a gear and she couldn't be a part of it any more. Her head was a mess and she was starting to worry about how much more she could withstand. She needed to get as far away from James as possible and spending time with her parents in Connemara would give her head space.

'Don't do this to me, Helena, please,' he had begged as she left the room, went upstairs to their bedroom and quickly packed a few clothes into a holdall before descending the stairs again. James had followed her out into the driveway as she was leaving. Although he was off his crutches now, he was still quite slow on his feet. 'Please, Helena, don't do this... I don't want to lose you – please – just come back inside... we can talk about this,' he had pleaded.

But they had talked about it over and over again and she knew nothing was going to change. There was nothing left to stay for; James wasn't going to back down. She would have to live with the guilt forever more about her role in all of this, but her involvement had to end here, she couldn't stand by and watch Milly be ripped away from her father.

'I'm sorry,' she had said, pulling the car door closed and reversing out of their driveway.

She stopped at the junction while the lights were red. She wiped her eyes and dripping nose with the balled-up tissue she had left in the drinks holder. Daylight was being stolen by dusk and the streets were growing shadowy. She noticed a gang of teenagers with hoods pulled up hanging around outside the petrol station. She watched them for a moment as they jostled with one another. She assumed it was just horseplay, but when one guy suddenly threw a punch at a smaller boy, she knew it was serious. He fell to the ground and the rest of the teenagers joined in, landing kicks all over his body while he lay crouched on the concrete, covering his head with his hands for defence. Before she knew what she was doing, she had pulled the car over, jumped out and ran across the forecourt.

'Hey!' she screamed. 'What do you think you're doing?' Her heart was racing as the gang stopped and turned to look at her. Panic flitted through her mind; what if they came for her next? She was relieved when they dispersed and began running off down the road. She hurried over to where the boy was lying on the ground. 'Are you okay?' she said, bending down to him. He had his hood pulled up and it was only when he turned his head to look up at her that she recognised his face. 'Callum?' she said in disbelief. His lip was bleeding and already his eye was starting to look puffy, where above it the skin had split into an angry gash. 'What's going on? Who were they?' she asked.

He remained silent.

'Come on, I'll take you home.'

He didn't protest as she helped him to his feet. He was quite unsteady as she led him towards her car. She opened the passenger door and sat him down inside. His whole body was trembling with shock. She opened her boot and took out her GP bag from where she had put it over two months ago now on the day she had been asked to take some time out.

'Here,' she said, coming back around to Callum and passing him a cloth. 'Keep pressure on your lip to stop that bleeding and I'll get that wound over your eye cleaned up.'

He winced as she began dabbing it with an antiseptic wipe before applying a bandage.

'Is your head okay? Did you get kicked there?' she continued, examining him when she was finished with his eye.

He shook his head.

'Right, let's get you home then.' She started the car, adrenaline still coursing around her body. 'Does your dad know where you are?' she asked as they drove along. He should only be finishing school around this time. But maybe he had a half-day, she thought.

Callum said nothing, just stared straight ahead. She realised he wasn't up for talking and they continued in silence. Eventually, she turned the car down Ledbury Road and pulled up outside Aidan's house.

Helena climbed the steps, with Callum trailing behind her, and rapped the knocker. He stood there with a hangdog expression on his face.

Aidan pulled back the door and his face creased with anger when he saw her. Helena knew she was the last person he wanted to see right now, given the arrival of the results the day before, but when he saw his bruised and battered son beside her, his face changed.

'What's going on?' he said quickly, looking at her, then to Callum and back to her again for an explanation. 'Where the hell have you been? I've been looking everywhere for you!'

'I found Callum in a spot of bother,' Helena began.

'You'd better come inside,' a pale-faced Aidan said.

The three of them walked through to the kitchen and Aidan immediately began checking Callum over.

'Will someone tell me what happened?' he demanded. 'Where were you?

'He got into a fight with a group of teenagers, they looked a bit older than he was.'

'Did you know them?' Aidan asked Callum.

'Leave me alone,' Callum brushed past him and they heard his footsteps climbing the stairs a few moments later, leaving them standing in silence together.

'I've checked him over and he seems to be okay,' Helena said. 'He has a burst lip and a nasty wound above his eye, but it's not deep. I've cleaned it out and hopefully it should settle down in a few days, but keep a close eye on him. If he shows any signs of sleepiness or confusion make sure you take him straight to A&E.'

'Thanks for bringing him home,' Aidan mumbled and silence fell between them. They both stood there, shifting awkwardly with nothing more to say.

'Right then, I'd better go,' Helena said, filling the silence. She began walking down the hallway towards the front door. She turned around as she stood on the step. 'Aidan – I'm sorry.'

Aidan nodded, his eyes taking on a mournful look once more.

'I'm sorrier than you will ever know,' she continued. She needed him to know just how much she regretted her actions. 'Actually, I'm heading away for a while... I'm going home to Connemara to see my parents, it's been a tough few weeks.'

Aidan nodded, implicit agreement. 'You think?' he replied, his tone heavy with sarcasm.

'For what it's worth, I've told James that I don't agree with what he is doing.'

'Why did you do it then, Helena? Why the hell did you start all of this? You're putting me through hell right now.'

She shook her head. 'I wish I could give you a proper reason, but I can't. I think I was in a spin after the crash and I needed to know the truth, but I didn't think it through properly. If I had known then what I know now, I never would have done it. I regret it so much. It doesn't matter what that piece of paper says,

Aidan, *I* know she's your daughter. No matter what happens, you'll always be her dad.'

'I wonder will the judge see it like that?' Aidan replied bitterly. 'James will have rights now…'

'I know,' Helena whispered. 'I've tried talking him down, but I can't make him listen.'

'She's already been through enough trauma to last a lifetime and now she's going to be pulled asunder in a tug-of-war, but I will fight for her – I will fight with every fibre of my being.'

Helena winced at his vitriol.

'You've done this to her, Helena,' he went on, stabbing his index finger in her direction. 'You!'

36

AIDAN

After Helena had left, Aidan climbed the stairs and sat down on the side of Callum's bed. He looked around his son's room, with its glow-in-the-dark stickers and the space rocket that Rowan had painted herself. At fourteen, Callum now thought the space theme was babyish and he and Rowan had been talking about giving the room a revamp before she died but it was another thing they would never get around to doing together.

Callum was faced away from him, looking at something on his phone. Aidan reached across and put a hand on his shoulder. 'Callum,' he began, pulling him back so that he had to face him. He took a deep breath. This conversation felt more important than all the others; he needed to get through to his son. He needed to make Callum see that if he didn't stop this trail of self-destructive behaviour, then he didn't know where he would end up. 'Are you going to tell me what happened today? Why did you walk out of school and who were those boys that you were hanging around with down at the petrol station?'

Callum remained infuriatingly silent.

'Who were they?' Aidan tried again and was met with stony silence once more. 'Well, if you're not going to tell me, then I'll have no choice but to go to the Gardaí and lodge a formal complaint and see if they can get to the bottom of it.'

'Just leave it, Dad,' Callum retorted.

'I'm serious, Callum.' Aidan stood up to emphasise the point. 'It's now or never. If you don't tell me what happened, I'm going straight to the Guards to tell them you were assaulted by those boys.'

Aidan knew by the flicker in his son's eyelashes that he had hit home. 'I don't really know them,' he shrugged his shoulders. 'They hang out down there.'

'But should they not be in school?'

'They don't go to school,' Callum retorted scornfully.

Aidan felt anger warming him up. What the hell was Callum doing hanging out with older boys who had dropped out of school? Suddenly, he heard Rowan's voice in his ear telling him to stay calm; the line of communication that had just opened between them was as fragile as gossamer and he knew that one angry word might sever it completely if he didn't keep his cool. He sat back down beside Callum on the bed.

'Are you friends with them?' Aidan asked, forcing his voice to stay level, even though what he really wanted to do was to shake some sense into his son.

Callum shrugged.

'Why were you at the petrol station?' Aidan tried.

'I dunno... sometimes I hang out with them there.'

'So why did these so-called "friends" hit you?'

'They were messing around and one of them grabbed my phone and I asked him to give it back, but he kept passing it over my head, so I hit him.'

'You hit him? You threw the first punch?' Aidan was horrified. He looked at his son sitting on the bed beside him; compared with the other boys his age, he was still quite small. He hadn't started his teenage growth spurt yet. Had Callum's anger clouded his vision so much that he had thought he would stand a chance going head-to-head against a group of older lads or had he just reacted instinctively, without weighing up the risks?

'What was I meant to do?' Callum protested. 'They had my phone!'

'So what happened next?' Aidan was fairly sure where this story was going, but he needed to hear it in Callum's own words.

'I grabbed it back off him, but he punched me and then they were all on top of me.'

'Do you know how lucky you are that a black eye and a burst lip are your only injuries? If Helena hadn't come on the scene, they could have beaten you to a pulp! These things can escalate really quickly, Callum – your safety is more important than any phone.'

'But I had to get it back! It has all my messages from Mam and my photos of her.'

Callum's words slammed into Aidan and his heart thudded to the floor. It all clicked into place.

Now he realised why his son had seen red when his phone had been taken from him. 'Oh, Callum,' he softened and held his son's face in his hands and for once Callum didn't push him away. 'When I got the call to say you were missing and I couldn't find you, I was so scared. I was terrified something had happened to you and I knew that would finish me off altogether. I'm worried about you. I know you're going through hell right now, but your mam loved you and she would hate to see you acting like this. I love you too, Callum – I love you with all my heart. I know it might not seem like it; we seem to be arguing all the time lately, but I love you so much,' his voice choked. 'I need you, Callum. And Milly and Jack need you too. We're stronger as a team; the only way we can get through this is together.'

A fat tear coursed its way down Callum's face. 'I'm sorry, Dad,' he began to sob, as his body sagged with defeat. His fight had left him. 'I just miss her so much; she was always there... standing in the kitchen making breakfast in her dressing gown or asking me how my day was when I came home from school – everything has changed. I don't understand why it had to be *our* family. It's not fair!' He lashed his foot angrily against the wooden frame of the bed.

'You're right, it's not fair, I feel the exact same way, but I've learnt that being angry doesn't change anything, it just eats you up. I got such a fright today, Callum, I've already lost your mother, I can't lose you as well.' Suddenly Milly flashed into his mind, that letter had changed everything, he could lose her too... He pushed it out again just as fast. He would fight for every last hair on that child's head to keep her with him, with the people who loved her and cherished her. This was where she belonged. He knew he was being a hypocrite telling Callum to control his anger because if James O'Herlihy was in front of him right then, he would smash whatever bones had not been broken in the crash.

'I just want it all to stop, Dad.' Callum looked up at him and began blinking back tears. 'It hurts too much.'

Aidan felt sorrow ball into a lump in his throat. He knew that this was grief in its purest form. Raw, painful and interminable. There were no assurances or promises he could give that would help. He knew because people had tried to do the same thing to him. Everyone meant well but no words could ever heal the brutal ache that seared your heart forever more. Callum was broken and there was nothing Aidan could do to fix him.

'Me too, son. Come here.' He pulled him in close and cradled his head against his chest just like when he had been a baby and he would fall asleep there, soothed by his heartbeat. He had come to an age where he usually shrugged off any form of physical affection, but he allowed Aidan to embrace him.

Rowan had always said whenever the children were acting out, that was when they needed the most affection from their parents; he had been the disciplinarian in their house while she was softer. Aidan used to think it was another of her hippy-dippy parenting philosophies, but now he could see what she meant. When had he last done this with Callum? When was the last time his little boy had cuddled in against him like this? Their first-born son; the baby he and Rowan had stared at with a mixture of awe and fear, as he slept in his Moses basket, his two hands balled into tiny fists on either side of his head. The little boy who had nervously clung to his hand on his first day of school. The same boy who had wobbled on his bike as he cycled by himself when Aidan had taken off the stabilisers, his cheeks plumped with pride as he called to Aidan, 'Look, Daddy, I can do it!' Aidan's heart had been in his mouth as he ran after him in case he fell.

'I'm sorry, Dad.' Callum began to cry as they held one another tightly.

'I love you so, so much, Callum,' Aidan whispered into his son's hair.

37

HELENA

Leaving Dublin the day before still seemed like a dream. Helena couldn't believe she had done it. After she had dropped Callum back home, she had driven on autopilot through the maze of chaotic, traffic-filled suburbs that surrounded Ledbury Road. Hot tears had spilled down her face and she couldn't seem to stop them. She had been too upset after everything that had happened; she was still shook after finding Callum battered and bruised and she knew she would startle her parents if she arrived unannounced in the middle of the night, so she had decided it would be safer to check into a B&B and then begin her journey from the east to the west coast of the island the day after.

Once on the motorway early the next morning, fields whizzed past in a blur of green. Her mind began to whirr with questions about the future. Her heart physically ached, as if James had taken it in his bare hands and twisted it until it was wrung dry. What was she going to do? Was her marriage over? What would happen to Milly? To Aidan? Around and around her head, they looped.

After a couple of hours, she bypassed Galway City and soon she had left the motorway far behind her and was driving along narrow regional roads. Low stone walls made by the bare hands of generations of farmers as they tried to rid their fields of the stone cut seams through the landscape, from which ragged sheep gazed at her with idle curiosity. The land full of rocky hillocks dipped and rose the further she drove into Connemara. In the distance, the Twelve Bens kept watch and the landscape took on an almost Jurassic feel as water rushed out of fissures in the mountainside after rainfall the night before while all around her was lush bracken with bright pops of heather and gorse.

A thick mist descended upon her as the Volvo climbed higher and she had to switch on her fog lights. She gripped tightly to the steering wheel and tried to concentrate on driving; although she knew it well, it wasn't the kind of road you could let your mind wander on. She drove slowly, meeting each twist and treacherous bend on the road with caution. Eventually, she emerged from the fog as the car snaked down towards sea level and she breathed a sigh of relief when she caught her first glimpse of the brooding ocean in the distance. Its ominous shade of petrol blue was streaked silver where it met the sunlight on the horizon and white cottages dotted the landscape as grassy fields rolled down towards the sea. The view never failed to take her breath away and she felt her heartbeat begin to slow. The village of her birth was calling her home.

She could still remember her nervous anticipation all those years ago when she had left Connemara to go to medical school in Dublin, at the age of seventeen. Her tummy had been full of butterflies as she left Ballycladdagh that day. She knew she would miss her parents and the way the sea sparkled on a warm summer's day or how the water in the bay glinted orange just before dusk fell. Dublin seemed so far away – almost like another universe to her, a girl who had spent her whole life in the west of Ireland.

Growing up in this tiny seaside haven, where everybody knew your name, had been idyllic. Although she hadn't appreciated it when she was younger, now as an adult she knew it had been a perfect place to raise a child. It was so much more peaceful than Dublin, with its traffic and noise and ever-present dangers. Helena always felt calmer here. Once she breathed in that sea air, she would feel her shoulders begin to drop, as if the worries that haunted her life at home couldn't penetrate her here. She had always thought that when she had her own children they would spend a lot of time here, especially during the school holidays. She had imagined carting her little family down for the summer, letting the children play in the crystal waters, running wild and free along the sand, watching them as they climbed over bladderwrack-draped rocks or fished in the pools beneath. She could picture them pulling back the carpets of sea moss looking for crabs or a starfish that might be hiding under there.

She and her brothers had played on the beach every day until the sun went down. They would go to bed with blistered shoulders and salt-streaked skin, but they were happy. Carefree. Those days seemed so long ago now.

She eventually found herself in the village, passing the pub, the local grocery store, and St. Jarlath's church where her parents attended mass every Sunday. Whenever she returned home, the place always seemed smaller than she remembered, as if it had shrunk in her absence.

She continued on a little further, eventually turning the car down a narrow boreen until she pulled up outside her parents' whitewashed cottage, *Ceol na Mara*. It was a traditional two-storey house with a central front door and a window on either side and three windows overhead. It had views over the sea from every room.

Helena silenced the engine and felt her stomach flip-flop as she realised she hadn't told her parents she was coming. What was she going to say to them? How would she explain it? She checked her face in the mirror. Her eyes were red-rimmed with the lack of sleep the night before and the make-up she had applied that morning was a mess.

She opened the car and breathed in briny sea air, letting it fortify her before walking up to the step. She took a deep breath and pushed open the door. Nobody locked their doors around here. 'Mam?' she called into the house so as not to startle her mother.

After a moment, her mother came flying out of the kitchen. 'Helena, *a ghrá*, what on earth are you doing here?'

'Hi, Mam.'

'Well, this is a surprise. Come on in.' She stood back to let Helena enter. 'Why didn't you ring to say you were coming?' This visit had clearly thrown her. 'Pat, look who's here,' she called to her father.

Helena followed her mother into the house, breathing in its familiar smell, a mixture between baking and salty air. She sat down in the kitchen, which was the heart of their home growing up. They prepared their food there, ate their meals there, did their homework at the table, clothes were aired on the shelf above the range, they watched TV – their lives revolved around this small room. They only used their main living room, or what her mother referred to as the 'good room', on Christmas Day.

Her dad entered the kitchen and threw his arms around her. She felt hot tears spring into her eyes, but she quickly pushed them back. She didn't want her parents to see her upset.

'I'll put the kettle on,' her mother Anne said.

'So where's James, you didn't bring him with you?' she asked a few minutes later as she set the teapot and three mugs down on the table, as well as a plate of freshly baked scones. She began pouring the tea for them.

'He's still recovering,' Helena said, clasping the mug between her palms, grateful for its warmth. 'He thought the journey might be a bit much.'

She saw her mother's face crease in concern and Helena was sure she caught her cast a furtive glance at her father. 'How will he manage without you?' she asked.

Of course they thought it was strange that she had left James at home when he still wasn't fully back on his feet, but her parents only knew part of the story. She hadn't told them about their fertility journey or that her practice had asked her to take some time out. They obviously knew about the crash, but they didn't know about the one-night stand or now this bombshell that Milly was actually James's biological child and not Aidan's. Her parents were quiet, country people – this kind of thing didn't happen in their world. It belonged in the pages of a red-topped tabloid newspaper, which they most definitely would never buy. Helena felt ashamed.

'He will be fine,' she said to appease them. 'He's flying around the place now. His physiotherapist is really happy with his progress.' But she knew that her mother could see right through her charade. For her to turn up out of the blue, leaving her convalescing husband at home, raised too many flags. Helena had never been able to keep any secrets from her.

'Well, it's a lovely surprise to see you, isn't it, Pat?' She turned to her husband. 'But I do wish you had told me you were coming, Helena…' Anne chastised. 'I haven't even put fresh sheets on the bed for you.'

'I'll be fine, Mam.'

'So how long are you here for?' Pat asked.

'A week, maybe… I'm not sure…' She just needed

some space for a few days to get her head together and then she would have to make a decision.

'Well, take as long as you need. This will always be your home.'

Helena swallowed a lump in her throat and worked hard to keep back the tears that threatened to spill over at any moment. Her parents clearly knew that this wasn't an ordinary visit home, but how could she tell them what had happened?

38

AIDAN

Aidan stayed sitting in the car outside his house and held his head in his hands. How was he meant to go in there and face the children? It would kill him to see Milly. He had just been for a meeting in Brendan Waters' office and things had gone even worse than he had expected. Brendan had wanted to discuss their next steps following on from the results of the paternity test.

'Thank you for coming in to see me today, Aidan.' Brendan had pumped his hand before taking a seat across the desk from him. 'I'm sure it won't come as a surprise to tell you that James's solicitor, Laurence Jones, has been in touch and they've mounted a case...' he had paused. 'I'm very sorry but... well... I'm afraid, there's more...' His voice had sounded stretched, like a catapult pulled backwards, causing Aidan's breath to hitch in his chest. He'd picked up a pen and twiddled it between his fingers before putting it down again.

'Go on,' Aidan had pushed, almost impatiently but feeling equally terrified for what was to come, wishing he could hold back Brendan's words forever.

'Well... there is no easy way to tell you this, Aidan, but James is seeking full custody. I know we had expected him to apply for access to Milly, but it seems he has gone a step further.'

Aidan had felt the world around him stop, Brendan's voice had faded into the background and all he could hear was an angry ringing sound in his ears. This wasn't happening. It couldn't be. Aidan had asked Brendan to repeat what he had said, he was sure that there must be a mistake. But, sure enough, Brendan had repeated those same cruel words. James wanted to take his child. It was outrageous. So callous. James was going for the whole shooting gallery. He wanted to snatch his daughter away from him like she was an inanimate object – like you might take back a book you had loaned someone or a coat that a friend had borrowed. But Milly was a child. She was his daughter!

As bad it had been losing Rowan, Aidan couldn't lose Milly too; he knew he would never have the strength to survive it, it would finish him off completely. And what on earth was he supposed to tell Callum and Jack if the worst happened? If James was successful in his challenge, how would he begin to explain something like that to them? They had just lost their mother; they couldn't lose their sister too. Hadn't they been through enough? He couldn't allow it to happen. He *wouldn't* allow it to happen. Aidan knew that he had to protect what was left of his family with every cell in his body. He would lay down and die for his daughter if that's what it took.

'I will need to get some direction from you on how you would like to handle it, whether you want to defend—' Brendan had pulled him out from the maelstrom that was circling inside his head.

'Of course I'm going to bloody defend it! She's my daughter for God's sake!' He had lowered his voice so that it was deathly calm before adding, 'I will fight for that child with every breath in my body.'

'I thought you might say that, but you have to realise, Aidan, that the results change everything. I can't see any judge denying a biological father access.'

'But Milly has been through so much.' He had stabbed his index finger against his chest. 'I'm her father. Me, not him,' he had added fiercely.

Brendan had avoided his eyes. 'It's not black and white any more, Aidan. As I explained previously, the UN Convention on the Rights of the Child recognises a child's right to know their parents—'

'Whose side are you on here, Brendan?' Aidan had demanded.

'I wouldn't be doing my job properly if I didn't point out what could happen. It's Solomon's choice, I don't envy the judge.'

'You're saying I'm going to lose her, aren't you?' Aidan had blazed.

'Calm down, Aidan, I'm not saying that; I just need you to be aware of the worst-case scenario. I do think there will be some element of compromise involved here though.'

'How the hell can I compromise? This is my child we're talking about here! What kind of a dad would I be if I stood by and watched her being taken away from me!'

'But on paper she's not your child, Aidan. James has rights too.'

Aidan had sat back in the leather-clad chair and gripped the armrests fiercely until his knuckles were white. 'So what are we going to do then?' Aidan had demanded. 'Without putting too fine a point on it, what am I paying you for, Brendan? I'm not just going to step aside and let him take my child!' He hated being confrontational, but these events had brought out the very worst in him. He couldn't just sit back and roll with it and see how they got on as seemed to be Brendan's stance. Someone had to fight for Milly.

'Well, we will of course be arguing that the disruption to Milly's life will be damaging given recent events, namely the loss of her mother, but Milly's biological father has rights and feelings too and it's most likely that James's team will argue that his rights have been infringed by the falsification of the paternity details on Milly's birth certificate. You need to be prepared to fight and, even then, it's unlikely that you will be happy with the outcome.'

Aidan had questioned how any sentient human being with feelings could allow Milly to be ripped out of the bosom of her family after everything that had happened to her, but Brendan had stated that the judge would want to be seen to be fair to all parties.

'So, you're saying that one day Milly could be living with the only family she has ever known and the next be taken away from us and sent to live with someone else? I'm failing to see how that could be in the child's best interests? Could you imagine how traumatic that would be for her?' He'd had a sudden image of Milly's red face, screaming as she was pulled out of his arms, or waking up crying during the night in a strange bed, wondering why Aidan wasn't there to comfort her. The thought terrified him. It was cruel; why should she pay the price for her mother's deceit? She was too young to understand this; it wasn't like he could prepare her; she would never be able to grasp it. Her world was simple – it was Mammy, Daddy, Callum and Jack, or at least it had been before Rowan died. 'Doesn't the person at the centre of all this matter? Doesn't what Milly want count for anything?'

Brendan had shaken his head. 'It wouldn't happen overnight, it would most likely be a stepped arrangement, starting with an hour here or there, probably with you present initially or perhaps in the presence of a social worker, then the time would build up gradually.'

'So even if the judge was only willing to allow James limited access initially, you're saying that, over time, he could build up a case for full custody?' Aidan had asked. 'Basically either way I'm going to lose her?' Brendan had seemed resigned to the fact that James was going to get some form of access to Milly – the only question was how much.

'Any decision made will be in Milly's best interest and although she is very young, they will try to ascertain her wishes.'

'How the hell can you do that? She's three – she just knows that I'm her dad, her understanding doesn't go beyond that!' he'd said in exasperation.

'Children are remarkably adaptable at that age, and I'd imagine that they will also involve play therapists specially trained in these matters.'

'Do you have children?' Aidan had finally asked.

'Well, no... I—'

'Well then, you'll never be able to understand,' Aidan had said, getting up and walking out of the office as temper overtook him.

As Aidan had drove through the city streets towards home, he was left with no doubt that he was going to lose Milly – if not now, in the future. He couldn't hold back the awful inevitability that he was going to lose his child.

He knew he couldn't stay sitting in the car forever, so eventually he took a deep breath, steeled himself and stepped out of the car. He made his way wearily up the steps to their house, where Gemma was staying with the children after collecting the boys from the school and Milly from the crèche.

'How did it go?' his sister asked, hurrying to greet him in the hallway as soon as she heard the door open.

He continued wordlessly into the kitchen and tossed his keys down on the island. The smell of baking filled his nose – it had been a long time since their kitchen had smelled homely like this. When Aidan had tried to bake cookies with Milly recently, he had ended up burning the dough.

'Daddy!' he heard Milly sing and she ran over

and collided with his leg, throwing her arms around him. There was no sign of the boys, he guessed they were upstairs in their bedrooms, hopefully doing their homework but probably hunched over their devices. Callum's behaviour had improved in the days since his run-in with the gang down at the petrol station and although it was early days, Aidan was praying he had finally turned a corner.

Aidan picked her up from the ground and held her in his arms.

'Me and Auntie G maded cupcakes. I maded one for you, Daddy.' She was already wriggling to be let down even though Aidan wished he could keep her there safe in his arms forever. She ran over to the worktop where baking trays full of steaming buns were cooling.

'They smell delicious,' Aidan said.

'Milly, why don't you go wash your hands in the bathroom and I'll see if they have cooled down enough for you to eat,' Gemma suggested.

'Okay,' Milly said, running off down the hall.

'Was it that bad?' Gemma asked, her whole face creased in concern.

Aidan nodded. 'According to Brendan, it's just a matter of time before I lose her.'

'Oh, Aidan,' she threw her arms around him and hugged him tightly. 'I'm so sorry.'

On his better days, he tried to believe that Rowan hadn't realised that Milly was James's child, but on days like this it was hard not to think that she had purposely deceived him by attributing the child's paternity to him sheerly because it was the easiest thing to do. Even though it had been a surprise when Rowan had told him she was pregnant, they weren't using protection, so it wasn't unexpected. They were married, they already had two children together, why would anyone suspect this baby might not be his? Or perhaps she was afraid to reveal the truth, knowing how their lives would have been unravelled so instead she had left that until after her death to be discovered. The irony of it was that if this situation had happened when Rowan had still been alive, Brendan had told him that Milly would never be taken away from her mother and the most James would probably have got was access, but instead it was Aidan who had to deal with this mess on his own and the very real fear of losing his daughter.

That night as he brushed his teeth before bed, the events of the day really hit him. The emotion – the fear – overtook him and he felt hot tears in his eyes. The reality slammed into him: he was going to lose his daughter. It was only a matter of time. Suddenly anger overcame him, and he lashed out at the vanity unit where all of Rowan's glass perfume bottles stood and swiped them from the shelf. The bottles landed with a crash on the tiles, some smashing instantly and releasing their musky aromas into the air.

Aidan stood looking at the shards of glass that lay all around his bare feet, where pale barley shades of liquid were running across the floor and he knew that dead or alive, if he lost Milly, he would never forgive Rowan for what she had done to them.

39

HELENA

Helena had seen every hour change on her smart watch that sat on the bedside table. She had been awake all night, her mind racing with worries and her stomach churning with guilt as the light creeping around the edge of the blind changed from deep navy to pinky-orange, until finally it turned bright morning white. She lay there and looked around her childhood bedroom where yellowed Sellotape still clung to the walls from her teenage days when she'd ripped posters of her crushes out of magazines and stuck them up, before pulling them down again in favour of someone new in the following week's edition. She could hear sounds of life in the kitchen and the smell of fried bacon filled her nostrils. Her stomach growled but she didn't have the appetite for food. She pulled back the duvet and climbed out of bed.

'Morning,' she said, rubbing her bleary eyes as she came into the kitchen.

'Helena!' her dad stood up and gave her a hug. 'Did you sleep okay?'

'Never better,' she lied, giving him a kiss on the cheek.

'Sit down there, love.' Her mum pulled out a chair for her and placed a plate full of rashers, sausages, black and white pudding, scrambled egg, tomato and beans in front of her. Normally she would be salivating over her mother's full Irish, but she didn't think she would be able to stomach it this morning.

'So how's James managing without you?' her dad continued.

Helena twirled her fork between her fingers. He clearly suspected something was wrong and was subtly trying to bring up the subject. What should she say? How would she even begin to tell them everything that had happened over the last few weeks, the fateful series of events that had culminated in her return to her childhood home?

'He's good,' she replied. The truth was, she had no idea. He had tried calling her several times, but she never picked up. It was better that way.

'Look, *a ghrá*, you would tell us if there was something wrong wouldn't you?' he broached.

'Of course I would, but you don't need to worry, honestly everything is fine,' she lied. 'I just wanted to see you both for a few days.' Helena cut down into a thick slice of bacon and brought a piece to her mouth to further prove that all was well with her. It tasted like cardboard as she tried to chew it.

'Well, how about we take a walk along the beach after you've finished that?' Anne suggested.

* * *

Later, Helena and her mother strolled along the amber sand of Ballycladdagh bay beneath the overhang of the cliff. The colours appeared oversaturated on that sunny morning; emerald green fields rolled towards the sea and a cornflower-blue sky blazed above them. The azure-hued waters of the sheltered bay would rival any Caribbean beach and the Twelve Bens were a beige silhouette in the distance. They walked along the beach, where up on the headland the ruins of old stone cottages, which had been abandoned during famine times, now lay crumbling towards the ground. Every now and then, they had to walk around a rocky outcrop behind which were hidden crystal-clear pools. Helena was only half-paying attention as her mother gave her the low-down on the village's comings and goings: who was getting married, who was sick or had recently passed away, and what family had fallen out over a will.

They reached a small inlet and they sat on a large flat rock, where Helena had eaten many picnics as a child. The winter sunlight hit their cheeks. Stringy seaweed was draped over nearby rocks and a carpet of sea-moss lay near their feet. Her mother unzipped her backpack and took out a flask of tea and some slices of home-made tea brack that she had wrapped in napkins. She handed Helena a tin mug and a slice of the sweet loaf. Her mother had had this routine for as long as Helena could remember. As a child, she would always produce a cake and a flask of tea from her bag as a reward whenever they went for a walk. Helena and her brothers had looked forward to the treat.

Even though she wasn't hungry, Helena took a slice, feeling grateful for her mother's ways; this little piece of childhood was exactly what her wounded heart needed right now.

'This is good,' Helena said, taking a bite of the loaf despite her wan appetite.

'Do you remember Grace Flaherty that you went to school with?' her mother asked, continuing on with all the village news.

'Uh-huh,' Helena replied vaguely.

'Well, I met her mother Maura in the shop at the weekend and would you believe she's having twins?' she said through a mouthful of cake. 'They were a long time waiting by all accounts.'

Helena's breath snagged in her chest. It felt as though her mother was testing her for a reaction. 'Good for Grace,' she managed to reply, trying her best to keep her voice level.

'What about yourself and James?' her mother threw the question out onto the sea breeze, leaving it to sit heavily between them.

Helena felt herself bristle. She hadn't told her

mother anything of their journey to become parents. It wasn't that she was trying to be secretive, but she hadn't wanted them to worry. She didn't think she could bear to see her pain reflected in her mother's eyes. That would undo her completely. She had always assumed it would happen eventually for them and no one would ever need to know about the heartache they had endured along the way. 'What about us?' she matched her mother's question with another one.

'Well, I guess I was wondering if, you know... you might be having a bit of trouble in that department yourself?'

Helena's heart began to ratchet. How could she begin to tell her? 'Trouble' didn't even start to cover it. Helena took a deep breath, knowing in her heart that the time had come to be honest. She couldn't keep things a secret from her mother forever. She had never been able to lie to her as a child; ever since she was a little girl her mother had been able to see right through her. 'You're right, Mam...' She paused to choose her words. 'Things haven't happened like we had hoped.'

'Oh love,' Anne linked her arm and gave it a tight

squeeze and Helena felt the weight of tears filling her eyes. 'Try to stay positive, miracles happen every day. I'll be praying for you in mass.'

Helena nodded gratefully. She couldn't bear to tell her mother any more about their heartache, how all the prayers in the world still wouldn't give her a much-longed for baby. How her arms ached with the need to hold her precious child and she had a physical ache in her womb where an infant should grow. 'I think we've gone past prayers, Mam,' she said sadly, 'but thank you anyway.'

'Is that what this visit is about? To do a little soul-searching?'

'I guess so.' She didn't want to get into the drama about Milly, she felt a huge sense of shame and regret for her actions. She didn't think she would ever be able to tell her mother about it, she felt awful enough without having to witness Anne's disappointment in her on top of it all.

'Are you and James okay?' her mother continued. 'Not being able to have a baby can take its toll on a marriage – you're too young to remember, but your auntie Úna and uncle Dan had a hard time of it before they had Katie. It's not easy.'

Suddenly the beach was leached of all its colour and when Helena looked up at the sky, she saw rain clouds had begun to encroach. Having grown up right on the edge of the Atlantic Ocean, she was used to how quickly the weather could turn on you without warning.

'To be honest, I think my marriage is over,' she admitted, feeling a wave of sadness floor her. It was one thing thinking it in your own head, but when you had to tell other people, it suddenly became very real.

'Oh love,' her mother pulled her into an all-encompassing hug and Helena folded into her arms like she was a small girl once again just as the skies began to open and the first pattering of raindrops fell.

40

AIDAN

The park was crawling with families. The rare, blue-sky winter's day had dragged everyone outdoors, wrapped up in coats, topped with hats and gloves to stave off the biting cold.

'Daddy, you look like a dragon.' Milly giggled at the little white clouds that fogged onto the air as Aidan breathed. She scooted along beside him, the large pom-pom on her woollen hat bobbing along with the motion. Jack and Callum were walking at a slower pace behind them.

They reached the playground and Aidan pushed open the gate and went inside. Milly threw down her scooter and ran off. Children zigzagged chaotically across the bark surface, narrowly avoiding colliding with each other, while parents winced at the near-misses as they looked on from the side-lines. He saw her climbing up on to a swing and he found a space on a bench and sat down.

They were slowly picking up the pieces of their lives and adjusting to their new reality without Rowan. The weekdays were a busy rush between school and work, then afterschool activities and homework, dinner and laundry, but they were muddling through and Aidan was so proud of his children. The situation with Milly was tormenting him though. The court hearing was set for two weeks' time – the week before Christmas – and Aidan was a mess. The stress was weighing him down. He couldn't eat, he couldn't sleep. His head was full of horror. He kept waking with nightmares that Milly was being taken away; she was screaming for him to stop it all, but in his dream his legs and arms wouldn't move – no matter how much he tried, he was frozen to the spot. Whenever he looked at his precious daughter, he couldn't believe they were in this situation. The pain slammed into him once more and he was broken all over again.

Christmas ads would play on the TV showing happy families gathered around the table celebrating the festivities and his heart would break as he realised Milly might not be at their dinner table next year. She would chat excitedly about what she was going to ask Santa for in her letter and Aidan's heart would twist at her innocence – her perfect trust in him as her father to protect her and to make things right almost crushed him every time he looked at her face. He felt as though they were racing against a clock – they were living on borrowed time – every day was a day closer to losing her. Was he doing the right thing by fighting for her? A part of his brain was questioning if it was fair to drag her into the centre of a messy legal battle and play tug-o-war with the child after everything that she had been through? But he also knew that he could never just hand her over to James. Aidan knew with every bone in his body that he had to fight; he had to do it for her.

The boys had headed for the roundabout and began messing around, seeing how fast they could spin one another. *Some things never change*, Aidan thought, smiling as he watched them fooling around together. Having Callum join them for the walk felt like nothing short of a miracle. In the days following the incident at the petrol station, Aidan and Callum had reached a truce of sorts. His purple bruising had now faded to a dirty yellow colour and so had his anger too, it seemed. Callum didn't slam doors or ignore him any more, he didn't avoid Aidan's eye and he had started to join them at the table to eat dinner once again. He gave Aidan a hand making the school lunches in the mornings, and he helped to dress Milly. He had apologised to his principal and Mr Leonard too and had even agreed to meet with the grief counsellor that Jack was seeing, which felt like a major win in Aidan's eyes. He hoped that by talking through his feelings in counselling, it might help Callum to deal with his anger. Aidan knew Callum had got a fright that night at the petrol station and although he was afraid to raise his hopes too much, he prayed that Callum had finally turned a corner.

A man clutching two takeaway coffees came up and handed one to what appeared to be his wife who was sitting at the other end of the bench beside Aidan. They exchanged an easy smile, a look of solidarity, as she took the cup from him, wrapping her hands gratefully around the warm cardboard. The simple gesture made Aidan's heart sore. He was still in disbelief at how the rug had been pulled out from underneath his life. To think that his family had once been like that; they had gone for family walks to the park, he and Rowan would get coffees from the little café that operated from the old Victorian bandstand while the kids sipped hot chocolate. He had once taken those easy, ordinary days for granted, but now he knew the fragility of life. He had seen up close and personal just how cruel life could be. How you could have your whole world around you one minute and then in the next it could be washed away, leaving it virtually unrecognisable.

'Come push me, Daddy,' he heard Milly calling over to him from the swings. He stood up, went over to her, and began to push her from behind. 'Higher, Daddy!' she demanded. She threw her head back and grinned up at him, those large blue eyes radiating her smile. Her dark hair fanned out on the air behind her.

Aidan's heart stumbled; she was so precious. What killed him was that she had no idea of how her world was about to change. When Milly had been placed in his arms for the very first time, this tiny, mewling bundle swaddled in white, Aidan had felt a huge surge of protectiveness for her. He had felt it with the boys too, but this was stronger – he had a daughter, and he felt an almost primal sense that he had to protect her from the evils of the world and now he was failing to do that. He couldn't protect her from what was coming down the tracks no matter how much he wished he could. He was so scared for what was to come. He'd never survive losing her. He stopped pushing and let the momentum keep her going.

'What's wrong, Daddy?' she said, turning around to face him, as the swing began to slow down. 'Why aren't you pushing me?'

Her face unravelled him, and tears pushed forward in his eyes. 'Nothing, sweetie, everything is good.'

'You look sad, Daddy, are you sad because you miss Mammy?'

'Well... yeah... sort of,' Aidan said, grappling for words, having been taken off guard.

'It's okay, Daddy, Mammy is in heaven now,' she said, repeating the same words he had said to her so many times to soothe her whenever she was missing her mother.

He moved around to the front of the swing and crouched down on the ground before her, using his hand to steady the ropes on either side. 'I love you so much, Milly, you know that don't you – no matter what happens I need you to know this.'

She began giggling. 'I already knowded that, Daddy, silly billy.'

She jumped down from the swings and tore off towards the spiderweb climbing frame.

'Daddy, look at me, me the itsy bitsy spider,' she laughed as she placed a foot on the rope and began climbing up along the web.

'Don't go any higher, Milly,' he warned as he followed her over.

She was already above his head, moving faster, getting braver and more daring with each step she took. She looked too small to have scaled such a height. She turned around and grinned at him, a daredevil set to her face. She bit down on her lip with determination and raised her foot to climb higher still, but it didn't connect with the rope and suddenly she was falling backwards through the air.

He heard a collective intake of breath from the other parents who were witnessing the scene unfold. She landed with a thump on the sand just feet away from him. She was lying at a funny angle; her neck twisted awkwardly.

'Milly,' he heard himself scream as he ran over and cupped his hands around her face, but she didn't respond.

'Don't move her!' another voice called, rushing over to him. 'She could have a spinal injury.'

Fear flooded through him. Sweaty palms, racing heart. This couldn't be happening.

'Somebody call an ambulance!' another voice shouted as they took off their coat and placed it over her small body.

'Milly,' he said, crouching down beside her. 'Come on, Milly, wake up, it's Daddy!' he begged, stroking the smooth skin of her face. He felt something warm on his palms and realised that his hand was covered in her sticky blood.

'Aidan – is she okay?' a familiar voice asked, crouching down on the ground beside him.

He turned around to see James there. His brain didn't have the capacity to wonder what he was doing there. His body was too full with fear to feel anything for him. Not hatred or anger. He was numb.

'I saw what happened,' James continued.

Both men were staring at the child lying broken between them. The precious child that they both wanted.

Callum and Jack were beside Aidan now staring down at the crumpled body of their little sister lying on the ground beneath them.

'Is Milly dead?' Jack asked, his eyes wide with fear.

'No, she's not!' Aidan said, sounding sharper than he had intended.

'Do something, Dad!' Callum roared at him. 'You have to do something!'

'She's going to be okay,' James reassured them. 'Your sister is a tough cookie.'

'But why won't she wake up?' Jack demanded.

'Where the hell is that ambulance?' Aidan cried. The wait felt like an eternity. Every second was stretched out before him like he was part of a slow-motion video. Chaotic thoughts scudded through his head: would she be okay? She had to be; he couldn't bear to think she wouldn't. How could this be happening again? He felt he had used up all his luck the first time around; somehow she had come back from the brink, but how could she hold on for a second time?

Eventually they could hear the wail of sirens coming in the distance and finally through a clearing in the trees, Aidan saw flashing blue lights and moments later the white shirts of two paramedics racing towards them.

'Stand back!' they shouted to the onlookers, putting order into the chaos.

The crowd moved back until it was just Aidan, James, Callum and Jack surrounding the paramedics as they worked on Milly. Aidan couldn't bear to watch at they checked her pulse and pulled back her eyelids to check her pupils for a reaction. They continued to check her over, before stabilising her with a neck brace. She looked so tiny as they moved her onto the stretcher and carted her towards the ambulance. A large scarlet stain marked the sand where her head had lain.

'Please tell me that she'll be okay?' Aidan begged.

'Come on, we need to hurry,' the paramedic urged, dodging his question.

'What about the boys?' Aidan said, panicked, torn between needing to take care of them and travel in the ambulance with Milly.

'I'll take them in a taxi, and we'll meet you at the hospital,' James offered.

'Thanks,' Aidan mumbled as he ran after the paramedic and climbed into the back of the ambulance.

41

HELENA

The wind whipped Helena's hair around her face and the waves rolled, licked and foamed far beneath her, sending up shoots of icy sea-spray to where she walked along the clifftop. Gulls and terns swooped and dived and cawed. She could see the craggy mass of Inis Mór in the far distance. She had always loved it up here. When she was a child, she and her dad would come for walks and he'd stop and stare out over the vast Atlantic and say, 'Next stop America.' It never failed to take her breath away. You had to be careful, picking your steps; she knew where the blowholes were and where it was safe to walk, but it was a place you could be alone with your thoughts –

you could shout and roar and scream onto the wind in anger or frustration and nobody would hear you. You weren't just at the very edge of Ireland or even Europe, up here, she felt as though she was at the very edge of the world. The sun was starting to set, and she knew she should get a move on if she wanted to be home before nightfall when the path would grow treacherous.

She felt her phone vibrate in her pocket. She fished it out and saw it was James calling her again. Her heart fell. She returned it to her pocket. She didn't have the energy to rehash the same conversation again. After a moment, her phone beeped with a text message. She took it out once more and read what he had sent:

It's Milly – please call me.

What was that supposed to mean? she wondered. Was he using Milly as a ploy to get her to answer the phone to him? Was it something to do with the case or something else entirely? She prayed James hadn't done anything stupid... But no... he wouldn't... would he? Crazy thoughts crashed around inside her head. She knew she would be tormented with worries if she didn't find out what was going on and so, with fumbling hands, she hit the call button as curiosity got the better of her.

'Helena – thank God.' She heard the panic in his voice as he answered on the first ring.

'What's going on, James? Where are you?'

'I'm in a taxi with Callum and Jack on my way to the hospital.'

'Callum and Jack?' she repeated in disbelief. Had she heard him right? 'Why?'

'It's Milly, she fell in the playground and hurt her head,' he said quickly. 'She's gone in an ambulance with Aidan, I'm taking the boys there now.' There was a crack in his voice.

She felt the hairs on her arms stand to attention. This didn't sound good. 'Is she okay?' Helena asked, knowing it was a stupid question. It was serious if Milly was being taken by ambulance, but she needed reassurance that the child would be all right. 'Was she conscious?'

'Please, Helena, just get here,' he said desperately and then he was gone.

She turned around and was facing straight into

the headwind. It howled and swirled and sucked the breath from her lungs. The last sliver of sunlight was left on the horizon. Her head was full of chaos: what had happened to Milly? Why had James been in the playground? And why was he the one taking Callum and Jack to the hospital? After everything that had happened, he was probably the last person Aidan would trust his children with. Nothing made any sense.

Helena's head was spinning as she made her way down the cliff path, picking her steps through the marram grass as carefully as she could, but still moving quickly in her desperate need to get back to her parents' cottage. Sea mist was starting to descend like a blanket and the village lights were fuzzy yellow in the distance. Fear chilled its way through her. She couldn't bear it if something happened to Milly. How must Aidan be feeling to go through this worry again so soon after the crash? And James too. Milly was his own flesh and blood. She was a part of him; he must be terrified.

'I have to go back to Dublin,' she announced breathlessly as she rounded the kitchen door back in *Ceol na Mara*.

'What is it? What's wrong?' her mother jumped up from the table in panic where she had been sitting with a cup of tea. Her father was probably out doing the cattle. 'Is James okay?'

How on earth could she explain this to her mother? How could she possibly begin to explain who this child was that had torn her and her husband apart? This child that was precocious and fun-loving and so wonderful in every way. Her eyes were drawn to the red glow of the Sacred Heart lamp which hung on the wall above the range. How many of her prayers had gone unanswered over the last few years? How much time had she wasted bargaining with a God that she wasn't really sure she believed in? *If he could just give her a baby, she would do anything, anything at all that he wanted.* And even though it felt futile, she found herself doing it again – *Please hold on, little one,* she prayed. She would do anything if he would just spare Milly.

'I'm sorry, Mam, I have to go,' she said, grabbing her keys and bag from the countertop and running out the door.

42

AIDAN

Dusk had fallen beyond the drizzle-spattered window which looked out onto the hospital car park. It felt like Aidan had been waiting for hours. He hadn't seen or heard anything since they had wheeled Milly's stretcher through a set of double doors and instructed him to wait in the corridor. Finally, he saw Callum and Jack running down the corridor towards him, with James who was carrying Milly's pink scooter over his shoulder, trying to keep up with them. He had forgotten all about it with everything that had happened. The boys smacked into his body with full force, telling him that this wasn't some awful nightmare that he was going to wake up from – this was real. He clung onto them, pulling them tightly into him. He was glad to feel the weight of their arms around him – they were the only things keeping him from sinking into the abyss.

'How is she, Dad?' Jack asked, his lips trembling.

Aidan shook his head. 'I don't know, nobody will tell me anything,' he said angrily.

'She'll be okay,' Callum reassured him. 'I called Auntie G,' he said. 'She'll tell Granny Aggie and Grandad Bill and Granny Sheila and Grandad Philip too.'

Aidan had totally forgotten to let them know with everything going on, but Callum had taken on the responsibility without needing to be told. Aidan looked at his son, who suddenly seemed to have matured overnight. When had that happened? Why hadn't he noticed before now? Was it the events of recent months or was this the normal child to teenage transition? 'Thanks, son,' he said, feeling a surge of pride for the young man that Callum was growing into. Rowan would have been so proud of him.

'Any update?' James asked, placing the scooter down when he had caught up with them. He had the audacity to look shaken by what had happened, and Aidan felt his fists curl into tight balls at his side.

'If anything happens to her...' Aidan began pacing. His fear was multiplying, like mitosis, filling every part of him and sweat prickled his neck.

James reached out to put an arm around him but thought better of it and let it fall down by his side again. 'Hey, she's going to be okay.'

Aidan knew he was talking in platitudes, filling the air with empty words because he didn't know what else to do. 'She has to be. I can't lose her too,' he replied.

He sat down onto the bay of plastic chairs that were attached to the wall in the corridor and held his head in his hands. How were they back here at the hospital again? None of it made any sense. He thought of Milly's daring smile just moments before she fell. Guilt wrapped itself around him like a python. Why didn't he sprint faster? He should have spoken sterner to her. Ordered her to get down from the frame. What other parent would let their three-year old climb so high, let alone one that was only just recovering from a serious accident?

'Here, thought you could use this,' James said,

handing him a coffee, bringing him back to the present. When Aidan looked up, he noticed that it was dark outside now and they sat under the bright glare of the artificial lights. Aidan hadn't even realised James had left. Time seemed to have taken on an ethereal quality, the minutes seemed to stretch out forever until they all fudged together. He saw Callum and Jack were sipping hot chocolates on the chairs opposite him. They were watching something on Callum's phone.

'Thanks,' Aidan exhaled heavily, clasping his hands around the cardboard cup but not drinking it. 'When are they going to tell me how she is?'

'It feels like she's been in there forever,' James agreed, taking a seat beside him as they both fell quiet.

Eventually there was a swish as the set of double doors opened and a nurse dressed in green scrubs with a plastic apron covering the front emerged.

Aidan stood up in front of her, blocking her path. 'Can someone please tell me how Milly Whelan is?' he demanded. 'I'm her father.'

'She's having a CT scan at the moment, Mr Whelan,'

'How long will that take?'

'We'll update you as soon as we can,' she replied as she continued out past them, telling him nothing at all.

Aidan began pacing once more. He noticed that the hospital had grown quieter as visitors went home and patients bedded down for the night. Ward lights were dimmed, and voices grew softer. His watch told him it was after nine o'clock. *Why the hell was it taking so long?*

He walked down to the end of the corridor and he saw Helena was coming towards him in the distance. He realised James had probably called her. Her hair was wild and windswept, and raindrops glistened on her waterproof jacket.

'Aidan, I'm so sorry – how is she doing?' she said quickly as the words tumbled from her mouth.

He shook his head. 'I don't know, nobody will tell me anything.'

He led her back towards the others and James jumped up as soon as he saw her, running towards her, pulling her in close.

'I got here as soon as I could,' she announced breathlessly as they embraced one another.

Aidan felt a pang of regret as all the pain of his loss was stirred up fresh inside him. His missed his wife, no matter what had happened between them, he really wished she was by his side right then.

'Why don't I go see what I can find out,' Helena offered, pulling away from James after a moment and looking at Aidan.

Aidan nodded.

'Helena will be able to talk doctor to doctor, she might be able to find out something,' James tried to assure him as they watched her heading back down the corridor. He placed a hand on his arm, but Aidan brushed him off.

After a few minutes, Helena returned shaking her head and Aidan's heart sank. 'I'm sorry, I tried my best, but nobody was able to tell me anything.'

She took a seat beside James on the bank of chairs opposite to where Aidan and the boys were sitting. They all sat in awkward silence, as they waited for news, punctuated only by the sounds of the overexaggerated shrieks of some YouTuber that they boys were watching.

Eventually a doctor in a white coat came towards him. He was a balding man, a little older than Aidan, with an open, friendly face. Aidan felt his breath stall as he tried to read his face for clues, but it gave nothing away. Aidan stood up on one side and James and Helena did the same opposite him.

'Which one of you is the father of Milly Whelan?' he asked, looking across the corridor at both men.

Aidan looked at James and James looked back at him as both men exchanged a look that said so much but told nothing of the pain they shared. He noticed Helena watching them both anxiously. Aidan felt his heart twist: how was the doctor to know the agony that such a seemingly innocuous question could cause?

The doctor was looking from one man to the other now, waiting for a response. 'Which one of you is Mr Whelan?' he repeated, with a note of impatience in his voice.

'He is,' James said after a beat.

'I have good news for you, Mr Whelan,' the doctor announced, directing his attention at Aidan. 'The results of the scan show that although Milly has sustained a linear fracture on her skull, there is no bleeding or swelling on her brain. We've cleaned the wound and dressed it. We will keep her overnight for observation, just as a precaution, but we expect her to make a full recovery.'

'Oh, thank God,' Aidan broke down. 'I-I thought I was going to lose her...'

'She's a lucky little lady. Not her first visit to hospital by all accounts... She's down this way if you'd like to see her.'

The five of them hurried down the corridor after him and entered a ward.

'Daddy!' she called as soon as he rounded the corner of her bed.

She was awake. Aidan felt relief flooding through him. Her lispy voice was the sweetest sound, like birdsong on a crisp winter's morning. 'How are you feeling, love?' He squeezed her hand tight. Aidan wanted to wrap her in cotton wool. Never let her more than a foot away from him again.

'I have a big plaster on mine head.' She raised her chubby hand to point to the bandage that surrounded her forehead.

'That's just your princess crown,' Callum said, laughing.

'Don't do that to me again, you hear, no more

climbing!' Aidan warned through a mix of laughter and tears.

He noticed Helena and James hanging back at the door watching them.

'Lena!' Milly cried as she spotted her. 'I was trying to be the itsy-bitsy spider, but I fallded.'

Helena smiled. 'How are you, sweetheart?' she asked, joining them at the bedside. 'You gave everyone a fright. Let's leave the climbing to the spiders from now on, yeah?'

'I'm so glad she's okay,' James said, coming up beside Aidan.

Milly wrinkled her nose when she saw him standing beside them.

Aidan nodded as awkwardness charged the air between them. He felt himself stiffen; although he was grateful to James for looking after the boys, the matter of Milly's paternity still loomed over them. What if James said something in front of the children? His head began throbbing, as the events of the day caught up with him.

'I appreciate you taking the boys for me today,' Aidan mumbled.

'Don't mention it, I'm just glad I could help...'

Aidan held his breath, waiting for something more; another blow or a dig was coming, he could feel it.

'We... eh... better leave you guys to it,' James said, looking at Helena after a minute.

The short-lived truce was over. Two men stood at Milly's bedside, each claiming to be her father, but they both knew only one of them could be.

43

HELENA

When they finally returned to the house, Helena was exhausted, but she felt wired and knew she would never sleep. They were both so relieved and overjoyed that Milly was going to be okay.

'Thought you might like this,' she said, handing James a glass of wine from the bottle that she had just opened. She rolled her shoulders back, trying to ease them out. They burned with tension and her neck ached.

'Thanks,' he said, taking it gladly. 'What a day.' He shook his head.

'What a few months,' she replied, joining him at the kitchen table.

'I was never so glad to see you when you arrived earlier. The longer it was going on, I wasn't sure she was going to make it...' his voice choked. 'I saw the whole thing happen; it was awful.'

'But why were you even at the playground?' She still hadn't had a chance to get the full story from him.

'I was walking through the park, doing my new exercises from my physio, and I spotted Aidan and the kids in the playground together, so I stopped to watch them for a moment. The place was packed, so they didn't see me. Aidan was pushing Milly on the swings, and she was laughing like she hadn't a care in the world. She looked so happy, Hel; you should see the way she looked at him – I had always hoped that our baby would have looked at me the same way when he got a little older... if he had lived.'

Helena felt winded, like he was pulling the pain from a place deep inside her, where she had buried it long ago. 'George...'

'Sorry?'

'I named him,' she said quietly. 'George is his name.'

James fell quiet as he digested this new information. 'That's a good name,' he said eventually, nodding his head in agreement. 'That day when we lost him... well, something died inside of me... I had his whole life planned for him, y'know? I was going to take him to football training, maybe I would even help out with the coaching for his team, then we'd go mountain biking when he was old enough. He would do well in school, we'd have to keep the pressure on to get him to study of course, but he'd breeze through his exams because he'd have your brains,' he smiled sadly. 'I would take him for his first pint when he turned eighteen and even though we were both men...' his voice choked with emotion, 'I'd never be afraid to hug him.'

Helena was stunned. She had thought it was only her that felt George's loss so deeply like a knife had scored her heart, but James had planned a whole life for him just like she had. And yet neither of them had spoken to the other about it. He had suffered so much too, he just showed it differently.

'When I looked at Aidan in the hospital today, he was broken. It reminded me of that same pain that we felt. I keep thinking back to that time and how awful it was and how sad I still feel about what might have been...' he continued. 'Seeing Milly lying on that stretcher changed something inside me today and coming so close to losing her, it's put everything into focus ... I was looking at it all wrong – I kept thinking about it from my point of view – about what *I* was missing out on and what *I* was being deprived of, but, you were right, I never stopped to think about Milly. I realised that it's not about me or Aidan or even Rowan – I got caught up in the battle and lost sight of the person who really matters here. How could I take her away from him? Her happiness is in my hands – I could destroy her life. She's too little to understand. How would I be able to look her in the eye, knowing I had taken her away from the only father she has ever known? She would think I was a monster. She would grow up hating me. I want her so badly, Helena, she's beautiful and precious, and everything I imagined a daughter of mine to be and more, but if I take her away from Aidan, she'll have lost two parents. I can't do that to her. I don't want to put her through any more trauma.' His voice choked. 'Even though it kills me to think about all I'm losing out on, getting to know my own daughter – my only chance to be a father – her happiness matters even more. I only want the best for her, and if that's with Aidan, then that's the way it has to be.'

Helena felt her heart stop. 'What are you saying, James?'

He suddenly began to cry, shocking her – it was the first time Helena had seen him overcome with emotion during all of this mess. Even in the hospital, at the height of his pain, he hadn't broken down like this. Despite everything that had happened between them, she couldn't help but move towards him and put her arms around him.

'When I watched her being carried off on that stretcher, I made a promise that if she came through, I'd stop all this. I can't go through with it.' He shook his head. 'What I'm doing to Aidan is wrong, I know it is, Helena. She's not some doll who can be split down the middle to keep us both happy. I was just so desperate, and I couldn't see a way out. It felt as though I was losing you; you were slipping away from me and I don't know...' He sighed. 'I guess I thought if I could just give us a child, I could fix us. Like Milly was some kind of plaster for our marriage. I know it sounds ridiculous and selfish and I hate that I thought like that, but I was angry with Rowan too – I still am – I think she knew this secret and yet didn't tell anyone. She caused all this heartache for so many people and now I've gone and made everything worse. I think that day of the crash she was going to tell me – I have to believe that she wanted to do the right thing and that's why she asked to meet me, but what would have happened then? Would we still be in this same situation we find ourselves in now?'

'Rowan isn't here to give her side of the story,' Helena said. 'Maybe she was frightened and just didn't know what to do and so she made a bad call. I don't want to vilify the woman when she is no longer around to defend herself and you're no angel either – sleeping with Aidan's wife behind his back was wrong – but I've also played a part in this, I have to shoulder my share of the blame too. We've all made mistakes, but we can do the right thing now – it's not too late.'

'I don't want to lose our marriage, I don't want a life without you in it, Helena. The last few days have been awful: I couldn't eat, I couldn't sleep – it's been hell. Life doesn't mean anything to me if you're not by my side to share it with. I love you. I've always loved you since you blew me away that very first day you walked into my shop.' A smile crossed his lips at the memory. 'I knew you were the woman I wanted to spend the rest of my life with.'

'Oh, James, what have we become?' She began to cry then as months of hurt and stress overtook her. 'How have we ended up here?' Through her work, she was well aware of the emotional and psychological impact that infertility wrought on couples, but she'd always thought that they were different. She believed that *they'd* be able to withstand it. Put their backs to the wind and survive the onslaught together, but she now realised it had driven a wrecking ball through their marriage and the worst part was that she hadn't even seen it coming. Their journey to become parents had broken them. Their desperation to have a child had clouded everything: their love for one another, their judgement about what was right and wrong. It had blinded her to the love she had for her husband. Helena had always thought that secrets were better off aired, but now she realised that some secrets were better off not being discovered. They could cause too much heartache and pain. Sometimes you were better off not knowing the truth. It was kinder that way.

They sat there for a long time, crying and hugging. When they got up to go to bed, everything seemed to sit better, like they had been trapped in a little rowboat, being tossed around by a storm and had been cast amongst the debris like flotsam and jetsam but now the water had settled again, and they were emerging damaged but stronger. She didn't know what the future held for them, but she knew they would take it on together.

'I need to tell Aidan,' James said.

She nodded and reached for her husband's hand and wrapped her own around it. 'We'll do it together.'

44

AIDAN

It was a chilly winter morning and a thick frost had covered the garden overnight, giving the world beyond the glass a magical feel. Aidan was in the kitchen, where the scent of the coffee he had just brewed filled the air. He needed it after the night they had had. Milly had been released from hospital after breakfast, and except for the bandage on her head and grazes on her face, it was almost as if the fall had never happened. She was spinning around the house now like a whirling dervish and Aidan was following after her every step, to make sure she didn't come to any harm.

'Woah, woah, woah,' Aidan chastised as she tried

to climb up onto a stool at the marble-topped island. 'No way, I want you on solid ground only.'

'Okay, Daddy,' she giggled and climbed back down onto the floor.

'So let's make these cookies,' Aidan clapped his hands together. She had been asking if they could bake cookies since she had arrived home and Aidan had agreed, reckoning it was a task she could do without coming to too much harm.

Milly began pulling her tiny apron over her head and he lifted her up onto the stool so she could see what was happening. Gemma had taken the boys back to her house from the hospital the night before and dropped them home earlier. Callum was watching TV while Jack was building Lego in his room and Aidan was looking forward to having a quiet day after the drama of the last twenty-four hours.

'This is the book Mammy uses.' Milly pointed out a cookery book with a dusky pink spine and Aidan lifted it down from the shelf and began flicking through its pages that were splattered with transparent greasy spots from batters Rowan had made over the years. He found the recipe but was having less success finding the ingredients. He pulled bags of flour and sugar out of the cupboard and began checking the dates, chucking the ones that were out-of-date into the bin.

Over recent days, he had found that mindless tasks like this were good; his brain could just switch off and not think about the court hearing that was looming like a spectre, keeping him awake in the dead of night as he worried about what was going to happen to them. Coming so close to losing Milly the day before had given him a glimpse of the pain that lay ahead if James was successful, and it was terrifying. If only he could switch his brain off – just for a second – from the horror inside his head, but the fear of losing his precious daughter was always there tormenting him. Although he was grateful to James for taking care of the boys yesterday, why had he been there at the playground? How had he seen the fall unfold; was it just a strange coincidence or was there more to it? He had said he was out for a walk, but Aidan couldn't trust anything that man said. It occurred to him with sickening dread as he'd lain awake at Milly's bedside the night before that James might try to use the fall as evidence in court that

Aidan was an unfit father. James could twist the whole thing to support his case if he wanted to.

The sound of the doorbell brought him out of his thoughts. 'Will you get that, Callum?' he called from inside the cupboard. 'We've no flour or chocolate chips,' he explained to Milly as he surveyed what was left. 'We'll have to go to the shop and get some.'

'But me want to make the cookies now, Daddy!' she protested.

Aidan sighed. 'I'll just—'

'Dad?' Callum interrupted him as he called from the hall. 'It's Helena and James.'

What the hell were they doing here? He didn't have the energy to deal with whatever blows they might send his way today.

His breath hitched in his chest and he felt goosebumps prickle along his arms. 'I'm coming,' he replied, quickly getting up from the floor. Were they going to try to ambush him at home? The children didn't know anything about the drama between them and he didn't want them finding out. He knew he wouldn't be able to shield them from it forever; their upcoming court hearing was drawing dangerously close, but he wasn't ready to do it yet. How would he even begin to tell the children something like that? How could he break it to them that the mother they had loved so dearly had lived a double life? He didn't want to tarnish what good memories they had left of her. They were children; she deserved to stay in their head as the woman who kissed away their tears and soothed their worries. That was all they had left of her and Aidan didn't want to rob them of that. They had been through enough.

He hurried down the hallway and saw them framed in the arch of the doorway. He flashed them a warning look over Callum's head, telling them not to start anything in front of the kids.

'How is she doing?' Helena began when Callum had gone back into the kitchen.

'She's okay, she got home this morning. Look, I'm grateful for your help yesterday, but you know you shouldn't be here. Anything you need to say can be put through my solicitor.' He raised his hand to close the door on them, but suddenly James stepped forward and blocked him.

Aidan balled his fists as white-hot fury overtook him.

'Aidan, wait,' James was saying. 'I really need to

talk to you. We're not here to cause any more trouble, I swear.'

There was something about his tone, a crack in his voice that made Aidan stop. He noticed that they both looked wretched. Helena's hair was unwashed and slung back in a ponytail, with loose bits falling around her face. Her clothes were all creased too. James wore a hangdog expression and his eyes were bloodshot.

'If you start anything, you'll be out on your ear before you know it,' Aidan warned, standing to the side and gesturing towards the living-room door.

They followed Aidan inside and shifted awkwardly. Aidan couldn't help but notice how different they were from the last time they had doorstepped him. James's bullish demeanour was gone and his 6ft 3in frame suddenly seemed smaller.

'Sit down,' Aidan told them.

As they sat down on the L-shaped sofa, Milly came into the room and they all held their breath as she ran towards Helena and climbed up onto her knee.

'Lena! We're making cookies,' she announced.

All eyes fell on his daughter, the very reason they

were all gathered here; the wonderful child caught in the middle, the child that they all wanted. James was looking at her in wonderment, like he was only just seeing what Aidan had seen on the day she was born.

Aidan looked across at Helena and saw tears filling her eyes. She had to use the back of her hand to wipe them away quickly.

'Callum,' he called out.

'Yeah, Dad?' He stuck his head around the door a few moments later.

'Could you take Milly to the corner shop and get flour and chocolate chips to make the cookies?'

'Sure,' he said, coming into the room and taking his little sister by the hand. 'Come on, Milly, let's get your coat on.'

'Make sure you hold her hand the whole time and don't let her run off,' Aidan warned.

He waited until he heard the slam of the front door a few minutes later before continuing. 'What do you want?' he asked in exasperation.

James looked over at Helena and she nodded at him. He took a deep breath. 'I wanted to say that I'm sorry – for everything—' he began.

'It's a bit too late for that now, don't you think?' Aidan blazed.

'Aidan, I've been doing some thinking... a lot of thinking actually... and I've realised that what I'm doing isn't fair on you or Milly.' He shook his head.

Aidan sat up straighter, wondering where this was going. Was James trying to soften him up before landing another punch? There was a 'but' coming somewhere, he knew there was.

'Aidan, we're sorry, both of us, for what we've done to you,' Helena was saying now, her voice audibly upset. She began rooting around in her bag and pulled out a packet of tissues. 'From the bottom of my heart, I know you'll probably never forgive me for my role in all of this, but I'm so very sorry.' She was fiddling with the packet, clumsily trying to take out a tissue.

'You might not believe me, but I want the best for her...' James's voice wavered.

'You don't have a bloody clue what's best for her!' Aidan interrupted him.

James and Helena exchanged a look.

'She belongs with you, Aidan,' James said quietly, so quietly that Aidan thought he had misheard him.

Aidan was speechless. 'What?' was all he managed to say.

'I'm dropping the case,' James continued. 'I can't do it to Milly. I've already instructed my solicitor that I won't be proceeding.'

Aidan couldn't process what they were saying. Was this some sort of cruel trick? Some kind of game they were playing? Was he supposed to take their words at face value, or was there an ulterior motive here? He had witnessed what they were capable of, how low they were willing to sink, how could he believe them? He looked over at Helena, who was dabbing at her eyes with the tissue but she couldn't keep up with them as tears streamed freely down her face.

'Is this a wind-up?' Aidan managed to say.

Helena shook her head. 'Aidan, James and I have been through an awful lot, I know it doesn't excuse what we have done to you, but as you know we were trying for a baby for a long time to eventually be told that it would never happen. Then the accident took place and when the question mark over Milly's paternity raised its head – I don't know...' She shook her head. 'I really never thought the test would show that you were not her dad. You have to believe me on that. I still don't know what possessed me to do it. I look back and don't even recognise myself. I'm not trying to make excuses for my behaviour, but I think not being able to have a child of our own made me do things I never thought I would be capable of doing.' She looked across at James. 'I think it made both of us do things we would never normally do.'

He saw tears fill James's eyes, which knocked him off guard. Aidan watched as he exhaled heavily before taking over from Helena. 'I'm sorry, Aidan... I just don't know what happened, I was like a man possessed. It's like I was blindsided. I saw Milly as my only chance to have a child and nothing could sway me from that, but I now realise I was using her to fix a problem in my life and I never should have done that. As much as it kills me to let go of my one chance to be a dad, I've come to realise that Milly belongs with you. Being a dad is a lot more than the DNA you share with someone – you're her father, Aidan, you always have been and always will be.'

Aidan was stunned. Although he felt relief as sweet as honey flood through him, how could he believe them after everything they had put him through?

'Why now? What's changed?' he asked in disbelief.

'I was in the park yesterday and I saw you pushing Milly on the swings. It was the way she looked at you – I realised that she would never look at me in the same way, no matter how much I loved her or tried to be good a father. She could never be mine… It's really simple; you're her dad, Aidan,' James said, his voice choked with emotion, and tears descended his face.

In a perverse way, Aidan actually found himself feeling sorry for James and Helena. Although they had betrayed him in the worst possible way and he hated what they had done to him, the hell they had put him through, in their own way, they too were victims in this tangled web of deceit.

'There is something that I wanted to ask you,' James continued after taking a moment to gather himself.

Aidan's heart fell just as quickly as it had risen. He knew there was going to be a catch. How could he be so naïve as to believe a word that came out of either of their mouths?

'Helena and I were wondering… well, if we could

be... involved in her life, I mean she would never know the truth obviously. I know we don't deserve that and you are welcome to tell us to get lost and that you never want to see us again, but we would love to be able to watch her grow up if you'd let us?'

CHRISTMAS EVE

AIDAN

Aidan opened the car door and stepped out onto the frozen earth. The boys unbuckled their seat belts and waited while he helped Milly out. He pulled her woollen bobble hat down over her ears and helped her to put on her mittens, then the four of them made their way across the path towards where Philip and Sheila were waiting for them. The leaden sky sat heavily above them. The stones beneath their feet crunched as they walked and the white-tipped grass was doubled with the weight of frost.

It was Aidan's first time taking the kids to the graveyard. Sheila and Philip wanted them all to gather there to wish Rowan a happy Christmas. Ever since they had told him of their plans, Aidan had been dreading it. He was worried that the reality of seeing his wife's name etched on the cold marble headstone that had just been erected would finish him off completely, but he knew he couldn't keep putting it off forever. It was time.

There was no avoiding the huge mother-shaped hole that was left in their house and the first Christmas without his wife was going to be extremely difficult. Christmas was a time for happy families and every time he heard a colleague in work excitedly chatting about their plans or heard 'War is Over' on the radio, it scored his heart because that was her favourite Christmas song. Rowan loved Christmas. She would bedeck the whole house. A huge garland would trail the bannisters of the stairs and a fresh holly wreath that she made herself would hang on their door to welcome any visitors. She would spend weeks leafing through recipes as she planned their dinner; how she was going to cook the turkey, whether they would have sprouts even though nobody ate them or break free from tradition and leave them off the menu altogether. She would bake mince pies and help the children to make a gingerbread house and the kitchen would always smell of cloves and cinnamon in the run-up to the big day. She would get excited as she ticked presents off her list and she always managed to find everything that the children had asked for in their letters to Santa. Aidan had left the Christmas shopping to her and would be as surprised as they were when they opened their gifts on Christmas morning.

He had put the tree up the day before and the kids had helped him to hang decorations, but it didn't look the same. It lacked the finesse of Rowan's touch. She would have had a colour scheme and used glass baubles and ribbons, whereas Aidan had just used whatever decorations he could find in the attic. Last year Christmas without Rowan would have seemed unimaginable but somehow they were emerging from the awful haze of the past few months and they were getting through it together and that was the most important thing.

'Sheila, Philip,' Aidan said as he drew closer to his in-laws. 'It's good to see you.' He greeted Sheila with a hug and shook Philip's hand, before Milly leaped into her grandfather's arms. Although Aidan and his in-laws would never be close, they seemed to have reached a truce in recent weeks. Aidan didn't know if it was because they were just keeping the peace for the sake of Christmas or maybe they had finally accepted that he was doing the best he could, but whatever the reason was, Aidan was grateful for the thaw in their relationship.

Aidan felt winded as he caught sight of his wife's name on the headstone and beneath it her date of birth and the date she had died, showing a life cut short. He bent forward and placed the bouquet of red roses he had brought with him onto the grave. He noticed there were other bouquets there too, their petals glistening in the frost. He lifted them and read the messages on the cards and saw they were from her friends.

'I thought we could all do with a little hot chocolate,' Sheila said as she bent down and opened a shopping bag, producing a thermos flask and several plastic cups. The steam rose into the air as she poured and Philip began handing them out.

'Here you go, Aidan,' Philip said, offering him one.

'Thanks,' he said as he curled his fingers around it. The warmth was welcome.

'Nana, will Santa come to Mammy in heaven?' Milly asked, taking a sip from her hot chocolate.

'Of course he will, he'll bring her something really nice,' Sheila replied, putting her arm around her.

'Maybe he bring her a neck-a-lace. Mama would like that.'

'She would, love,' Sheila replied with a sheen of tears in her eyes.

Aidan looked at his daughter whose cheeks were now rosy from the biting cold and a semicircle of hot chocolate stained her top lip. He felt a lump stick in his throat. When James and Helena had called around and explained that they were stopping the proceedings, Aidan had been afraid to believe them, but when Brendan Waters had confirmed it, the relief had flooded through him. Initially, when James had asked if they could be a part of her life, Aidan had felt outraged by their audacity, but the more he'd thought about it, the more Aidan had come round to the idea. If he let James and Helena be a part of Milly's life but on his terms, he was the one in control. He needed to keep James on side and this felt like the best way. There was the very real fear that if he denied James access to Milly, then he would get fixated on the idea of gaining custody of her again. He had decided he would allow them to watch Milly grow up but keep them at a safe distance. So he had invited them over for Christmas morning drinks so Milly could show them what Santa had brought. He didn't know what the future held for any of them, but it felt like a tentative step forward from a nightmarish few months.

'Shall we light a candle for your mum?' Sheila asked as she reached for Callum's gloved hand and gave it a squeeze. She took a candle and a lighter from her bag and lit the wick, before placing it down on the grave.

Aidan placed his hot chocolate down on the graveside and reached for Milly and Jack's gloved hands and held them within his own. Then Milly reached for Callum's other hand, and Philip, seeing the five of them holding hands, joined with Sheila and Jack so that the six of them were all linked in a circle. Philip began to sing 'Silent Night' and was soon followed softly by Sheila, then Milly joined in even though she didn't know the words and then Jack and Aidan followed suit. Callum looked momentarily awkward before finally singing with them too.

As they reached the high notes, Aidan felt the weight of tears push into his eyes and he squeezed Milly and Jack's hands tightly, somehow hoping it could stop them falling down his face. Suddenly a single snowflake fell gracefully through the air before them and they all raised their faces to the sky, where plump flakes were starting to fall, landing on their cheeks and carpeting the ground around them. Milly broke free from the circle and reached out and caught a flake on her mittens. She giggled as it melted on the wool. The boys ran off after her and Aidan watched his three children as they laughed and played together in the snow. He looked at his beautiful children that Rowan had given him, his beautiful family.

'Happy Christmas, Rowan,' Aidan whispered. 'Sleep in heavenly peace.'

EPILOGUE

Sunlight shone through the leafy branches of the gnarled oak tree where they all sat at a linen-clothed table beneath its shade. The triangles of bunting that Helena had strung around the garden flapped gently on the breeze. Children's laughter rang out as they chased each other across the lawn.

Baby Theo was in James's arms, kicking his pudgy little legs, his chubby pink face peeping out from beneath his sunhat. Every time she looked at them together, Helena's heart swelled so much in her chest that she thought it might burst out through her ribcage. She still had to pinch herself that he was hers. He was at that adorable chubby stage that babies reached around their first birthday, but she knew it would all fall off him once he got walking over the next few months.

She had never felt such contentedness. She had always imagined how it would feel to be a mother, but even in her wildest fantasies, it hadn't been like this. She had watched Theo come into the world in a whirlwind as if he couldn't wait to meet her. Their surrogate Anna had kept them involved during the whole pregnancy and none of Helena's fears or worries about using another woman to carry their child had been realised. Anna already had two children of her own and had finished her family and now she wanted to help others. It had taken Helena's naturally cautious personality ages to trust her; she was waiting for the catch in Anna's altruism, but it never came. Anna had been selfless throughout the pregnancy and had kept them involved the whole time. Helena really felt she was sent to them by angels.

The midwife had handed Theo to Helena first; they had planned it that way. Helena had asked Anna if she wanted to be the first to hold him, but Anna had told her that the baby should be held by his mother first. So she had taken him gingerly from the midwife, his tiny face red furious and roaring in complaint about having been evicted from his home of the last nine months. As she'd looked down at him nestled in her arms, she had noticed instantly that his nose had the same aquiline shape as James's – a good strong nose, she had thought – and as his eyes had opened up to the wonder of the world, she had recognised the familiar almond curve of her own eyes.

One of her biggest fears about using a surrogate had been that it might feel strange when she didn't carry him herself or because she wasn't the one to give birth to him, that the bonding process might be slower – or maybe not happen at all – but those fears were unfounded; she had taken one look at Theo and known he was hers to love. It was as if everything in her life to date had been leading up to this moment, like she had been waiting the whole time to meet him.

Now, as she looked at her beautiful boy, she wondered how she had ever rejected the option of surrogacy. She wished she could have realised this years ago, it would have saved them so much pain. But she had learned that sometimes you had to travel the hard road in this life to get to the place you were destined for. She and James had been shaped by their scars and by some miracle they had emerged stronger than ever before. Nobody knew what the future held, what suffering or happiness lay on their life path, but in that moment, Helena was so grateful for all of it; the pain and anguish, even the grief, because it had led them here. If they hadn't gone through all of that heartache, they wouldn't have had Theo. And he was perfect. So, so perfect.

'It's cake time!' she announced as she placed the cake down in the centre of the table. Her parents, Anne and Pat, and Theo's other grandparents, Breda and Kevin, all gathered around their grandson. Callum, Jack and Milly came tearing across the grass, with Milly chanting 'cake, cake, cake!' She was nearly six now and would be going into Senior Infants soon. Callum scooped her up and swung her around. She giggled until he put her back down again. At nearly seventeen, Callum had grown into a broad-shouldered man of over six foot tall and had just been selected for the senior cup rugby team in his school. Aidan had told her that he was working hard in school and it was difficult to believe that he was ever the troubled young boy that she had once brought home to Aidan.

'Jack, would you lead us?' Helena asked when everyone had gathered round. She watched as his small chest plumped out a little as he picked up the guitar that went everywhere with him these days. Music was his passion and he had told Helena that he was writing his own songs.

Helena watched Aidan, his whole face lit with pride as Jack began to strum the opening chords of 'Happy Birthday' and they all sang along with him. Aidan had recently taken the plunge and started his own consulting business and it seemed to be working out well for them all. He had a steady stream of clients and so could pick and choose what work he took on, which gave him more flexibility with the kids. They had emerged from their nightmare and, although they would never be the same again, Helena could see the signs that they were starting to heal.

When they had finished singing, she struck a match along the side of the box and lit the single candle on the cake that she had made for her son.

'Milly?' James asked. 'Will you help Theo to blow out his candle?'

Her face lit up as she bent her head in beside Theo's. Helena quickly lifted her phone from the table and managed to capture a photo of Milly's cheesy grin in beside Theo's dribbly-mouthed smile. They didn't know that they were half-brother and sister. Helena wasn't sure if they would ever tell the children, but she knew that if they ever did, it would be Aidan's decision, not theirs. It was a secret that would stay between the three of them.

'Can I get you another beer?' James asked Aidan.

'Go on then.'

They were very grateful to Aidan, who had kept them involved in Milly's life. He had invited them to her last birthday party and they had spent an hour in the house on Ledbury Road with them for the last two Christmases. Helena knew they certainly didn't deserve it, after everything they had put him through, so they appreciated opportunities like that to be a part of Milly's life. They were like a special aunt and uncle, but as far as Milly was concerned, Aidan was her dad and they all knew that was the way it was going to stay. Helena was glad he had accepted their invitation to join them in celebrating Theo's first birthday. Since they had had Theo, Aidan had softened towards them; perhaps he no longer saw them as a threat. They would never be best friends, there was too much history between them, but they were civil to each other and Helena was so thankful for that.

Having Theo had shed a new light on things for James and Helena; they now understood with a searing remorse what they had put Aidan through. Becoming parents had opened up a whole new world for them; they realised that what came with such a chasm of love for their son was a terrifying fear that somehow it could all be snatched away from you. The thought of someone coming in and trying to take your precious child away was the worst nightmare imaginable.

James lifted Theo beneath his armpits and handed him over to her. She placed a kiss on his velvet-smooth skin, like she was meeting him for the first time all over again. He still took her breath away every time she laid eyes on him. At last she had everything she had ever dreamed of. Her family. Her world. Her happy ever after.

ACKNOWLEDGMENTS

To Hayley Steed and Hannah Todd from the Madeleine Milburn Agency, thank you both for your help and guidance with this book. Hannah, your belief in me and my writing means so much and I look forward to working on many more books with you.

To my wonderful editor Caroline Ridding who really makes me drill down into the story and also to Amanda Ridout, Nia Beynon, Claire Fenby, and all at Boldwood. You are brilliant at what you do and I love working with you. To Jade Craddock for her copy-edit, I really appreciate your detailed eye and to Emily Reader for her fantastic proofread.

To my family, both Finnertys and Van Lonkhuyzens, for all their constant love and support.

To all my dear friends too, for always cheering me on. A special mention for fellow author Janelle

Harris. Our walk-and-talks always help to keep me sane.

To all the booksellers, bloggers and libraries for their support.

A book would be nothing without readers, so to everyone who had picked up my book, thank you. To those who contact me with lovely messages and kind words, you'll never know how much those messages mean.

Lastly to my husband Simon for his support and our beautiful children, Lila, Tom, Bea and Charlie. You are without doubt the best things I have ever created. I am so privileged to be your mother and I adore you all beyond words.

MORE FROM CAROLINE FINNERTY

We hope you enjoyed reading *A Mother's Secret*. If you did, please leave a review.

If you'd like to gift a copy, this book is also available as an ebook, digital audio download and audiobook CD.

Sign up to Caroline Finnerty's mailing list for news, competitions and updates on future books.

http://bit.ly/CarolineFinnertyNewsletter

The Last Days of Us, another tender story of hope and forgiveness from Caroline Finnerty, is available to order now.

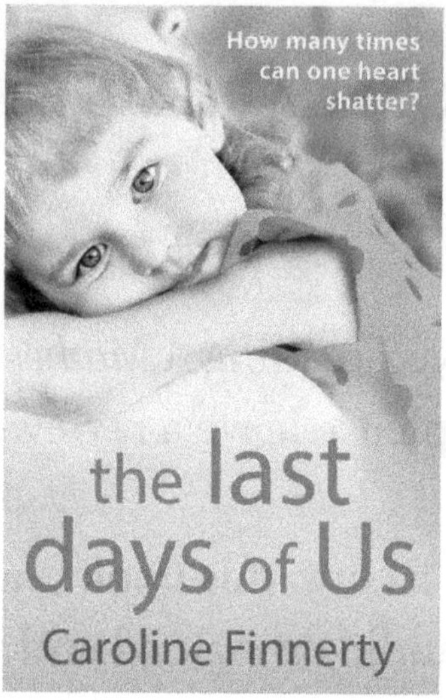
How many times can one heart shatter?
the last days of Us
Caroline Finnerty

ABOUT THE AUTHOR

Caroline Finnerty is an Irish author of heart-wrenching family dramas and has published four novels and compiled a non-fiction charity anthology. She has been shortlisted for several short-story awards and lives in County Kildare with her husband and four young children.

Visit Caroline's Website: www.carolinefinnerty.ie

twitter.com/cfinnertywriter

facebook.com/carolinefinnertywriter

instagram.com/carolinefinnerty

goodreads.com/carolinefinnerty

bookbub.com/profile/caroline-finnerty

ABOUT BOLDWOOD BOOKS

Boldwood Books is a fiction publishing company seeking out the best stories from around the world.

Find out more at www.boldwoodbooks.com

Sign up to the Book and Tonic newsletter for news, offers and competitions from Boldwood Books!

http://www.bit.ly/bookandtonic

We'd love to hear from you, follow us on social media:

facebook.com/BookandTonic
twitter.com/BoldwoodBooks
instagram.com/BookandTonic

Lightning Source UK Ltd.
Milton Keynes UK
UKHW040805150222
398717UK00003B/123

9 781801 625364